IN HIS SIGHT

IN HIS SIGHT

ANNA POWELL

SALT & LIGHT CO.

Copyright © 2025 by Salt & Light Co.
Littleton, CO
All rights reserved.

This is a work of fiction. Some locations, businesses and landmarks referenced in the story are real; however, the characters, organizations and events portrayed are fictionalized. Any resemblance to actual persons, living or dead, or to real events is coincidental or used fictitiously.

No part of this book may be reproduced in any form or by any electronic or mechanical means, including information storage and retrieval systems, without written permission from the author, except for the use of brief quotations in a book review.

Paperback ISBN 979-8-9939569-0-9
Hardcover ISBN 979-8-9939569-1-6
eBook ISBN 979-8-9939569-2-3
Library of Congress Control Number: 2026901890

Edited by Kristen Kavan

Cover design by Anna Powell

For Dan,
my biggest cheerleader and the steady anchor
beside me through every season.

And for Sawyer, Holden, and Wesley,
who made every word worth writing.

In His Sight **is inspired by true events.**

"And we know that in all things God works for the good of those who love him, who have been called according to his purpose."

— ROMANS 8:28

1

PROFESSOR HOOVER

Professor Joseph Hoover sits at his desk pondering his classes at Midland College this year. Not the subject matter (communications), nor his schedule, nor the curriculum. He's laser-focused on one thing: *Piper Hawthorne*.

Four metal poles and a hard plastic top make for more of a table, really. He had planned to buy a wooden desk with more character after he settled into his Chicago apartment, but here he is, still working at his makeshift desk a year and a half later. The cream-colored plastic rectangle is hardly visible beneath the books and papers scattered about, not to mention the three computer monitors spanning its length. One thing he did invest in, however, is his chair. He knew he needed one of those reclining executive chairs with a footrest, because comfort is key when it comes to his hobbies, and he didn't think twice about purchasing it.

It's not a habit he's proud of, but he often finds himself falling asleep to the hum of his computer harmonizing with the pings of his geo-location tracking system. Perhaps he should be more concerned about the crumbs and grease stains making their mark on the gray polyester fabric. Leather was just too expensive.

If you ask Hoover about his apartment, he'll tell you he found it through fate, or through his undeniable determination to get exactly what he wants. He had the option of having it furnished, which he jumped at. Sure, the four-drawer dresser is a bit cookie-cutter, and having a double bed as a grown man in his forties isn't ideal, but why buy furniture if he doesn't have to?

Admittedly, the bones of his apartment have suffered a bit. The sink has a slow drip, and the paint is chipping in a few places, but the last thing he wants is maintenance paying him a visit and becoming aware of his personal life.

He's a visualizer, so his goals, most of which are rather intimate, are in plain sight, printed out and taped to the walls here and there. "Manifesting," he calls it.

Once he wins her over, there'll be plenty of time for apartment tune-ups.

Heck, they'll probably move somewhere together, and this will all be a moot point.

He skims through the student directory and stops when he sees her. He thinks back to his very first day of teaching. The moment she walked into his classroom for Communications 301 is still ingrained in his mind. She was late and frazzled as she found her seat, but she had a warm, gentle aura that was palpable and immediately drew him in. Her straight blond hair fell just above her chest, her pinpoint dimples were undeniably contagious, her hazel almond eyes mesmerizing.

He was captivated and couldn't help himself, like a puppy trying to wait for a biscuit. He still can't. Yes, he knows he's older than she is, and yes, he's her professor at a Christian college, and quite frankly, she's way out of his league — yadda, yadda, yadda. But she's graduating soon, and then age is but a number. His chances with her, he'll confidently, perhaps a little too confidently, leave up to destiny.

He tries opening a new tab in his browser, but without thinking, and as if on command, or more likely out of habit, finds himself scrolling through Facebook until she pops up on his feed. His heart thumps fiercely in his chest like a bass drum. This is what she does to him.

He abruptly gets up, throws on his almost worn-through leather loafers and his favorite navy crushed-velvet blazer (always velvet, regardless of season), and decides to go for a walk along Chicago's Lakeshore Path to take in the changing leaves. Maybe if he walks long enough, he'll get distracted and forget about her...unlikely, but maybe.

2

GUT INSTINCT

Piper Hawthorne's feet pound the pavement. She can feel her heart thud with each pass. She closes her eyes and lets her lungs expand as wide as her body allows. Running here is freedom in every sense. The air is crisp and smells like autumn; it ignites her being.

One of the things she likes best about coming home to Wisconsin on college breaks is this: running through her parents' neighborhood, smack-dab down the middle of the road. Alone. Free. Safe. For a single young woman, that feeling is exhilarating.

There are about twenty houses, each resting on three to five acres of land, so it's peaceful, and you have to work to see a neighbor's home.

The main drive is flanked by tall grass and pine trees that extend as far up as you can see before you're forced to blink away the blinding sun. The breeze is audible and relaxes her soul.

I probably shouldn't even be running right now, she thinks, wiping the snot tickling the edge of her nostril. Ever since transferring colleges her junior year — yes, she left one of the nation's top party schools for one of the most conservative, Midland College — running has become her thing. Partly because anxiety has sunk its ugly roots, and partly because her beloved roommates have introduced her to a whole new approach to being skinny and looking good. Both are a lot and take up more mental space than they should. She runs because it's an escape for her mind and good for her body.

Piper's run is interrupted by goosebumps spreading down her neck as she nears her parents' house. She darts her gaze left and right, searching for the source. She slows to a walk and spots her — a doe, standing still, watching her with unblinking calm. Her golden body is defined by delicate muscle.

Deer freeze when caught off guard, the way they do under headlights at night. This doe wears that same stunned stillness, but Piper spots two polka-dot-painted fawns tucked behind her and knows she's only protecting them.

Piper recently had to write a communications essay on human reactions and did a deep dive into two of her biggest struggles: fear and anxiety. In the process, she learned that people have four fear responses: fight, flight, fawn, and freeze.

Fear begins in the amygdala, the part of the brain that processes emotions. When the amygdala is activated by possible danger, it elicits one of these fear responses, the one we believe will keep us safest.

To fight is to try to attack the threat. To flee is to try to escape if the danger can be outrun. To fawn is to try to please whoever is triggering the fear to prevent them from causing harm. To freeze is to be as still and quiet as possible until the danger passes. The freeze response is the brain's attempt to avoid detection, as fear shuts down the body's ability to move.

Piper likes to think she'd be a fighter.

The mama deer is still frozen as Piper picks up her pace, rounding the bend that leads her home. She slows to a walk again, noticing the tall grass shifting left and right, the pine trees reaching up to the sky, with ombré needles on their way to becoming burnt orange.

She opens the front door, throws off her shoes, and barges into the kitchen of her parents' colonial-style home, heading straight for a box of Kleenex. She blows and blows and blows her nose.

Her mom, fresh from a shower with still-wet, black-as-night, shoulder-length hair, stops unloading the dishwasher and takes it in.

"Are you sure you should be running, Piper?" Concern spreads across her forehead.

"No days off, Mom. I'm fine, I promise. Google said running with a sniffle is actually good for you because it can open your nasal passages."

"Who? I wouldn't call whatever that just was a sniffle," she mutters while stacking bowls.

Piper's phone rings, interrupting her on her way to the pantry. *Professor Joseph Hoover,* it reads. Her brow furrows. *Why would he be calling me?* She quickly thinks through a shortlist of reasons — *He needs something to complete my internship credit... he's missing something to finalize my grade for my Comm Senior Seminar...or...it's an accident?*

An outgoing introvert, Piper tries to avoid situations like this at all costs. She's the life of the party when it comes to her friends, but her professor? No thanks. Yet still, as a type A perfectionist, Piper can't ignore the call even if she wants to.

The only reason Professor Hoover even has Piper's number is because, on the first day of Comm 301, he sent around a sheet of paper for everyone to fill out and share their cell phone numbers and he, in turn, shared his. He tries to be the texting type of professor. The reality is, none of his students see him as remotely cool. He's widely known around campus as the lonely, socially awkward professor who tries too hard and is painful to converse with, but gives out A's like bubble gum.

"Are you okay? Who is it?" Piper's mom notoriously reads her like a book.

Piper answers her phone and takes a few steps away. "Hello? This is Piper," she says pointedly, trying not to show how annoyed she is.

"Is this the one and only Piper Hawthorne? Wow, I'm so happy you answered. I, ah, just, ah, wanted to check in to see how your fall break is going."

What? Is this actually why he called? Doesn't he have more important things to do? Don't be rude, Piper, she reminds herself. *He may be weird, but he is the one grading your papers.*

"Umm...okay. That's why you called? It's good; break is great. Can I help you with something?"

There's a pause on the line before he clears his throat and continues, "Do you have a cold, Piper? I can't help but notice you sound a little congested."

"Umm, yes, I have a cold..." Piper rolls her eyes and daggers them at nothing in particular in the distance.

"Oh no, I'm so sorry to hear that. The reason I'm calling is because I have a book for you. I was just sitting here thinking about you and realized I'd forgotten to give it to you before break. So I grabbed a pen and paper to send it to you, but then realized I don't have your address. Are you at your parents' house?"

"Umm, yes, I am...at their house." That feeling is back. Goosebumps spread across her neck. The hairs on her arms awaken, and a chill runs through her body. Piper shudders and brushes it aside.

"I'm ready when you are. Can you share your parents' address? I'll pop this in the mail straightaway."

"Their address...umm...okay, sure." Piper gives him their address, against all lessons she's ever learned. But he's technically not a stranger. *Was he really just thinking about me, though? Whatever that means. Gross.* Her skin prickles.

"What are your plans over break?" He acts casually, as if they normally converse like this.

"My plans? I don't really know...just hanging out with my family, I guess." *He is so awkward. Why is he asking me this?*

"Okay, well, this should do it. Listen, Piper, I wish you nothing but health and peace. I look forward to seeing you after break." Hoover distances himself from the phone in a huff.

"Okay, thanks. Bye." Piper blurts it out, throwing her phone on the counter as if it's a spider she needs to kill.

"What was that all about?" her mom asks, confusion gripping her gaze. "Who needed our address?"

"That was Joseph Hoover, my Comm professor," she sighs. "He's a little socially awkward, but he's an easy grader, so here we are. He's sending me a book."

Piper's mind flashes back to the last email he sent her before break.

From: Joseph.Hoover@Midland.edu
To: Piper.Hawthorne@Midland.edu
Date: October 7, 2008 4:12 p.m.
Subject: Apologies

Piper,

I want to apologize because you were sharing something important about school and I just bolted like a barbarian for the train. Only now I realized that I think you were sharing something about difficulty in class work. You should know you have already passed the internship, and I am just waiting for them to make the grade sheet available online. I have no doubts in my mind you will do well in your other Comm classes. Are the English classes not going so well? Could you please let me know what's going on? Is there anything I can do to help you? Please let me know. God has blessed you with an amazing mind and I have no doubt you will ace your classes.

If you need a sympathetic ear, you should know I am your well-wisher and will go to bat for you to the ends of the earth.

Always at your service,
Hoover

A self-proclaimed overthinker, Piper keeps replaying *"I will go to bat for you to the ends of the earth"* in her mind. *Why does this feel so off?* she wonders, with a shiver.

She pictures Hoover — his skinny, pasty-white frame, hunched shoulders, and worn black slip-on shoes that are begging to be replaced. She can see the acne scars on his cheeks and the sunken-in eyes that are so dark brown they look black. The fact that he's a Christian is the only thing reassuring to her.

Two more months. Just push through for two more months, and come graduation, this will be a thing of the past, she reminds herself.

"Piper." No response. "Piper." Silence. "PIPER," her mom shouts, commanding attention.

"What, Mom? Gosh, you scared me." Piper looks up from the tunnel she's been sucked into while scrolling through Facebook on her laptop a few days later. Lying on her parents' plush, paisley-brown, overstuffed couch, with a fleece blanket engulfing her body, Piper is on the verge of dozing off. Something about being home does that.

"Piper, you got a letter in the mail," her mom repeats, snapping Piper back to reality.

"I got a what?" Confused, she scrunches her forehead.

"You got a letter...in the mail." Her mom hands her a white envelope.

Weird, Piper thinks to herself as she looks at the card, wondering who on earth would send snail mail to her parents' house when she technically hasn't lived there in more than three years.

Hoover, she realizes, her stomach tightening. *Ugh, why did I give him their address?*

Piper hoists herself up so she's sitting, opens the card, and is met by an illustration of two pieces of bread. They each have skinny stick arms and the daintiest brown outline. The first piece of bread has a plate next to it with a pad of butter, and the second is saying, *"Feel butter!"*

She opens the card, and a flowery *Get Well Soon* Starbucks gift card falls out. It has "$20" written on the back.

> *So sorry you're sick, Piper. Hope you get some rest and feel better. Treat yourself to some coffee or tea while you're on the mend. Can't wait to see you back at school soon.*
> *-Hoover*

Piper's eyes bulge. Her throat tightens, and her stomach turns over. *Just think for a minute,* she tells herself, so as not to get worked up over nothing. *Hoover called me a few days ago and was going to send me a book. He made it sound like it was ready to go. And instead, he sent me a card he clearly wrote after we talked... with a gift card for coffee?*

Feeling blindsided, she wonders, *Did he just do a bait and switch to get my parents' address? That seems like a stretch...or does it?*

"Is this weird, or is it just me?" she calls out to her mom, who's now in the adjoining kitchen. "Professor Hoover sent me a letter and a Starbucks gift card to make me feel better. He called me last week, you know, and said he was sending me a book. And this letter, well, he must've written it after our call, when he found out I wasn't feeling well. I mean, this is kind of weird, right?"

"Yeah, it's weird, but you said he's a little off, right? He's probably just bored and lonely, Piper."

Piper thinks about it a minute more, stifling the growing knot in her stomach, and agrees, if only to feel at ease.

3

PROFESSOR HOOVER

Professor Hoover makes himself a cup of coffee. His go-to order is as eccentric as he is: one hefty dash of sugar, four tablespoons of heavy whipping cream, and a squirt of honey. He stirs it for far too long.

His cup, a once-white Midland mug with two nickel-sized chips around the rim, is his daily staple. He sits on his couch, an overstuffed mahogany-brown leather loveseat he found on Craigslist, and pulls out the binder.

A penny pincher, Hoover taps his left foot, unbothered by the fact that his big toe protrudes through his gray cloth slipper. He's aged more than he'd like to admit these last few years. His black hair is thinning, and the etchings around his eyes have deepened. Ever since he met her, life has felt strained by his desire to have her all to himself, with the complications that come with her being a student.

He's a creature of habit and grasps for control in all areas of his life. Despite growing up in Missouri, he's developed an affinity for velvet blazers, slacks, and anything remotely comfortable. Fashion is the last box he checks when buying something new, which rarely, if ever, happens. He'd rather save his money for his future and, even more so, the future with her that he's been dreaming up in his spare time.

He was raised by his older sister, Myra, who still lives in Missouri. His mother died when he was three from a sudden respiratory virus that landed her in the hospital on a ventilator, which she never recovered from. His childhood led him to be a dreamer. Not that his upbringing was bad; he just grew up yearning for the love that can only come from a mother and became resentful of how busy his dad and sister were, even though they were just trying to survive.

There's one day left of fall break, and truth be told, he has too much time on his hands.

I'm reviewing her work to make sure I have a comprehensive overview of her accomplishments for her senior seminar capstone grade. I must be comprehensive, he thinks.

He's been diligent about making two copies of everything.

This will make for the best end-of-year surprise when I gift her with her copy, he thinks.

He lands on her essay personifying the thing she struggles with most: *Growing Pains of Internally Stretching Myself*, his favorite piece to date. She wrote it for the creative writing class she took from him. He wasn't supposed to teach that class, but when he learned that Professor Clark needed to take a leave of absence for family matters and that Piper was enrolled, he jumped at the chance.

It was the perfect opportunity to really get to know her. Hoover's class assignments were based on what he was most interested in discovering. He'd even received a glowing review from the department chair for the creativity and vulnerability he drew from students.

Hoover skims his bony finger over the pages. Her biggest fears, her greatest dreams, they're all here.

4

COLLEGE CONSERVATIVE

Fall comes and goes, and this year, winter is especially frigid. Piper feels strange being the lone ranger still attending college while all her friends have graduated. It's like she's doing the splits, with one foot on campus and one stretched as far as she can go into the so-called real world.

Her grades have slowly yet steadily declined because of her public relations internship at Harmon Consulting. She's been working closely alongside her boss, Kate, for the last year and a half. Once Piper got a taste of doing meaningful work she's passionate about, she found it hard to care about linguistics and elective credits. She also has a tough time saying no to Kate.

Kate is charismatic and fun, outgoing and unapologetically herself. She wears designer everything (Jimmy Choo and Chanel being among her favorite brands) and has opened Piper's eyes to the glamorous, fast-paced world of PR. She has thick, red-tinged hair that falls just past her shoulders and porcelain skin marked with freckles. Her energy is electric when she enters any room.

In many ways, Piper is indebted to her. Before this internship, she had zero experience, and Kate took a chance on her. And so, Piper has worked her butt off to prove herself worthy of this job. All she wants is more — more work, more experiences, more challenges, more responsibility to continue proving herself.

Piper is an introvert by nature, and this job has broken her in all the best ways. It has forced her out of her shell, to come into her own, and to carry herself with poise. Kate's motto, instilled in her from day one, is to *act like you can*, even when you have no clue what the hell you're doing. Piper has done exactly that, and it's worked like a charm.

Piper drives down Yale Street through the college campus in her white RAV4 and, this time, feels sentimental about it, like a mom reflecting on her child exiting the years of toddlerhood all too soon. Graduation is a week away, and while the real world has been calling her for quite some time, the beginning of a new life chapter means saying goodbye to another, and goodbyes are always hard.

She decided to transfer to Midland College after growing tired of the shallow relationships, constant partying, and lack of direction she felt after two years at a state school. What she yearned for were friends who shared her faith in Jesus, could hold a conversation, and had an educated worldview. Midland led her to exactly that.

There are, of course, some things about Midland she won't miss. It's an extremely conservative environment. After agreeing to attend, every student signs a covenant agreement that includes rules such as no drinking (regardless of age), no tobacco, no drugs, no sex, and no dancing outside of college-sponsored events, to name only a few. Not that Piper is upset she can't indulge in some of these things; she's just looking forward to not feeling like she's living under a microscope. There are students at Midland who literally tell on one another for committing an offense.

There's another thing, a saying, *ring by spring,* that Piper finds painfully annoying. Because, truthfully, so many women actually chase it. There's this stigma that if you don't find a Christian husband while at Midland, you're doomed to a geriatric pregnancy or, even worse, celibacy. She's never understood it, because it feels like, in many ways, her life is just beginning. And so, Piper finds herself going against the status quo.

She drives past the chapel, first-year dorms, and student rec center, taking in the vast white brick building of Orchard Hall, nestled atop the college's only hill. One of her favorite memories is from her first weekend at Midland.

She finagled her way into living in the Brady Apartments, where most juniors lived, and avoided the dreaded "transfer" dorm thanks to her older brother, Dave. He had graduated from Midland the year before she transferred and connected her with a girl he knew who was the same age. One thing led to another, and Piper ended up rooming with her friend Laura, who remains one of her closest girlfriends to this day.

Thank goodness I ended up in an apartment my first year here, she thinks, imagining the people she would've been forced to befriend otherwise.

During that first weekend, after moving in and getting settled, there was a black-and-white–themed dress-up party hosted by a group of girls who lived in an off-campus house. Everyone got dressed up for the party. Piper wore an A-line black jersey dress that skimmed her knees, with a wide white elastic body-hugging belt and white platform sandals. Laura helped her tease her blonde hair so it was full of volume, and she wore it back in a side ponytail.

They arrived, and by all accounts, you'd think it was a real college party — except, of course, there was no liquor. The music was bumping so loudly you could hardly talk. Bodies of anyone and everyone in the junior class who was remotely cool were plastered against one another, making it an all-out sweat-fest despite all the windows being cracked open. Between people yelling in an attempt to have a quick catch-up about how their summers went, the living room was one big dance floor. Diet Coke, Sprite, root beer, and LaCroix flowed like beer and vodka.

Piper was known as the "new girl" and had the time of her life getting a lay of the social landscape and meeting new people. She could tell there had been a handful of people drinking because she could smell it on their breath, but she didn't dare break the rules straight out of the gate. She was totally sober. And yet, it didn't keep her from climbing atop a wooden table to dance with her new friend, Laura.

The two girls pushed themselves up and giggled as they shook their booties. Before they knew it, the table, which she later found out was an antique, came crashing down, unplugging the lamp that was their only source of light and taking the speakers with it, cutting the music. It had been dramatic and embarrassing at the time, but now it just makes Piper laugh.

Truth be told, Piper had her fill of college partying, even at Midland. The first time she drank alcohol there was in the comfort of her own apartment. Laura was turning twenty-one, and it felt like they had to celebrate the milestone, even if it was in secret. So they bought a bottle of Malibu and had a girls' night complete with candy, Jell-O shots, and coconut rum mixed with Dr Pepper. It was very classy.

They took hilarious photos to document the evening and woke up sworn to secrecy. *It's a miracle we never got caught for all the times we went out,* she thinks.

Piper drives over the train tracks that mark the school's boundary, pulls into her driveway, and snaps back to reality as her trip down memory lane comes to an end. She and Laura are still roommates and share a single-family townhome just outside of campus, but only for a few more months. Laura is getting married in the spring and will be moving out, and Piper is still deciding what to do.

She's torn between finding a place within the comfort of Midland and venturing to Chicago to get a studio apartment on her own. Her stomach churns just thinking about the excitement and fear that would evoke. *But how fun it will be to live alone in the hustle and bustle of the real city.*

She gets out of her car and notices a huge pile of dog poop in the middle of the sidewalk right in front of her house. Better than last week, when she actually stepped in it.

Whyyyyy? Why can't people clean up after themselves?! she fumes, looking around as if she'll catch the culprit.

The thing Piper has learned about people is that they're all human. And, by nature, humans are flawed.

5

PROFESSOR HOOVER

Professor Hoover wipes the beads of sweat beginning to drip down his temple and forehead. Now that his widow's peak is becoming more pronounced with age, there isn't much hair left to help soak it up. He's thought about starting something like Rogaine but feels he's much too busy for that kind of commitment.

He's just finished an eight-mile speed walk along Chicago's Lakeshore Path. Lately, he's been experiencing panic attacks, and exercise seems to be the only thing that clears his mind. He just can't stop thinking about *her*. Walking is the only thing that centers him, regardless of season, mostly because he loves people-watching and finds those along the path wildly amusing. He also loves knowing that exercising is a hobby he and Piper share. When the opportunity arises, he can't wait to connect with her and talk about it.

He guzzles a glass of ice water, takes a lightning-fast shower, and throws on his favorite hole-laden T-shirt and gray pajama pants. Then he turns on his desktop computer. All three screens come to life simultaneously, like previews at a movie theater.

The time has come, he thinks. *She's almost done with finals by now...and, most importantly, I need to get this off my chest. I'm going to do it.*

He heats up a prepackaged microwave meal consisting of rice, beans, ground beef, and cheese. He opens Microsoft Word between bites and begins —

Piper, he types. *I hope this letter finds you well. May the God of Heaven and Earth bring you peace as you read this. I am a man of peace and am asking for God's providence to intervene in my life.*

His fingers take over as if of their own accord. This letter has been written on his heart since the moment he laid eyes on her, and has been haunting his mind for weeks on end. Fingertips clacking recklessly against the keys, he lays it all out, leaving no sentiment behind.

He breathes a huge sigh of relief. *That should do it,* he thinks, knowing he'll finally sleep soundly tonight.

"I almost forgot," he mutters, a grin spreading across his ghostly pale face, "the most important part."

Subject line: *Please read this email only if you are done with finals,* he types.

With one click, he presses Send. He reclines his chair and relaxes to the steady thrum of his computer, waiting for sleep to come.

6
THE CONFESSION

Since transferring, Piper's rounding out what she lovingly calls her *victory lap*, finishing just in time for Christmas. She tried to get the school to let her walk the stage and receive her diploma early with her friends back in May (for the photos, of course), but they wouldn't allow it because she still had a handful of credits left. She even filed an appeal, and they still wouldn't budge.

Piper's mom had the genius idea for the family to come up for spring graduation anyway, to celebrate with all of Piper's friends and their families. She brought Piper's older brother's blue cap and gown so Piper could match everyone and take part in the never-ending photo sessions to prove she did, in fact, graduate — eventually.

Piper has her head down in her Comm Senior Seminar textbook, trying to review notes before her very last college exam tomorrow, but she finds herself rereading every other sentence, realizing she's retaining nothing. One final exam is all that stands between her and freedom, and the anticipation is all-consuming.

She already has her job lined up, which makes what she's

studying feel even more meaningless. She's going to stay on with Kate and join her full-time at Harmon Consulting. The office is just a few miles from Midland, outside Chicago, though Kate is toying with the idea of moving the office into the city. It's all lining up better than Piper could have planned.

Piper's thoughts are interrupted by the all-too-familiar ping of her inbox, a welcome distraction from the humdrum of final communication rhetoric.

Her eyebrows furrow as the name *Professor Hoover* flashes across her screen. Instinctively, the hairs on her arms rise with careful curiosity. The subject line reads: *Please read this email only if you are done with finals.* A chill runs down her spine.

Despite feeling frozen in time, her fingers move as if they have a mind of their own.

Click.

Piper,

I hope this letter finds you well. May the God of Heaven and Earth bring you peace as you read this. I am a man of peace and am asking for God's providence to intervene in my life.

Please accept my apologies for bringing this up in a letter and not in person. Piper, I am begging you to listen to my personal story.

I have been experiencing severe panic attacks lately. Just this week, I was on my knees crying like a baby because of something weighing heavy on my heart. I collapsed yesterday and was about to collapse today as well. This was my turning point, when I realized that I have to be honest about the circumstances in my life. I think you'll agree, there is freedom in confession. It did not occur to me until recently that I have been repressing something for the longest period in my life.

For context, on the first day of school in the fall semester of 2006, I requested one of my students to shut the door because I was ready to begin the instruction of COMM 301. A few minutes later, the door opened and I didn't know if I was looking at the face of an angel or of a human. I said to myself 'Dear Lord, she must be an angel.' She was, of course, a student and she gracefully took her seat despite being late. She was the last student to enter the class.

Since I am placed in a position of trust and responsibility, I told myself that I would only be a brother in Christ to this young lady whose spirit emanated a radiant beauty and transcendent joy that made a deep impression on me. I promised myself that I would care for her the way the Lord wants me to care for her and other students, and not in any other way.

I tried my best in every conceivable way to not let my feelings get in the way of my duty. I really tried my best and I hope people (and more importantly you) will believe me when I say that. I worked so hard at doing everything that I can, given the circumstances of my life, to care for this young lady only in the proper sort of way. Despite desperately wanting to, I never even asked this young lady out on a date.

My conscience kept eating at me and I repressed the spirit. To forget about this special lady, I started going out on dates with other ladies that I met in other settings. I never did anything wrong on any of the dates, but my spirit kept gnawing at me. Something told me that my life would never be at ease until this young lady knew that I cared for her.

I stopped going out on dates and most of the people around me wondered if I was gay. Wearing velvet jackets (which I'm sure you've noticed, is my thing) in the Midwest didn't help my case either. Please forgive my levity while I am trying to share something of this nature. I often use humor as a defense mechanism to keep me sane.

I tried to be brave, put on a bold face and treat this young lady only as a sister in Christ. But a few days ago, I had my first serious attack. I was on my knees blubbering like a fool and asking the Lord to show me mercy and grace. I realize that I wanted to make a confession, I want to come clean and come to grips that I cared for this young lady not just as a sister in Christ but that I cared more for her. I want her to know that I am more than willing to care for her with my actions what I am struggling to express in my words. I want her to know that I will be there for her. I will be her servant and do everything in my power forever and ever to make her happy.

The young lady, I should tell you, Piper, is my better in every respect. She is superior to me in every conceivable sense of the term. You are probably wondering who this young lady is. Piper, I must tell you that you know the name of this young lady. This young lady is you.

    Piper jolts up from her chair like she's just remembered a missed appointment. She sprints to the nearest bathroom, barely making it in time to empty the contents of her stomach. She can't remember the last time she retched.

    It's not until her stomach is completely emptied that she stops, her arms draped over the cold porcelain bowl. After she's sure she's done, she slowly rises to her feet. Her body has lost control of itself as her amygdala fires into overdrive, and she shakes uncontrollably from head to toe.

    She wraps her arms around her body, offering herself a sliver of comfort as she robotically walks back to her desk. The last thing she wants to do is read another word from this deranged human formerly known as her professor, but she can't stop herself.

It is you, Piper, who has been the gem of my life, my island of sanity in the ocean of my abyss. I promise you that I will never give my heart away to anybody else who walks through the door of my classroom ever in my life. Never, I promise. Not even in my thought life.

Piper, I must confess that I care about you. Give me the chance to care for you with my actions, and I will be the happiest man in the world. If you want me in your life, I will be there for you. I pray that you will let me know so that I can start planning our first official date.

Thank you so much for being gracious and reading this letter. My spirit is relieved.

Always, your servant in Christ,
Hoover

Piper's thoughts are deafened by the thumping in her chest. *What on earth is happening?*

Sweat pools under her arms. She grasps her mouse with fumbling fingers and clicks back. *Refresh. Refresh.*

The email is still there.

She reaches for her phone with trembling hands and hits "Home."

It rings...and rings...

Come on, answer.

Her mom picks up.

"Hey, Mom, can I talk to Dad? I need to talk to him!" she shouts, not even realizing it.

"Is everything okay?" her mom asks, concern thick in her voice.

"Honestly, no...I just really need to talk to Dad. Now, Mom, I need to talk to him now. Is he there?" Piper hears her call out, "JOHN!"

"Piper, are you okay? What's up?" Her dad's voice cuts in. Piper never calls and immediately asks for him, hence everyone's confusion.

"Dad, something awful just happened," Piper says between shallow breaths. "I don't know what to do. I need your help."

"Piper, are you okay? What's going on?" His voice escalates, worry muddling his tone.

"I just got a really disturbing…really weird email. From one of my, um…from one of my professors. He just confessed he's in love with me. In the creepiest way possible."

Tears start falling, sliding down her cheeks and into the air, steady as rainfall.

"Dad? Did you hear me? I don't know what to do…I'm freaking out. I mean, I have my last final tomorrow…and it's a Comm final. What if he sees me?! I promise you, I promise you I don't like him. I've never even hinted at…"

Piper's words trail off, her mind cycling through a Rolodex of classroom encounters, running through the classes she's taken with him. That first day of class he referenced, when she was new on campus and utterly lost looking for that room. How he was her internship leader. How she and her friends started a PR club, and he oversaw it.

She can picture his pasty, porcelain skin, his routine lineup of crushed velvet blazers, and can hear his weak, meek, raspy tone ringing in her ears. Bile rises and burns the back of her throat, and she gags.

"Can you send me the email so I can read it and have some context for how concerned we need to be?"

"Yeah, I just sent it to you."

"Okay, got it. Just hang on here with me while I read it."

Piper is a mess of snot, sniffles, and broken breaths.

A few minutes pass…painstakingly long ones.

"Piper, you there?" Her dad's voice cuts back in.

"Yeah, Dad, I'm here." Clearly, she's a heavy-breathing, blubbering mess.

"Piper, I'm going to handle this. I'm calling the college administration first thing tomorrow to get to the bottom of this, to keep him away from you, and to make sure you're safe. You don't need to worry about a thing. We're going to make sure this creep is nowhere near you. I've got this. I will protect you."

"Please, please don't do anything crazy. I don't want this getting out around school. I just want to get through my last final exam, and then we can figure out what's next. I can't even think about this until it's over."

Yet in reality, I am so disgusted...this is all-consuming.

She knows her dad. He's the equivalent of a possessive black bear when it comes to stuff like this. Nobody messes with his daughters, and clearly the line was crossed.

"Okay, Piper, I hear you. Just trust me and let me handle it. I know it's hard, but this is the last thing you need to be worrying about. I'll be praying for you and your final exam. If you want to talk about this at any time tonight, just call. We're here — always. You know that."

"Thanks, Dad. I'll try not to obsess over this, but, I mean, it's wreaking havoc on my mind. Gah, I just don't get it. Why would he ever send this to me? He's a socially awkward teacher...not even a remote hint I could ever be into him. And now I come to find out he's been a freaking closet creep this whole time?!"

"It's normal to be feeling this way, Piper. That's part of the process when life throws a curveball at you unexpectedly like this." He takes a deep breath. "I don't know what to say other than I'm really sorry you received this. I'll do anything to protect you and will make sure it's handled. We love you."

"Thanks. I love you too." Piper ends the call and just sits, staring off into space.

After more time has passed than she realizes, she gets up from her desk and heads downstairs. Much to her relief, she sees Laura's car out the front window, which means she must be home. She knocks on her bedroom door.

"Come in!" Laura calls cheerily. She's changing out of her work clothes, her back to Piper. "I can't wait to tell you about the day I've had at the office. Let me tell you, work life is not as glamorous as I thought..." Laura pulls on an oversized T-shirt to match her baggy home sweats, then turns to face Piper. "Oh my gosh, are you okay?! Forget about my day, what in the heck is going on with you?"

"I...I...I don't really know where to start. It's a nightmare, Laura. You can't make this up."

"Okay...start at the beginning of whatever this situation is so I can follow."

"Just — read this," Piper says, handing Laura her laptop with the email open, taking up the whole screen.

Laura reads, her eyes bulging, lips pursing, and head shaking as if on rotation. "I know this may sound dense, but this is from Professor Hoover, as in the professor we've taken countless classes with to get A's and started a PR club with. That Professor Hoover? The socially awkward, shoulders-hunched dude who sits alone and stares off into dreamland in the cafeteria?"

"Yes, yes, and yes. That's the one. The one it feels like we know so well, and yet don't know at all. I am freaking out, Laura. I mean, what if I see him? I have my last final tomorrow." Piper closes her computer. "What on earth made him think I would ever, in a million years, be remotely interested in him? I am so grossed out and feel so dirty and disgusting, I can't even explain it. I want to clean myself of this, and I don't know how."

"I hate to say it, but in my core, I feel like I knew he was a creep. I just need a second to wrap my mind around this." Laura throws herself back on the bed. "What is he thinking? Piper, I am so sorry he sent you this messed-up, freakishly weird email."

She pauses, processing everything, before continuing, "As if you'd ever give him a chance?! Okay, let's game-plan. What are you going to do now?"

"Ugh, I don't know. I was trying to study, but now that's a lost cause. I can't think of anything but this. I called my dad, and he's going to call administration tomorrow to try to help me get some sort of protection from Hoover's obsession. I'm hoping they'll take some kind of action, maybe even fire him, so this doesn't become anything bigger than it needs to be."

"That's great. I think that's a great plan," Laura says, filing one of her light pink, manicured nails. "So really, our goal right now is to get your mind off this. No one better to help you with that than me." She laughs. "I haven't eaten dinner yet, and I was legitimately going to have cereal because I'm exhausted. Safe to say you're drained from being hit with that train wreck. Okay, I'm making the call. We're having Life cereal, whipping out the Peanut Butter M&Ms, and binging *Sex and the City*. What do you think?"

"Yes, please. Thanks for taking charge. My brain is mush. That sounds perfect."

The girls head downstairs and get to work pouring two heaping bowls of cereal, drowning the sugared squares in milk before cozying up on the couch.

Despite trying her best to get lost in the show and Carrie Bradshaw's enviable fashion choices, Piper's brain is a mishmash of racing thoughts. It's stuck in a loop, replaying encounters, emails, and run-ins. The time he asked her to lunch to discuss a project, and she felt weird and said no. The time he invited a handful of Comm students to his apartment for a holiday gathering (also a no). The time he offered to give her his old couch and treadmill. The time she was walking from her apartment to class and felt like someone was following her and turned around to see him. The time she was studying alone in the library, and he asked if he could share her table.

And the time she baked him cookies to say thanks for overseeing her internship...*Oh my gosh, what if that's what made him come on to me? Was it the stupid, overdone cookies I baked?*

She replays every instance, realizing how these normal, yet not-so-normal, professor-student encounters had been coming from such a gross place in his mind. She feels tainted by the pictures he painted with his words. And confused. *Did I bring this upon myself?* She's certain she didn't. She never did anything to mislead him.

Yet how is she here?

7

PROFESSOR HOOVER

Professor Hoover typically gets ready in utter silence, focused on the mission at hand or with *Fox News* murmuring in the background. Not today. Today, he's blaring music throughout his entire one-bedroom apartment. He started with the Beatles, moved on to Frank Sinatra, and now he's jamming out to "I'm A Believer."

With confession comes freedom, and he's never felt more liberated or more hopeful.

He puts on his usual go-to black slacks but, on second thought, decides to switch things up. He changes into a pair of cream linen slacks. He's only ever worn them once before, and that day was a great one, so it just feels right. *When she approaches me, I want to be memorable*, he thinks.

He puts on a crisp white button-down shirt, tucks it in, and layers his dark-as-night navy crushed-velvet blazer on top.

Not usually one to do his hair, today he warms some pomade between his fingertips and makes a few passes through it until he looks polished. He sprays on two squirts of musty cologne, one on his neck and one on his wrist, then kicks his feet together with a spin.

He remembers leaving some spare change in his pants from the day before and pauses to find it. He opens the cookie jar on his counter and tosses in $1.83. He smiles, satisfied to see how far he's come since starting to save his daily change. Hoover's a cash guy. While most people seem to despise change, the more the merrier for him.

He found the cookie jar about a year ago while walking through HomeGoods and knew he had to have it the second he laid eyes on it. He's been saving for a diamond ring in preparation for the future that lies before him. The jar is half full, which means the time is getting near.

He guzzles the last of his coffee, unbothered by the way the chipped mug scratches his lip, and calls it good.

"Today is going to be a great day! Piper, I can't wait until you are all mine. I'm going to make you the happiest woman to walk this planet," he says aloud, winking at himself in the mirror before grabbing his worn caramel leather briefcase and shutting his apartment door.

8

IT'S HANDLED

Piper stirs, and even for an early bird, she can tell it's early.

She pats the alternating shiny-and-matte stripes of her golden comforter until her fingers find her phone.

4:30 a.m. Great.

She blinks away the last bits of sleep, and her mind takes off at a full sprint, replaying the email she received, just as it did through every hour of her restless night.

Her imagination won't stop creating scenarios — bumping into Hoover on her way to her last Comm final; him confronting her, demanding an answer to his email. In one, he got down on one knee, pleading for a chance, humiliating her in front of onlookers. In another, she was trying to focus on her exam when her name blared over the loudspeaker ordering her to report to Hoover's office.

Each nightmare was more vivid and more unbearable than the last.

Piper forces herself to get out of bed. She foregoes her usual run to the gym for a living room Jillian Michaels workout video. Anything to avoid a potential run-in with Hoover. It's no surprise that Laura is still asleep. Like most people, she doesn't start work for a few hours.

Piper takes an extended shower, the water scalding but therapeutic. She'd planned to wash and style her hair today but, on second thought, doesn't have the energy. Besides, she wants to look anything *but* cute.

She gets ready haphazardly with a few swipes of concealer and mascara. She gives her roots a quick spray of dry shampoo, then runs a brush through her warm, blonde hair.

She throws on some clothes and walks with her head down toward her last final exam.

It isn't until she's halfway to the Writing and Communications Center that the irony of her red-and-white striped thermal shirt hits her. She's a walking *Where's Waldo,* and all she can do is pray her seeker doesn't spot her.

Piper texts her dad.

> Headed into my last final. Let's chat after.
> Love you.

She glances at her watch. It was a gift from her grandma for her high school graduation. Each of the grandkids was presented with a TAG Heuer watch on their special day. The one Piper picked out is timeless, with a silver band and a mother-of-pearl face. 9:00 a.m. on the dot.

She puts her phone on mute. As she walks into the WCC, she finds herself torn between scanning the hallways and staring at the ground. She settles on making a beeline for her classroom and tries not to make eye contact with anyone or anything.

"Piper."

She thinks she hears someone call her name from a distance. Her heart races, and a chill slithers down her spine. She cautiously looks up but doesn't see anyone. Her heart momentarily settles. *I need to chill out. The fact that I'm hearing things is next level.*

"Piper."

She hears it again and quickens her pace. This time, she's positive someone just called her name.

"Piper, hey there."

Piper slowly lifts her eyes from the ground and comes to an abrupt halt at the sight of velvet. *Oh no, it's happening,* she thinks. The saliva in her mouth disappears, and blood rushes to her cheeks, a trait she despises about herself.

"Hello," Piper says quietly, her brain desperately trying to formulate a strategy. She lands on only one conclusion: pretend she hasn't read the email. She clears her throat. "Hello, Professor Hoover. If you'll excuse me, I'm just on my way to my last final." She gives him a tight-lipped smile.

"Oh, err — okay." He pauses. "Say, did you, um...did you... have you checked your email recently?"

Piper's heart slams in her chest so hard it physically aches. *Get out as fast as you can,* she thinks, trying to play it cool so as not to create a scene. "My email? No, I haven't. I mean, I haven't since...since yesterday morning. Just been so focused on studying, as you can imagine," she lies, looking away.

"Right on, that makes sense. I sent you an email, so let's connect on it after your final."

"Oh, okay. Yeah, I'll take a look."

Despite feeling as if her feet are cemented to the floor, she walks away. Just like that.

She can faintly hear him call out, "Bye, Piper!"

Piper steps into the nearest women's restroom and locks herself in a stall. She rests her forehead against the frigid metal door, squeezes her eyelids shut, and tries to control her shallow breathing. *My nightmare just came true. What in the hell was that?*

She finds herself hyperventilating and forces deep breaths

in, holding the air between each inhale and exhale. *I can do hard things,* she reminds herself. *I will get through this.*

She fights back the tears that threaten to fall and unlocks the door.

My last final exam. Here we go.

Piper quietly takes her seat in the classroom, closes her eyes, and fills her lungs to the brim. *I've got this.*

Her heart races like a staccato beat, and she struggles to steady herself as her mind replays every angle of their interaction.

Her thoughts halt as Professor Lawrence, a short, stubby man with a full mustache and a shiny bald head, clears his throat to command the room.

"Congratulations, seniors," he says, projecting his voice like an engine's roar. "This should be, for most of you, your very last examination. While I'm sure you can't wait to race out of here to what some may consider freedom, I encourage you to take your time. Read each question slowly, and don't rush the writing portion."

He pauses, attempting to look each student in the eye, a process that takes far too long before continuing. "Without further ado, you may begin."

A hypothetical sixty-minute timer begins. Piper feels the weight of the pressure cooker she's been placed in, because while she normally tests well, her brain is nothing more than slush.

She finds herself rereading each question three or four times before mechanically penciling in the A, B, C, or D bubble below it. She doesn't even care if she gets them right. Suddenly, this grade feels as important as remembering what she ate for breakfast.

Piper decides to strip herself of the pressure of perfection and starts filling in bubbles faster, relying on intuition instead of what she knows to be true.

She skirts to the writing portion of the exam and is met with the following prompt:

Detail a communication technique you will apply from your Midland Communications rhetoric following graduation.

While Piper wants to go on a rant about why she can't possibly share this right now, given that her communications professor is the very one who has robbed her of wanting to apply anything from Midland to the rest of her life, she settles on writing about how the power of knowing your target demographic can shape your message and win your audience.

Piper scribbles a full three paragraphs and calls it good. As soon as she writes the final period on her page, she gets up so abruptly that she draws attention from the students sitting around her. She offers an apologetic smile and proceeds to drop her paper on Professor Lawrence's desk.

"Good luck, Piper," he whispers, taking her by surprise and pulling back her jet-set pace. "You don't need it, but I'm excited to see you do great things."

"Thanks, Professor Lawrence. I appreciate it." Piper half-smiles and turns, never looking back.

After quietly closing the door behind her, Piper bolts out of the WCC so fast you'd think there was a prize for being first to finish.

She gasps for air when she slams open the double doors and takes a minute to just breathe and collect herself.

She pulls her phone from her pocket and is brought back to reality. She has a text from her dad.

> Call me when your final is over. No rush.

She calls him immediately, and he picks up on the first ring.

"Dad, hey, my final is done. But I saw him. Before my final. It was terrifying. I need to get out of here. I feel like we need to do something, though. What am I supposed to do?"

"Hey, Piper. I'm actually here, at Midland. Sitting outside the provost's office as we speak."

"Wait, what? The who?"

Her dad goes on, "I'm sure we're in the same boat. I couldn't sleep and hit the road at 5:30 this morning. I called the administration on my way and explained I had a student emergency that needed immediate attention until I finally got the name of who we need to talk to — Provost Bryce Jones.

"When I got here, I asked around until I was directed to where his office is located, and now here I am, sitting outside it. I've been here for about an hour and a half. His assistant said he's booked for the day and that I needed to make an appointment, but I told her I needed to speak with him about a drop-dead serious matter involving a professor and my daughter and that it was going to happen today.

"I told her I was happy to wait, that I didn't care how long it takes. I don't care if it takes days…I'm not leaving until I speak with the provost. So that's where I'm at, Piper.

"I know you didn't want me to take any action without you knowing, but I'm your dad. I love you, and it's my job to protect you. I need to know this matter is going to be addressed…and that Professor Whatever-His-Name-Is leaves you alone and gets the message loud and clear."

A few stray tears start to glide down Piper's cheeks and she wipes them away. "Thank you, Dad. Thanks for being here with me. Where can I meet you?"

"Meet me on the second floor of the Student Center. You don't have to sit here and wait with me. I'm sure you have more exciting things to do, but it would be great to give you a hug and see your face."

"Of course. I'm on my way." Piper quickens her pace. Relief floods her soul, knowing she's not alone in this and that her dad is here in person.

She briskly walks to the Student Center and up two flights

of stairs. She's breathless and starting to break a sweat as she rounds the corner and sees her dad sitting in a leather armchair. She can see the worry imprinted in his eyes as he makes eye contact with her and stands for a hug.

"I'm so sorry this happened to you, Piper. I'm just truly sorry," he says, enveloping her in his arms.

"It's okay, Dad. It's going to be fine," she says, trying to reassure them both.

Just then, they look up to see a mousy-looking woman with a brown bob, a long blue jersey dress, and black flats open the door in front of them.

"Provost Jones will see you now."

Piper and her dad exchange hopeful eyes.

They both stand and walk through the door into the office of Provost Bryce Jones. It's not a large room, but it's immaculate and meticulously arranged.

He stands from behind his desk, looking far too wiped for how early it is. His day isn't going to get any easier. His neatly coiffed silvery hair is starting to come undone, like the rest of him, and the front pieces are beginning to droop.

"John Hawthorne," Piper's dad says pointedly, returning an outstretched arm to shake.

"Hello, my name is Piper," she says, her tone just above a whisper, making only brief eye contact.

"How can I help you today?" Provost Jones asks expectantly.

Piper's dad plops a printout of the email on his desk. "This email is what I'd like to address. My daughter, a student at your institution, received this disgusting email from one of her professors, a person in a trusted position, last night. The night before her final college exam.

"As you can imagine, we've all been a wreck for the last fifteen hours. None of us have slept, and my daughter has been filled with fear as the recipient of such a note."

The provost looks down and skims the letter, his head

shaking in disbelief, his eyes ever so slightly widening as he reads the unwanted words now forever singed into Piper's mind.

"Mr. Hawthorne, Piper, I'm sorry you're dealing with this situation and for the stress it's caused you. Here's what I can tell you — had this email been sent this morning, after Piper's last final exam, there would be nothing I could do to help, because she would no longer be a student under our care.

"Because this was sent last night, when she was still technically a student, it's a violation of Joseph Hoover's contract and, therefore, an issue we'll address. I would like to hear Joseph's side of the story, to be fair. I'm going to request twenty-four hours to consult with my leadership team about next steps, and I'll loop back with you. Is that agreeable to you?"

"No, Bryce, no, that's not agreeable to me," John says, his voice raised. "Do you understand the severity of this situation? My daughter is fearful and scared, and this needs immediate attention — as in today. This professor needs to know that not only was this email unwanted by my daughter, it was inappropriate.

"He's in a position of leadership and trust, and this has gone far beyond what's acceptable. Your school prides itself on faith and excellence, and I expect this to be handled as such. Joseph needs to be fired. We expect nothing less."

"I understand your frustrations and concern, Mr. Hawthorne. I am, however, unable to make such decisions on my own and will need twenty-four hours to consult my team so we can come to a decision. There's nothing I can do between now and then, but I assure you, this will be handled appropriately. I can't say whether or not Professor Hoover will be fired, but we'll be in touch."

The provost stands, signaling that the meeting is over.

John rises, his irritation and disappointment unmistakable. "I'll be awaiting your call. If I don't hear from you in twenty-four hours, you're going to have an even bigger problem to deal with."

Provost Jones extends a hand for a shake, but John turns and walks out of the office. Piper quickly skirts after him.

"Piper, listen," her dad says quietly once they reach the hallway and he's had a moment to compose himself. "You should take it easy this weekend, lay low. I'm not saying you have anything to be worried about. I just think you should play it cool and avoid any chance of running into this Joseph fellow until we get some direction."

"Yeah, of course," she says genuinely. "I'm on the same page. Promise me...promise me you'll call me as soon as you hear from the provost?"

"Of course I will. You want to go take a minute and grab some lunch?" he asks.

"Yes. I'm starving."

The next twenty-four hours crawl by agonizingly slowly. Every time Piper's phone rings, she sprints to answer it, heart racing. She can only imagine the level of disappointment in her voice for whoever's on the other end.

That is, until her dad finally calls.

"Hello, Dad?" she answers quickly, sitting at her kitchen table and looking out at the backyard, grass so long it's almost embarrassing.

"Hi, Piper," he says, sounding wiped. "I just talked to Provost Jones. I don't have much information to share, but I promised you I'd call you first."

"Details, please. Tell me everything you can," she says, anxiously awaiting the scoop.

"The provost just called me and basically told me they're handling the situation. He wouldn't confirm if Joseph Hoover was being fired. In fact, he told me I wasn't showing any Christian compassion, that this man should be given a chance to make good on his mistakes. Can you believe that?

"Essentially, all he said he was allowed to tell me was that this Hoover guy is getting help and that you won't hear from him anymore. That's it."

The frustration in her dad's voice is tangible. Piper can only imagine how tense their conversation must have been.

"Well, that's not what I was hoping for either. It's actually crazy the more I think about it. My favorite English professor was fired this year for getting a divorce. Fired! His marriage, his personal business, which none of us even knew about, got him fired. Yet Hoover can be a total creep and continue to teach, and be a threat to me and girls all over campus? This is insane!"

"I'm sorry. Unfortunately, I don't think there's much else we can do," he says through gritted teeth.

"Thanks for going to bat for me. I appreciate it more than you know."

"Let's just keep in close touch," he says. "I don't need to know your every move, but let's check in once a day, just so we know you're doing okay."

"Deal."

Piper hangs up and takes a deep breath. It doesn't feel entirely behind her, but at least things seem to be moving in the right direction…as much as they can.

If nothing else, Hoover must have gotten the hint by now.

She hopes she's right.

9

PROFESSOR HOOVER
TWO YEARS LATER

Professor Hoover stands at the window of his newish studio apartment in Chicago's Gold Coast, watching people come and go from the building below bundled up head-to-toe. He'd specifically requested an east-facing unit for the view of the lakeshore, but in truth, all he cared about was having a direct line of sight to the building's entrance.

It's 7:40 a.m., the time Hoover predictably sits down at the round table in front of his bay window on weekdays to slowly enjoy his coffee and keep watch. He sees a blonde walk out the building's front doors, and his heart skips a beat.

No. Not her, he thinks to himself.

He checks his watch. Too early.

He's arranged his teaching schedule to start at ten and end at three thirty, just enough time to catch the train in and out of the city and still indulge his favorite routines: sipping coffee (or whiskey, depending on the hour), reading the newspaper cover to cover, and watching for Piper like a hawk circling its prey.

He pours another cup, quickly opens his apartment door to grab the newspaper, and darts back to his perch. *There she is.* He almost missed her, an utter disaster in his mind. It had happened once before, and the uncertainty of what she was doing threw off his entire day.

He stares, transfixed, taking in her every move — the way she brushes her hair over her shoulder, searches in her bag for sunglasses, and stares off toward Lake Michigan. The way she glides instead of stomps like every other morning commuter. She's wearing dress pants, flats, and a black, tailored, knee-length coat. *She must have meetings today,* he thinks, piecing together as much as he can from what he knows to be true. He's seen her in similar attire enough times to know she keeps a pair of heels in her bag, which she'll change into as she nears her office.

He watches her every move until she disappears from view. The rush of endorphins hits; his pulse steadies.

Like Groundhog Day, but in the best way possible, he settles in with his fresh cup of coffee and newspaper.

Exactly forty minutes until he has to leave, too.

They're both creatures of habit. One of the many things he adores about her.

10

TAKEN BACK

TWO YEARS LATER

The last two years have flown by in a blink. Piper has finally moved from the comfort of the Midland suburbs to bustling Chicago and into her very own studio apartment in a high-rise along the city's stunning Lake Shore Drive.

Her place is tiny but perfectly cozy for one, about the size of a cramped hotel room. A small section of floor tile defines the kitchen area, with a handful of cabinets and a narrow rectangular island. Her bed, of course, shares the space, but there's just enough room for a pint-sized couch to host a guest or at least create the illusion of separation.

Aside from being conveniently located within the city and just off her favorite running path overlooking Lake Michigan, another perk is that her building has a small commissary on the main level. What really sold her, however, is the twenty-four seven security, with a doorperson always on duty. While she's long recovered from Hoover's creepy email, she still wants that added measure of safety living alone.

Thankfully, Kate's PR agency has grown, and she too has

moved her office downtown to the city's River North neighborhood. Piper's commute is a breeze. To get to and from work, she walks a handful of blocks to the Red Line, takes it three stops to Grand, then walks four more blocks. She finds walking to be a therapeutic way to start and end her day.

Piper now leads Kate's hospitality division, a huge step for someone just two years out of college, but she can't bring herself to say no to any project that lands on her desk. As such, she's been gifted with more work and more responsibility. She wouldn't change it for the world, though her dating life is, well...quite non-existent.

Piper has begun to hone her PR specialty: restaurant and nightlife openings and events. She and her team throw parties where the who's who shows up to see and be seen; they land restaurants and swanky cocktail spots in the press; and they promote athletes and celebrities spotted dining at her clients' venues, after inviting them there and orchestrating the entire meal behind the scenes.

Pitching and coordinating live TV cooking demonstrations with chefs, as well as offering up clients as experts on the city's hottest culinary trends, are all part of a day's work. Over the past two years, she's become well networked and has learned to thrive in the fast-paced, no-nonsense world of drumming up news coverage.

Today, however, has been one of those less-than-ideal days, the kind where a client gets upset about how a headline is written and rips Piper a new one, as if it were her fault. The thing is, once a story is live, asking for a change that isn't fact-based is basically taboo, and a reporter definitely isn't going to rewrite it. Her client seemed to think otherwise, and Piper got the brunt of it.

She can't stop replaying their conversation in her mind during her commute home.

She gets off the Red Line at Clark and Division and trudges

up two flights of grimy steps, trying to avoid the smells of sweat and urine that inevitably waft by until the darkness of the underground merges with the fresh, cold, albeit smog-laden, air above.

She walks up to State Street, as she does every evening, and is met with an intersection of choice. To the left — home. To the right — countless options. But on this particular evening, a manicure is beckoning her. It's been a long week, and there's no better way to unwind.

She pivots right, and her leisurely walk is abruptly interrupted in front of Barnes & Noble. She freezes instinctively for a moment to take in her surroundings. She can't tell if it's her gut intuition or just pure adrenaline, but her eyes laser-focus on an unmistakable face.

He's hiding behind a wide-spread *Wall Street Journal*. She couldn't mistake those pasty, divot-covered cheeks, beady eyes, or that hunched posture even if she tried.

Her heart slams against her ribs, screaming for oxygen, her brain suffocating for lack of understanding. She looks away as quickly as her eyes had caught on his shiny forehead. Turning her head, she cranes it east, toward Lake Michigan.

She hasn't seen him since the day she bumped into him on her way to her last final exam. Piper is sure he didn't see her now.

But what if he saw me? Would a sighting reignite his obsession? Was this a chance encounter or a ritual he's been practicing all along without me knowing?

Memories rush at her in a violent blur, pinballing their way through her head as her feet remain frozen in place, superglued to the cement. Each memory triggered by that fear-filled, heebie-jeebie feeling deep in her core.

She's so distracted that she begins walking home on autopilot, dodging cars turning right on red through the crosswalk.

Her body moves, but her mind is elsewhere. She reaches for her phone to call her mom.

Her mom answers on the third ring.

"Mom, you will never believe what just happened." Piper doesn't even wait for her to get a word in. "I just got off the L on my way home, like I do every day after work, and I'm standing at the corner of State and Division when I see none other than *Hoover* sitting in the window of Barnes & Noble, reading a newspaper. How insane is that?!"

"Wait a minute. Did he see you? Where are you now? Did you make eye contact?" Her mom spitfires the questions in rapid succession.

"Mom, no, he didn't see me. I'm one hundred percent positive he didn't see me. I was on my way to get my nails done, but…" She pauses, remembering that's what she'd been doing. "Now I'm just walking home. I'm so creeped out, even if he didn't see me. I mean, what are the chances of that, Mom?! Do you think I should be concerned?" Her tone begs for reassurance.

"If he didn't see you, which it sounds like you're positive he didn't, right? Then I think you're fine. I know I usually say there are no such things as coincidences, but this I actually do think is a random sighting."

Okay, phew. Piper feels her chest release a huge breath, freeing the pent-up adrenaline racing through her veins.

"I'm just going to go home and relax. Today was a long day before this even happened. We're working on the opening plan for *The Eiffel*, that new French restaurant and upstairs club I was telling you about. It's exciting, but the bar is so high and our clients are so tense, my brain is fried. I'll call you tomorrow, okay?"

"Okay, sounds good. You know I like to check in, just to make sure you're safe and well. So keep me posted on how you're doing. Love you."

"Love you too," she says. *Click.*

Piper changes her mind. She unlocks her phone and texts her best friend and colleague, Chloe.

> SOS. I just saw HIM. By him, I mean my creepy professor, Hoover. Are you free for a debrief?

Chloe replies right away.

> OMG!!! Yes, free. Let's meet. Bar Taco in 10?

> See you there.

Chloe and Piper both live in the Gold Coast, and Bar Taco is their go-to spot to meet up. It's convenient, they serve the best guacamole, and their skinny margaritas don't taste so skinny.

Piper turns and doubles back the way she just came, but walks four extra blocks to avoid Barnes & Noble and any potential run-in with Hoover. Better to have peace of mind than risk bringing his attention back to her.

When Piper steps into Bar Taco, the familiar hum of conversation and the smell of lime and sizzling fajitas hit her all at once. She spots Chloe at a high-top table near the window.

Chloe waves the second she sees her. "I already ordered you the usual. Tell me everything."

Chloe is preppy, composed, and always put together. A platinum blonde who exudes style and effortless class.

"Okay, you can't make this up. I wish you could, because I can't believe this is resurfacing after two years. I got off the L at Clark and Division like usual, walked to the corner, and there he was, my creepy old professor, sitting in the window of Barnes & Noble reading a newspaper."

"I'm not trying to question you, but you're one hundred percent sure it's him?" Chloe asks, eyebrows raised.

"Yes, it's him. Here, let me Google a photo real quick. This isn't someone you'd mistake." Piper pulls up the first image that appears on the college's faculty page. It's Hoover, wearing his signature navy velvet blazer with a black button-down underneath. His wispy dark hair is brushed to one side so that it looks done, but really all you see is scalp. His eyes bulge, and his half-smile reveals yellow-tinged, slightly crooked teeth.

"Okay, yes," Chloe says, leaning in. "I see what you mean. Ugh. I just wish it wasn't so. But you can't argue with that. Also, not to make light of this, but how on earth did he ever think he remotely had a chance with you?"

"I know, it's all just ick." Piper laughs in spite of herself, surprised as her cocktail straw hits dry ground. "Okay, that margarita went down way too smooth."

Their server appears right on cue. "Another round?" she asks, smiling knowingly.

"Yes, keep them coming," Chloe giggles.

"Okay, tell me something about your life. I can't talk work, and my current news is equally disturbing and depressing," Piper says.

"Okay, well, I haven't mentioned it yet, but...I just joined that new dating app, Tinder," Chloe admits, beaming. "I've got to mix things up. I can't date a client, I'm not dating anyone from high school, and it's just too hard to meet people fortuitously."

"*Yesssss*! I'm so excited for you. Show me this app. I've heard of it, but how does it work? Is this something I need to join?"

"Piper, yes. You need something going on in your life outside of work. Just download the app, let's set up your profile, and you can decide tomorrow morning if you want to delete it."

"Deal."

An hour, a third margarita, and two baskets of chips later,

the girls have gotten completely lost in judging guys on the app. They've established a system: if someone is hot (a ten) but has a cheesy profile, it's a no (swipe left). If someone is average (a six or seven) but has a great job, it's a yes (swipe right). And if someone's an eight with an average job, that's also a yes. Suffice it to say, Piper's going to have a lot of messages to catch up on in the morning.

"Okay, it's late. Ten is way after my bedtime, let's be honest. I may regret all of this tomorrow, but thanks for taking my mind off things," Piper says, standing and grabbing her bag.

"Piper, this is the least I can do. We're in this together. Let's share a cab home so I know you're safe."

Chloe hails a taxi, and the girls ride home in silence, each lost in her own thoughts, trying to make light of the night. When they reach Piper's apartment complex at Lake Shore Drive Residences, she exhales a sigh of relief.

"Thanks again. See you bright and early." Piper gives Chloe's hand a squeeze before climbing out. She stumbles slightly, catching herself against the door before closing it. Once steady, she glances over both shoulders, scanning the quiet street.

Inside, she nods to the doorman and heads for the elevator. She presses *Up*, then *18*. The soft hum of the lift and the faint buzz in her head from the drinks make her feel both tired and strangely alert.

When she steps into her apartment, the weight of the day hits her. She rests her forehead against the cool steel of the door and closes her eyes.

Something tugs at her chest, a cocktail of emotions she can't quite name. *Am I nervous right now?* she wonders, changing into sweats and tossing her bag aside. *Why am I so on edge? Sure, I saw Hoover, but he didn't see me. Am I...dare I admit it...scared? I have nothing to be afraid of.*

She curls up on her couch, gazing out at Lake Michigan, its

inky expanse spotted with city lights like stars scattered across water. Usually, it calms her. Tonight, it doesn't.

Piper closes her eyes and whispers, "Lord, calm my heart. I'm scared, but I don't want to be. You are the ultimate protector. Please grant me the peace that surpasses all understanding that can only come from You. May I feel Your presence in this moment and know it is You, and only You, who watches over me."

11

PROFESSOR HOOVER

Professor Hoover looks out over Lake Michigan and feels a pang in his chest, almost like an elephant has abruptly taken a seat on it. He gulps for air, and his heart sprints like someone racing a 100-meter dash. He's trying to pinpoint what's causing it, even though, in his subconscious, he knows.

He's tried to tuck away that one thing that brings him guilt, the thing he stuffs way down into the depths of past memories that shall never be retrieved.

He tracks Piper's every move.

That, in and of itself, isn't what he feels guilty about. No, what he's doing is necessary, essential for her well-being. So he can take care of her if something happens, protect her as he watches from afar.

He's beginning to realize he was sent to do this, his life's mission, if you will, and tracking her is simply part of the job.

He tries not to take advantage of knowing her whereabouts. Has there been the occasional time when he's done a drive-by at a bar's closing time when she hasn't come home yet? Sure. Actually, he has developed the habit of meticulously tracking her whereabouts on weekends. And maybe he has a habit of waiting in the lobby at a dark corner table, dressed incognito if she stays out past midnight. But that's to make sure she's safe and making pure choices.

There was the one time she came home with some spiffy-looking guy at 3 a.m. It took everything within Hoover not to confront him...or punch him. He promised himself he wouldn't slip up like that again.

The truth is, once he came face-to-face with his feelings for Piper way back when, he knew he couldn't let her go. She was something special. And special things are to be cherished. And so, before he admitted his feelings to her in that email, he downloaded an app on her phone so that he could track her.

That is what he feels guilty about, for opening her phone and going through her stuff without her knowing. All he wants is open communication someday, and this feels like the wrong start, which pains him.

Hoover chuckles, reminiscing back on that day. During the last final exam she took from him, he required all students to give up their phones. He passed a basket around, and in they went. Hoover sat in the back of the classroom during the examination, and as he suspected, darling Piper was so trusting she didn't even have a passcode on her phone. And just like that, a sweet beginning of Hoover knowing her whereabouts blossomed, giving him peace of mind and a new life mission: to win her over. By the grace of God, she hasn't yet gotten a new phone, which causes Hoover anxiety just thinking about when that day comes.

He stares at the glow of his three massive computer screens, holding his breath as the moving dot labeled *Piper,* in what he assumes is a taxi, makes the final turns home.

Thanks for being a good girl tonight, my sweet Piper. We both need a good night's sleep, my darling.

His timing exact, Hoover races to the window, night-vision

binoculars in hand. He lifts them to his eyes just as a taxi pulls into the building's turnabout. A blonde stumbles out, looking a bit tipsy, which is always a little disappointing. She's younger than he is, after all. He can't expect her not to have any fun.

Hoover's mind settles as he watches her disappear into the lobby beneath him. He's finally regaining his confidence to make another move. He just needs the right moment to show itself.

12
WORK TRIP

Piper yawns as she waits in line at airport security. It doesn't matter how early you arrive or what day of the week it is, Chicago O'Hare Airport is always mayhem. She looks over as Kate scrolls through the emails she accumulated overnight.

The two of them, Blondie and Rouge, as they affectionately call themselves, are headed to Los Angeles to meet with a restaurant client who wants to throw a party uniting Chicago celebrities in LA. Piper lives for stuff like this, mixing up her day-to-day and traveling to sunnier parts of the country.

They make it through security with their carry-on bags and head to their gate, B32.

"Want to grab a mag on the way?" Kate asks, eyeing a newsstand.

"Say no more." Piper veers to the side and enters Hudson News. She grabs a copy of *Us Weekly*, *People*, and *Women's Health* and pays with her work AMEX, another perk of work trips.

A bag of gummy worms and two vanilla Starbucks lattes later, they sit at their gate waiting to be called to board.

Piper can't shake the feeling that she's left something behind, and she racks her brain for what it might be. *Underwear, shoes, pajamas, cute outfits, heels, workout clothes, gym shoes, makeup, curling iron, toothbrush — I've got it all.* She starts to think through a shortlist of what she forgot to do before leaving her apartment that morning. *I have my curling iron, so I definitely didn't leave it plugged in. I locked my door. Wait, did I lock my door?* Piper pictures her final steps. *I'm sure I locked my door. Huh.* She brushes off the feeling and chalks it up to being an overprepared Type A personality. She just can't help it.

Finally, a flight attendant calls the attention of all "A" passengers, and Piper and Kate take their place in line.

With a 6 a.m. flight, the duo both agreed to wear comfy leggings and pack dresses to change into at LAX. Regardless, they still look chic with manicured nails, full makeup, and designer Chanel bags. Kate has fully taken Piper under her wing, and Piper has gladly expanded her designer horizons to fit the bill.

Piper follows Kate onto the plane, and they sit next to one another in row 10, seats A and B.

"You do whatever you want on this flight, Blondie. I'm going to get some beauty rest. I was up last night with two of my kids, and Lord knows I need it." With that, Rouge puts on a black silk sleep mask and is out.

Piper partially feels obligated to work, considering she's sitting next to Kate, but first, she cracks open *People* to catch up on the latest celebrity dirt.

An hour and a half later, Piper feels her head go limp as it slumps forward with a turbulent bump. She forces herself awake and opens up her laptop.

The pilot announces that they're about to make their final descent. *Perfect timing. At least I'll be working when Kate wakes up.*

The plane smoothly lands thirty minutes later, and Kate and Piper immediately turn on their phones.

Piper's first message is from Chloe.

> Were you expecting someone at work today? Some guy just stopped here asking for you… he said he's looking to open a club or something, and it was so flipping weird. Call me when you can.

Piper abruptly turns to Kate, her eyelids spread wide. The hair on her arms stands up straight as she stares off into the distance.

"Are you okay?" Kate asks. "You look like you just saw something awful. What's going on?"

"I need to get off this plane. Chloe. I need to call Chloe."

"Okay, all good. Listen, nothing we do is this important. As I always say, PR doesn't save lives."

"No, it's not that, it's…it's…I don't know what it is, but I need to find out."

Piper sprints off the plane, grabs Kate, and ducks into the nearest lactation pod for some peace and quiet.

"What on earth is going on that we need to be here of all places?" Kate says, confused.

Piper ignores her and dials Chloe.

"Tell me everything," Piper blurts the second Chloe picks up.

"Hi, hello, you make it to L.A. okay?"

"Spill it!" Piper yells, her heart pounding against her chest.

"Okay, this is what happened. At 8:30 a.m. on the very dot, someone buzzed up. Initially, we thought this was strange because no one had a meeting scheduled, and, well, it's 8:30 a.m., and we're all just arriving and trying to enjoy a hot minute with our coffee, as you know. We look on the monitor screen, and it's some tall, lanky white guy, so we assume it's Amazon. Lord knows they deliver at all hours of the day and night. Next thing we know, some dude walks onto the floor and asks for you, Piper. But it's like he knew you weren't here. I can't really explain it...like he asked for you but already anticipated we'd say you were on a work trip. While we were answering him, he was frantically looking around the office as if to pinpoint your desk on the open floor. And when he did, it's like he got off on knowing. Sorry, I don't have a better way of explaining it than this, but it was creepy. Like, I had goosebumps."

"Aaaaaaah!" Piper screams. "I don't want to make an assumption, but just tell me more. What did he say? What did he look like? I need more."

"Okay, after that insanely weird arrival, he proceeded to walk closer to your desk, and get this — he picked up the photo of your family and studied it. At this point, I stopped him and asked him what he was doing. Only then did he realize how weird he was acting, and it's like he became self-aware. He cleared his throat in this gross way, almost to buy himself time to get his thoughts together. He started very vaguely saying he was trying to open a new nightclub and was looking for PR support and thought you would be the best fit. Then he corrected himself and said he meant Harmon Consulting would be the best. But when we asked where the nightclub was, he had no info, no address, no concept...nothing. Which is why we were all like, *what in the hell is happening?* As for what he looks like...tall, lanky, thinning dark brown hair, deep-set brown eyes. Oh yeah, and he wore khaki pants and, like, some dark velvet-type jacket. Who wears that in March? I don't want to make any assumptions, Piper, but does this sound like..."

Piper cuts her off. "Yes, it's Hoover. There's no question. It's Hoover, and he's trying to...I don't know what he's trying to do. Great. What do I do now?"

"Okay, whoa, whoa, whoa," Kate interrupts. "This mother-f-er showed up at work this morning? Okay, I'm calling building security for one. For two, Chloe, you need to send an email to everyone on staff with a photo of him and make sure that they do not let him in again, under any circumstance. Number three, I don't have one, other than we've got you, Piper, and we won't let anything happen to you."

"Gah, okay, I think this is a good plan for starters. I just have to think through what else I need to do to make sure this doesn't happen again." Piper says, lacking confidence.

Why on earth would he show up to work? What if he shows up again and I'm there? What's going to happen to me? Piper's heart races.

"I hate to be the boss, but we have a meeting in thirty and we need to change and freshen up and get there. Chloe, make it happen, and let's talk later."

Piper hangs up and robotically goes through the motions of life, a shell of a human who knows just what to do and when. When to laugh, when to smile, when to connect with clients. She's gotten really good at pretending she's okay. She's physically present for their day of client planning, but mentally, not there at all. Her mind can't stop racing through the what-ifs, the whys, and the *what-the-hell-do-I-do-nexts*.

At dinner that night, Kate broaches the subject. "How are you doing, Blondie? Like, really, truly, how are you doing? You did great today. I just want to make sure you're feeling good after this morning, and knowing we're headed back tomorrow."

Piper offers a deep sigh. "I'm okay. I'm just confused and distracted and mentally ruminating about what on earth Hoover was doing and why he's back."

"Back? What do you mean by that? Maybe today was just a fluke, weird thing, and you won't see him again."

"I would love it if that were the case," Piper admits. "I don't want to be naïve about this. I want to assume the best, of course. It's just...I saw him last month, Kate. And now this? I have a bad gut feeling. I'm trying to justify these sightings, but it's becoming a little much to be just a coincidence."

Piper doesn't want to say what she's really thinking out loud and give life to what she fears is true.

I'm terrified Hoover is intentionally following me. How else would he know my whereabouts? Is there such a thing as a coincidence to this extent? I don't see him for two years and suddenly, he's there. I think he's stalking my every move.

Piper stops herself before her thoughts get the best of her.

"Wait, what? Why didn't you tell me? Spill it."

"Well, for one, you're really busy. And for two, because I hate giving an ounce of attention to him. Ugh, okay…I was on my commute home, taking the normal route I take every night after work. I got off the L at Clark and Division, and there he was, sitting in the window of Barnes & Noble reading a freaking newspaper. He didn't see me, though. I know he didn't. I haven't been too worried about it. But now this…this is just throwing me off. Clearly not a coincidence, so what is it then?"

"Gosh, Piper, I'm so sorry. I didn't even know. I'm sure you've been worrying about this literally all day." Kate takes a sip of her white wine. "Okay, let's all be on guard. Our office is being vigilant. You can continue to be hyper-aware of your surroundings. Let's let things settle and see how this plays out. And if it makes you feel better, I will happily file a police report or do whatever you need to support you."

"Thanks, Rouge. I mean it. I really appreciate it. It's complicated, because what would we even file a police report for… seeing someone? There's nothing tangible I can report. It's like he knows how to play the game and skirt around it."

Piper pauses, deep in thought.

"I never would've guessed that the day we met, when I was wearing slacks and a button-down, we'd end up here."

Piper pictures how clueless she was, showing up dressed like she was interviewing to be a bank teller. Kate laughs.

Piper laughs too, even though it feels forced, because deep

inside, her gut is whispering that watching her back won't be enough to keep Hoover's pursuit at bay.

13

PROFESSOR HOOVER

Professor Hoover leaves the offices of Harmon Consulting with a sense of accomplishment. He was having a really difficult time not knowing Piper's whereabouts at work and just needed to confirm a few things to calm his mental space.

He feels adrenaline pulse through his veins, causing him to triumphantly flex his scrawny forearms. "I just wish I had been more prepared," he mumbles to himself. Normally, he'd spend days preparing for an encounter like this...plotting every detail, rehearsing every move. But this morning unfolded on a whim. When he saw her wheel a suitcase out of their apartment complex and hail a taxi, instinct overruled logic. He knew he had to seize the moment.

He reflects on his interactions at Piper's office while rolling her bubblegum-pink gel pen back and forth between his palms. Stealing it from her desk was nothing short of thrilling. Piper's colleagues were so dumbfounded when he picked up her family's photograph, they didn't even see him slide her pen into his pocket.

His only regret was when the stark blonde pointedly asked

about his nightclub concept and location, and the whole blah, blah of it, that he was so thrown off it put him at a loss for words. That, and he was distracted, trying to drink in as much of Piper's presence as he could. She wasn't there today, of course, but touches of her were — her folders neatly arranged on her desk, her blue Post-its with scribbled notes, a tan sweater left behind, all remnants of her. What he really wanted to do was pick up that sweater and hold it up to his nose and breathe in her scent, or sit in her chair and pretend to be her for a few minutes. Thank God he stopped at picking up her photograph and stealing her pen. The desires of his heart, coupled with his wild imagination, almost got the best of him.

Now what? The thought pounds in his head. *It's time she remembers who we are.* He needs to be closer, close enough that she can't ignore him. *Piper Hawthorne will want me. She has to. We're bound, the two of us.* He feels his pulse quicken. *I'll make sure she sees it. I'll make myself impossible to forget.*

14

NOTICE ME

Piper is sprinting to finish getting ready for a night out. She has girlfriends coming over to pregame before they all head to a birthday party for a guy she only vaguely knows. The CliffsNotes she's been given by Chloe — his name is Ryan, he's in finance, and he's ridiculously attractive. Chloe was friends with his roommate in college, and when you move to the city, one way or another, everyone reconnects.

Typically fit with indecision, Piper lands on a classic mini black dress with spaghetti straps and nude high-heeled pumps. Spring is flirting with the city and she's all in. She exudes sexy sophistication and is glad all her working out pays off once in a while. She brushes one dash of shimmery golden shadow on each eyelid, swipes a final coat of mascara, and applies soft coral lipstick.

Her cell phone rings, and she presses 1, notifying the building doorperson her guests can be sent up. Per usual, she's ready just in time.

Without even waiting for a knock, Piper opens the door. "Hi, hi, hi!" she shouts, giving hugs and side-cheek kisses to Chloe and Emily.

Piper grabs three wineglasses without even asking what the girls want to drink. They're typically on the same page that wine goes with every occasion. Three generous pours later, she hands them out and clinks a resounding cheers.

"I can't remember if I mentioned, but Ryan is newly single. You know, the hot guy whose birthday party we're going to. He's a catch if anyone is interested in exploring that situation," Chloe says between sips.

Piper purses her lips, and the corners of her eyes crinkle. "I mean, if something were to happen, I certainly wouldn't object," she laughs.

Piper has a three-date-max policy. She'll go out with someone up to three times before deciding whether it has potential. Any more than that, and a formal breakup conversation is required. Three dates or fewer, though, still fall safely within the confrontation-free zone.

"Emily, what's the latest with you and Tom?" Chloe is typically one to dig right into the juicy details.

Emily and Chloe are childhood family friends turned grown-up best friends. They're similar in that they both have fun, outgoing, direct personalities, will do anything to help a friend, and exude elegance and grace.

"Oh, you know, just stuck on the on-again, off-again train. Currently we're 'off,' and honestly, I don't even know what I want aside from space and time to figure my life out. Aka, Ryan is all yours, Piper."

Piper watches Emily, trying to decipher the earnestness in her confession. She feels like it's her turn to share something. "The truth is, I've been single for longer than I'd care to admit, have no potential guys in my life, and at this point, feel like I'm on track to be married to my job. Every time I go on a date, there's something that throws me off. The last guy did this laugh thing that I couldn't get past. Shallow, sure, but dealbreaker. The one before that had a drinking problem, and the guy before that was hot as heck, but his personality was the equivalent of talking to a cardboard box. The similar thread in all these instances is me. Maybe I'm the problem," Piper says, half-joking.

"There are instances where 'it's not you, it's me,' but trust me, you are not that. You just haven't met the right guy. That's a real thing. Plus, it's good you're so picky," Emily admits.

"I've actually been on a handful of dates recently, mostly average, but I just met a guy this week, and we're going out again tomorrow night. His name's James. He's a day trader from the East Coast," Chloe admits with a sly grin.

"Girl, yes, that's exactly what I would picture for you," Piper exclaims, taking a generous swig.

Upon realizing each of their glasses is already running low, Piper goes to open another bottle of Sauvignon Blanc but opens the door to an empty cabinet. "I swear I had two more bottles of wine left. You ladies hang here. I will be right back, legit five minutes. I just need to run downstairs and grab another bottle."

Piper trades her heels for flip-flops to expedite the trip downstairs. She speed-walks to the elevator and painstakingly awaits its doors to open. She's clipping at such a pace, she can feel her cheeks flush but finally makes it down to the commissary on her building's main level.

She grabs two bottles of Kim Crawford and, realizing she's starving, gets distracted by the irresistible snack selection. As she's perusing the offerings, she can't help but catch a glimpse of someone through the aisle and immediately gets goosebumps, like her body is trying to sound an alarm. *It can't be,* she tells herself, keeping her wits about her to see where this person has gone. Her anxiety has been slowly escalating, and she can feel the jolt of cortisol tracing her veins. She quickly settles her indecision and grabs a pack of whole wheat table crackers, a package of rosemary crisps, sharp cheddar cheese, and a $20 package of nuts. She's laser-focused on finding the person she just skimmed for some reassurance and to calm the feeling that *it's not him.*

Piper edges to the end of the market's mini-aisle and peeks around the corner, suddenly aware she looks like she's in full stealth mode. She gasps when she sees him. *Hoover. Here. Right now.*

She quickly turns around, bumping into an elderly lady and startling her. "I'm so sorry," she frantically whispers. She walks as quickly as she can to the checkout, not glancing anywhere but straight ahead. The next minute of her life feels like an eternity as the credit card machine takes its sweet time processing her payment.

Finally, she hears the system *bing* and takes off in a full-on run to the elevator. She closes her eyes in unison with its doors and rests her head against the ice-cold metal wall, taking deep breaths to steady her racing heart.

He didn't see me, she thinks to herself. *There's no way he saw me. I was in there for three minutes max. But why the hell was he there?*

Piper's thoughts are interrupted as the elevator doors open on her floor. She steps out and can feel her knees start to shake, holding her panic.

She pounds on her door with her fist without thinking, and Chloe answers.

"Woah, are you okay? All that banging sounds like the plumber just showed up or something," Chloe laughs.

"No, I'm not okay. I mean, yes, I'm fine. I just..." she trails off, replaying what just occurred in her mind.

"Wait, seriously, are you okay, Piper?" Emily questions.

"I just...I just saw him. Hoover. He was in the market. But he didn't see me. I'm sure of it. I was so fast, and there's no way he saw me. I'm just confused. I don't get it. Why do I keep seeing him?"

Piper busies herself opening and pouring a new bottle of wine.

Am I sure he didn't see me? Piper questions herself, feeling like she can't even trust her own intuition anymore. *I was so fast; there's no way. But why do I feel like he's trying to seek me out? It's almost as if he's watching me.*

The room is so quiet you could hear a pin drop. Chloe and Emily continue to look at her with concerned eyes.

Chloe breaks the silence. "You saw him...again? Piper, what in the world? What are you going to do?"

"I'm not going to do anything." She looks away and blinks back tears, her heart pounding so hard she can feel it in her throat. "He didn't see me. I'm positive he didn't see me," she repeats, as if saying it enough times will make it true. Her mind flashes back to the way his head tilted, how his eyes seemed to linger just a second too long. *No, stop.* She shakes her head, forcing a shaky breath. "I'm just going to chalk it up as a coincidence and try to forget about it. I'm going to have fun tonight... that's what I'm going to do," she says, though even she can hear the tremor in her voice.

"Okay, so you saw him one time getting off the L in February, and now in your commissary. And you don't think that's weird?"

"Well, yeah...and then you and everyone else saw him at work," Piper says with hesitation.

"You what?" Emily asks. She's one of those girls who can make a cardigan sexy, with a few buttons undone, black skinny jeans, and knee-high boots.

"Yeah, he showed up at our office last month when I was on a business trip with Kate. It creeps me out for sure. But he's never actually seen me, and I don't want to draw attention to myself, so for now, I'm just letting it go."

"Piper, you need to be careful. This guy seems a little...I don't know, off? I mean, the way he picked your family photo up off your desk and studied it was straight-up, can't-deny-it weird as all heck. It gives me goosebumps just thinking about it. No normal, sane 'new client' would ever do that. Coincidences, maybe, but seeing someone this many times two years after he sent you that gross email still seems intentional," Chloe says matter-of-factly.

"Yeah, I guess you're right," Piper admits. "But what am I going to do...turn him in for walking nearby? I can't really do anything about it. As long as he doesn't talk to me or try to spark things up, I'm just brushing it off. On that note, who wants a shot?" Piper asks, grabbing a bottle of Grey Goose vodka. It's out of character, but the wine isn't cutting it after what just happened.

The girls look at her with a little hesitation but give in. "Me," Chloe says. "Yeah, let's do it!"

Piper pours the shots without giving herself a chance to think twice. "Okay, on three — cheers! One...two...three," Piper yells, stifling all emotions. The girls clink and tip back their shot glasses in unison.

A few minutes later, she can feel the warmth hit her cheeks, and her mind starts to get fuzzy.

"Alright, ladies, let's head out." Piper leaves the slew of glasses, wine bottles, and snacks spread across her countertop.

The girls grab their coats and walk out of Piper's apartment building as fast as they can, without looking back.

―――

The cab slows to a crawl as Piper, Chloe, and Emily attempt to read house numbers until they find the one that's their destination. They finally spot it: a stunning brick three-flat in Chicago's Lincoln Park.

"Is this Ryan's actual house?" Piper inquires.

"Yeah, I think it is. Dang, his job might be better than I thought," Chloe remarks.

The girls walk up and Chloe opens the door. They're met with music so loud it overwhelms their senses. The room is crammed with people milling about, yelling to talk above the bass.

"Let's head out back," Chloe yells. The girls follow suit.

They head to the back door and find, to their relief, that there's a whole crew outdoors where the music is at a manageable level.

"There he is," Chloe points. She leads the way with confidence, and the three of them approach Ryan.

"Chloe!" he shouts, giving her a hug. "So glad you could make it, it's been too long. Teddy, look who's here!" Teddy is their mutual friend from college. While Chloe makes the rounds, Ryan turns his attention back to Emily and introduces himself. "Hi, I'm Ryan," he says, offering a handshake.

Emily, distracted by everything going on, shakes his hand, mumbles something about how nice it is to meet him, and walks off toward Chloe.

Ryan turns to Piper, and their eyes lock. *I feel like Chloe didn't do justice telling me how good-looking he is,* she thinks to herself, caught off guard. A pause that lasts three seconds too long ensues before Piper snaps to and clears her throat. "Piper," she says, with her arm outstretched, "I hear it's your birthday. Happy birthday, Ryan."

He shakes her hand. "Have we met before? You look so familiar."

"I don't think we have, but who knows," Piper laughs.

"Let me grab you a drink," Ryan says, again holding eye contact as he looks down at Piper long enough that her stomach starts to flutter.

"Okay, sure. I'll take a glass of champagne," she says, adding, "to celebrate you." She cringes inside, not knowing where that comment came from. *Thanks, vodka,* she thinks to herself.

He smiles at her, revealing a dimple on his left cheek. His rich brown hair flows back before fading, and Piper can't resist. His chiseled jaw is made even more attractive by his dark brown, dove-like eyes.

"So, Piper, tell me about yourself," he says. "Tell me something real...none of this surface stuff I've been hearing all night."

"Okay, let me think." She pauses, a trill of adrenaline flooding her system. "I work in public relations. I work with Chloe. We do a lot of really cool restaurant events and openings...throw parties. It's a dream job, but I work way too much. I don't have much of an off-switch. I love fitness and working out. Running along the Lakeshore Path is my favorite way to start a day. I have a fear of being alone for the rest of my life. And I love Mexican food," she admits, her lips forming a smile.

"I feel like you just described me," he laughs. "Except my job isn't nearly as cool as yours. I sit at a desk, crunch numbers, and eat dinner at the office four out of five nights a week because I'm there too late." He pauses. "Piper, what do you think about changing that, you and I? Say, next week, we peel ourselves from our computers and grab dinner?"

Piper isn't sure if it's the alcohol speaking for both of them or what, but this situation feels too good to be true. "Yeah...I'd like that. I'd like that a lot."

"Okay, it's a deal. I need to go make a lap, but I'm going to find you again. I have more questions for you," he says, his dimple showing itself off again.

Piper turns and walks off to find Chloe, chugging her champagne and refilling it with a bottle sitting atop a high-top table nearby.

She doesn't see Chloe or Emily anywhere, so she decides to head inside and find a bathroom. After waiting in line for what feels like an eternity, but is really just five minutes, she locks herself inside and takes a minute, uttering a silent squeal. She pees, freshens her lipstick, and finishes off her champagne before walking out in search of more. Typically, Piper is one to have a three-drink maximum, but tonight, all bets are off.

She walks through the main room, still thumping with beats blasting, searching for a refill, and gets lost in the music, swaying her hips, hands held high. She forgets that she was looking for her friends or even more champagne and finds herself carefree for who knows how long.

The next thing she knows, she feels hands on her hips. She turns, wide-eyed, to see who would dare make a move but quickly relaxes when she finds Ryan beside her. "I've been looking for you," he whispers in her ear, his eyes looking as tipsy as she feels inside.

"I want to see you again. What night can I see you this week?" he says, tickling her ear with his lips.

"Wednesday! Can you do Wednesday?" Piper yells so he can hear her above the music.

"Yes," he mouths, pulling her closer. They sway in unison with the beat, his arms around her waist, and hers around his neck. Piper drinks in the moment and briefly acknowledges that she can't remember the last time she felt so carefree.

The song ends, and Ryan grabs her hand. He leads her through the crowd of sweaty bodies to the back, down the steps, and outside. It's quieter than it was earlier.

Hand in hand, he walks her to a bench and sits down. He pulls her onto his lap. "I'm not usually this forward, Piper," he says with a grin. "For one, I've had way too much to drink, you know how birthdays are. And for two, I can't explain it, but I'm drawn to you. I want to get to know you."

Despite her buzz, Piper is momentarily taken aback by his forwardness. "Didn't you...didn't you recently go through a breakup?" she can't help but ask.

"Oh, that...yeah, I did. But honestly, it was over long ago. One of those should've-ripped-the-cord situations that never felt like the right time and dragged on for far too long. I assure you, I'm not using you to cope. I just think you're beautiful, we have a lot in common, and you seem different from most people I've met before."

Piper's heart slams in her chest. She looks away, only to have Ryan ever so gently pull her chin back so she's making eye contact with him.

He starts to close the gap between them, and before she realizes what's happening, their lips are locked. His hand slides into her hair as their tongues intertwine. He tastes like vodka and strawberries.

Piper is totally lost in the moment when Chloe yells from across the yard, "Piper, is that you?"

Piper and Ryan pull apart. He rests his forehead on her shoulder, catching his breath.

"Yes, it's me," Piper calls back, laughing.

"Okay, you two lovebirds, it's 1 a.m., and we need to get the heck out of here."

Ryan leans in and whispers, "Thanks for coming tonight, Piper. I know I'm kind of a mess, but I loved meeting you and can't wait to see you again soon."

Piper pulls back and smiles. "Me too."

"Let me get your number. Type it in my phone." He hands it to her.

She taps in her number, biting her lip, still smiling. Then she stands and finds Chloe and Emily.

"Loved meeting you, Ryan," she says as she starts walking toward the front of the house.

She glances over her shoulder. Their eyes meet. Ryan's gaze lingers on her from across the yard.

"What on earth was that?" Chloe asks, wide-eyed and grinning.

"I have no idea." Piper puts her head in her hands. "I don't know how that escalated so quickly, but I'm not complaining about it. Also, I'm sleeping at your house tonight. There's no way I'm going back to my apartment building in this state after my run-in with that creep earlier tonight."

"Yes, come to my place. Sluuuuumber parrrty!" Chloe shouts. The three of them stumble to the cab that's shown up to take them home.

They arrive at Chloe's Gold Coast condo, and Piper throws herself on the couch, not bothering to change out of her dress. She hears her phone buzz and checks it, curious who would be reaching out at this hour.

> Hey Piper…it's Ryan. So great meeting you tonight. Thanks for coming out to celebrate. Can't wait to see you Wednesday.

A smile spreads across her face, and it's the last thing she remembers before drifting off to sleep.

Five hours later, Piper cracks open her eyes as the sun beams down on her from Chloe's expansive walk-out patio door. She lifts her head and looks around, remembering where she is. She quickly comes to as she glances at herself, still wearing her dress from last night. Her head pounds like stomping feet and begs for water. *Not closing the curtain was my last mistake of the night,* she thinks to herself.

She stretches her body and forces herself to sit up. Mascara is caked to her eyelids, something that doesn't happen often. Piper thinks back on her night, and a smile spreads over her face as she remembers Ryan. She opens her phone and breathes a sigh of relief upon confirming she does, in fact, have a date on Wednesday and didn't dream that up.

Given that it's only 7 a.m., Piper uses her phone to call for a taxi. She needs to get herself together and knows it could be a bit before Chloe stirs. Unlike Piper, she probably pulled her blackout curtains tight like any responsible weekend partier.

Piper arrives at her apartment building twenty minutes later. It's not until she stands in the lobby awaiting the elevator that her heart rate spikes. It transports her back to last night, and she can feel the panic wash over her body as she shivers. *Hoover*, she thinks to herself.

Piper proceeds to hit the elevator button religiously, as if it will make it come any faster. Finally, the doors open, and she breathes a sigh of relief that she's alone.

She quickly makes her way to her apartment and slips the key into the lock as fast as she can. For whatever reason, the speed at which she does things makes her feel safe.

Piper can feel her heart quicken with no sign of slowing down. This always happens after a big night out. But taking in her spotless apartment brings a small sense of relief as she drops her clutch on the kitchen island.

Wait a minute. Piper freezes. *Didn't I host the girls last night? Yes, I definitely did.*

We pregamed here. And then...the whole Hoover thing happened.

She walks herself through the night, fighting the fog of exhaustion clouding her memory. *We drank wine, took shots, hailed a taxi. Did we clean up after that? No...we didn't. I'm sure of it. So how on earth is my place this clean?*

Piper tiptoes through her apartment, her heart racing. She opens a cupboard — wine glasses, spotless and neatly lined up. Shot glasses, tucked in the bottom drawer to the right. Another cupboard — leftover crackers. The fridge — cheese sealed in a baggie in the bottom drawer.

"Okay, everything is perfectly put away. I need to stop getting in my head," she says, trying to reassure herself. "But I am one hundred percent certain we left a mess."

She grabs her phone and texts Chloe.

> Chloe, did we clean my apartment before we went out last night?

Much to Piper's relief, her phone pings almost immediately.

> Ugh, sorry, no, I don't think we did. That cheese is probably so ripe. Sorry, girl.

Piper types back.

> I knew it. I was just retracing my steps and needed confirmation.

Chloe questions right away.

> Why are you asking me this? ... Want me to come over and help clean? I totally can...just say the word.

Piper dials Chloe.

"Chloe, my apartment is spotless."

"What do you mean, it's spotless?" Chloe asks, confused.

"We just agreed we left it a mess, and it's spotless. Do you know what this means?"

A shiver runs through Piper's body.

Piper is met with silence and can't take it another second. "Hoover, Chloe. Hoover was here," she whispers, despite wanting to scream, as if whispering will prevent her from being overheard.

"Oh my...oh my gosh, Piper. How could he get into your apartment? It's not like the guy has a key." Chloe sounds like she's grasping for something reassuring.

"I have no clue. What else could it be? I mean truly, think about it. I've been seeing him all over town. I ran into him last night, and now this? He probably saw me down there buying all those stupid crackers and the wine and put it all together and…ugh." Piper pauses. "I am freaking out, Chloe. I think I'm going to get sick."

"Breathe deep, girl. Just come back over. Take a shower and change and gather yourself. Spend some time here today."

"Honestly, I feel sick…I feel sick from last night and sick from this whole situation. It's entirely too much for me. I'm going to force myself to go out and buy some security cameras. I need evidence so I can have something against him. Everything he does, by all standards, makes me look crazy. He comes around me but doesn't talk to me. Even now — what am I going to do? Go to the police station and tell them to write up a report that I have a clean apartment? I'm going to buy cameras and prove that this lunatic is after me."

"I'll meet you, Piper. Just tell me where."

Piper walks to her closet and pulls out her softest sweatpants and an oversized T-shirt, finally changing out of her dress.

"Best Buy. In Lakeview. I'll see you there in thirty."

"I'm on it. Changing as we speak."

Click.

Piper longs for someone to tell her everything's fine, so she turns to the One her parents taught her to call on since childhood — God.

"Please, God…send me peace. Give me clarity for everything happening in my life. I'm freaking out about Hoover. Please make him stop. Keep me safe, and let me rest in Your presence."

She zips her purse. The air shifts, subtle and cold, just enough to raise a prickle along her spine.

She's not as alone as she wants to believe.

15

PROFESSOR HOOVER

Hoover pours himself a glass of cheap scotch with one round, baseball-sized ice cube in it. He places a Frank Sinatra vinyl on his vintage record player, moves the tone arm, and cranks the volume knob as far up as it will go.

He sits on his loveseat and closes his eyes, feeling the beat thrum through his body. This is his tried-and-true recipe for forced relaxation when breathing techniques and walking the Lakeshore Path won't cut it.

He breathes in and mentally counts to four, holds for another four, then exhales to a four-count. He takes a large swig and blinks his eyes open.

"These run-ins aren't cutting it," he mutters into the empty room. "I've made no progress." His hand tightens into a fist. "She's a bright girl...obviously. So why isn't she noticing me? Looks like it's time to step things up."

He pulls out his black leather-bound notebook and turns to the page bookmarked "Piper's Habitual Daily Whereabouts — WEEKDAYS ONLY." It's an ongoing work in progress, of course...months upon months of painstaking, admittedly enjoyable research.

5:30 a.m. Workout or run
Run on Lakeshore Path, three miles out and back / 50-minute elliptical and strength workout in workout room

8:00 a.m. Morning commute to work (Clark & Division L Red Line to Grand; walk to office)

8:25 a.m. Grab coffee at Honey Roasters on the way

1:00–1:30 p.m. (give or take) River North 10-block walk (only when schedule permits)

5:30 p.m. Evening commute home (Grand L Red Line to Clark & Division)

5:55 p.m. Walk from Clark & Division to Lake Shore Drive Residences

Evenings: Occasional work event, girls' night, or late night out

That's when it clicks. He takes another swig, unknowingly spilling scotch down the front of his oversized white T-shirt, the fresh stain joining the yellowed marks beneath his armpits.

I'll go to the workout room before her. Every day this week. Until we overlap. That tiny room is so small — she'll have no choice but to acknowledge me. Face me. Interact with me. I could use a little extra pump myself anyway.

He finishes his glass and gets up to pour another in silent celebration.

16

SURVIVAL MODE

Piper can hear her alarm blaring through her dream but is too zonked to care. It's been calling to her for a few minutes before she finally rolls over and hits stop. 5:25 a.m. — still dark out.

All she wants is to keep sleeping, but the thought of starting her day with a workout wins out over thirty more minutes of already-broken sleep.

Hoover, she thinks, remembering the fear that took root over the weekend. She drags herself out of bed, pulls on her workout clothes, grabs her water, and locks the door behind her. *Surely endorphins will ease the feeling that I'm going crazy.*

She rides the elevator to the ninth floor and walks the length of the hallway, passing blasé framed pictures of floral arrangements on the wall separated by steel apartment doors, until she reaches her destination: the workout room. Calling it a gym would be giving it too much credit. The workout room is, quite literally, a square box, even smaller than her tiny apartment.

She opens the door and is surprised to find the lights already on. It's all about twos in that room — two rows of exercise machines, two of each treadmill, elliptical, and stair master, with a small rack of hand weights in the far back corner. Some days there's one other random person from the building in there, but most days, it's just Piper.

She steps on the foot gliders of the closest elliptical and, naturally, takes in her surroundings. There's a man to her right walking briskly on a treadmill. He's bald and looks super fit. On the treadmill next to him, there's another man. Despite just waking up, as if on command, her heart skips a beat and she stops breathing. *Hoover.*

She knows it's him without even fully seeing his face. It's pitch-black outside, lit only by the spotlights dotting the shore of Lake Michigan. She can see his eyes in the reflection of the rectangular glass window looking out. His lanky legs stride at a snail's pace as they repetitiously hit the spinning black belt, like someone who never runs. He's not athletic and clearly has no interest in staying fit.

Her mind is on overdrive, blazing with panic as she tries to comprehend what's happening, while her body refuses to cooperate. Her feet feel as heavy as cement, yet her legs somehow keep pushing the elliptical on their own. Her hands grip the long black poles, moving without conscious thought.

Time seems to stop. Piper's gaze drops to her legs, her stare so sharp it's as if she's willing herself invisible. *Maybe he won't recognize me like this,* she thinks. *If only I can hide my face.*

Why on earth is he here? What do I do? I don't understand why he's here.

She keeps her head down, heart pounding.

Has he seen me? Oh my gosh — my reflection. In the window.

It's a huge pane of glass, and it's dark outside. She can see his reflection, barely, but just enough to know — *he's definitely seen me.*

What does he want from me?

The realization chills her. It's nothing short of terrifying.

His treadmill comes to a stop. Piper looks to her left, turning her neck as far as she can, staring at the blank, cream-colored wall. She needs to hide, but there's nowhere to go. She's utterly stuck.

Without turning to look, Piper can tell he's watching her. She hears him fill a cup at the water cooler and guzzle it slowly. She doesn't even need to glance over because she can feel his eyes burning into her back.

Then, finally, the door shuts. He's gone. Piper gasps for air, realizing she'd been holding her breath the whole time.

One thing is now crystal clear: *He lives in my building.*

When she thinks the coast is clear, a few minutes later, Piper slips out of the workout room, sweaty though not from exertion, and shakily hurries to the elevator. Her heart is still pounding by the time she reaches her apartment on the eighteenth floor.

As she approaches her door, she nearly trips over something resting on the black doormat. She stops short, retracing a few steps, and peers down. Her breath catches.

There, neatly placed in the center, is her favorite chocolate peanut butter protein bar, tied with a red bow.

Her pulse spikes. Her heart aches for respite; it's beating so fast it hurts. Panic races through her veins.

How did this get here?

HOOVER.

She thinks back to twenty minutes ago, trying to replay her exit for the gym. *This wasn't here when I left. I'm sure of it. Which means it was placed here within the last twenty minutes.*

Hoover.

It was Hoover.

He knows exactly where she lives.

Piper scrambles to open her apartment door with urgency as the reality of everything dawns on her all at once. She immediately dials her parents.

Her mom answers on the first ring. "Piper, it's so early. Is everything okay?"

"Mom, I just saw him. He's here." she huffs.

"What? Saw who — where?" she blurts, groggy.

"Mom, I went to do my usual morning workout in my apartment building, and he was there. Hoover was there, Mom, on the treadmill. And then there was this bar on my doorstep, my favorite bar, when I got back to my apartment." Piper tries to process what she's saying as she speaks aloud. "Do you know what this means?"

"Wait a second. I'm trying to walk through everything you're telling me."

"Mom, Professor Hoover lives in my apartment building. And he knows exactly which apartment is mine."

Silence.

"Mom, did you hear me?" Piper asks, fear gripping her voice.

"Piper, this is really serious. Let me get your dad...one second...Okay, we're both here. Can you tell your dad what you just told me?"

Piper repeats herself. "He lives here."

"Piper," her dad says, "I don't know what to think yet. Here's what I'm going to do. I'm going to call the college provost and find out where he lives. We need to confirm where he lives, and we'll go from there. Do me a favor and don't walk to work today. Drive or take a cab or have a friend come get you. Play it safe until we know what's going on."

"Okay, sounds good. I have a really busy day at work, but I'll call you later." *Click.*

Piper feels a tiny sense of relief having shared her burden with her parents. She finishes getting ready and calls a taxi. Going through the motions of life provides a sense of normalcy where there is none.

She finally gets dropped off at work in a cab, sprints into the building, and steps off the elevator on the third floor breathless, practically running into Kate.

"Well, hello there, Blondie. What on earth is so pressing that it requires a full-on Friday morning sprint?"

Kate's smile turns to concern as Piper loses the fight against the tears that immediately slide down her flushed cheeks.

"Tell me what's going on. What is it?" Her voice quivers.

"I saw him. This morning. I saw him in my workout room. When I walked in, he was already there. And then there was this bar, my favorite bar, just sitting on my doorstep when I got back, like he placed it there for me. Kate, it's finally become unmistakably obvious. Hoover lives in my building," she admits, wiping her nose.

"Piper, listen," Kate advises in her signature tone that commands the authority of any room. Kate looks sleek and sophisticated, dripping in nude Jimmy Choo pumps, a matching Chanel bag, and a navy Hermès scarf. Quite the opposite of Piper, who threw on the first thing she could find — baggy jeans, a tucked-in white T-shirt, and flats.

"Here's what you need to do. We don't know what this creep is up to, and we need to make sure you and everyone who works here are safe. I need you to draft an email for me to send around the office, warning people — again — not to let him into the building. Anyone who buzzes needs to be screened before we let them in. Include a photo of him. I have to hop on a call...let's talk after," she says, giving Piper a reassuring hug.

Piper moves robotically to her desk, unpacks her bag, and opens her laptop. She can feel the curious eyes of her colleagues on her, making her want to crawl back into bed. Not her bed in her apartment, but the one at her parents' house, because her apartment no longer feels like her own.

From: Piper@harmonconsulting.com
To: Kate@harmonconsulting.com

Date: April 16, 2011, 9:20 a.m.
Subject: URGENT: SECURITY EFFECTIVE IMMEDIATELY

Work fam,

Piper is dealing with a situation that requires us to increase our security efforts. Without going into detail, effective immediately, we are implementing a new security check before letting anyone into our building. If someone buzzes, you need to check the video monitor to get eyes on who is trying to come up, and also get verbal confirmation, before letting anyone in.

*Below, please find a photo of Joseph Hoover, the man we are taking extra precautions around. Some of you may recognize him, as he's been to our office once before. If you see this man, or anyone who looks remotely similar to him, **do not** buzz them in.*

Notify Piper and me immediately so we can contact the appropriate authorities.

Please direct any questions to my assistant, Cheryl.

Thanks,
Kate

Piper clicks and sends Kate the draft. Two minutes later, the email is in Piper's and everyone else's inbox, begging to be opened.

Piper is so on edge she doesn't even realize she's been biting her cheek until she tastes blood.

She hears chatter in the office and wheels her chair around. Sophie, the graphic designer, and a few colleagues are chatting and look up at her.

"We remember this guy," Sophie says, looking at Piper with

heartfelt eyes. "From that trip you took with K to California. I think Chloe already told you, but he showed up asking if we were taking on any new clients and inquiring about who he could meet with. I remember it specifically because the whole interaction was weird. He was looking around the office while we were talking, trying to take something in, pausing around your desk. It's like he had no clue what kind of business he was opening when we asked for more information."

Piper sits down. She feels the warmth drain from her cheeks and thinks she might pass out.

17

PROFESSOR HOOVER

Professor Hoover groans as he pulls an 18 x 24 whiteboard out of the depths of the storage closet in the back of his apartment. He walks it over to his living room, resting it against the wall. He cuts the tag off the just-purchased hammer and takes a nail out of a plastic container.

He hammers three times, securing the nail in the wall, and hangs the whiteboard. Slightly crooked, but it will do. He pages through his binder until he finds her senior school photo and tapes it to the top center of the board. Beneath it, he writes in thick black marker —

Mission: Make Piper MINE. Then he begins outlining a series of action items, each carefully bullet-pointed beneath the heading:

- **Daily morning workout run-ins.**

"Today went well," he says aloud, tapping the marker against the board. "She definitely noticed me. I know she's a creature of habit. I think I'll make this a regular thing for me. For us."

- **Midday walks by Harmon Consulting.**

"Just to scope things out, of course. Possibly have a coincidental run-in if the stars align. What's meant to be will be," he chuckles, the sound echoing in his apartment.

- **Engage Piper with an email.**

"I just need to figure out the proper timing on this. It didn't go well the first time."
Okay. Next time I see her around her office, I'll exchange pleasantries, and then I'll send this as a friendly follow-up, he thinks.

- **Welcome her home one evening.**

Convince her to come over to my place. Or charm her into inviting me over.

- **Court her**

Flowers, homemade meals, surprises, dates — every day.

- **Badda bing, badda bang.**

"Fill cookie jar to the brim," he says grinning. "Buy the ring of her dreams. The rest is history."

Hoover rests his marker on the board's ledge, grabs his velvet blazer, stuffs his mini notebook in his jacket pocket, and heads out to run a few errands before he's off to watch Piper's every move all over again.

18

GET OUT

Piper is at a loss for what to do with herself. Everyone in the office is milling about being productive, while she's stuck in what feels like a trance, replaying her morning over and over in her mind as if it will bring answers. She can't focus, nor does she care about anything not related to her current situation.

Upon realizing she's staring at a blank computer screen, she decides she needs to do something and calls her apartment building management.

"Hello, Lake Shore Drive Residences, this is Alicia speaking," mumbles a young woman, her voice drowned out by shuffling papers.

"Hi, Alicia, my name is Piper, and I'm a current tenant of yours. Listen, I have a very weird request. It's a long story, so I'm going to cut right to it. One of my former college professors is stalking me, and early this morning, when I went to the workout room on the ninth floor, I saw him in there." She can hear her own voice quiver. "I guess what I'm asking is if you can tell me if he lives in your building. I need to know what I'm dealing with here as I'm trying to sort out what's happening."

She holds her breath, fighting back the urge to cry, desperately clawing for composure.

"Oooookay. Hmmm. First, I'm sooo sorry you're dealing with this. Second, I'm honestly not really supposed to legally discuss tenant information. Let me see what I can do. What's this guy's name?"

"Joseph. Joseph Hoover." She sounds nice, between gum chomps, at least. *Please, please help me. Lord, please help me.* Piper's body shivers as she waits.

A few minutes pass. "Piper? Thanks for holding. Listen, I can't tell you much, but I can confirm that he lives in our building. His lease started in August. He's lived here for eight months."

Silence.

What did she say? Eight months?! Hoover has lived in my building for eight months?! How could I be so naïve and stupid? How did I let this happen? How did I not see this reality?

"Piper, you there?" Alicia asks.

"Yes, yes, I'm here," she says between shallow breaths. "I understand you can't tell me his unit number, but can you please tell me if he lives on my floor, or close to me?"

"Let me check. No, Piper, he doesn't live on your floor or close to your floor. I'm really sorry. There's not much I can do, but if you do end up pressing charges, please let us know, and then we can make things happen on our end to keep you safe."

That's reassuring...kind of. Piper places her head in her palms, feeling disappointed in herself for not putting this all together sooner, and also so mad at her circumstances.

"Thanks, Alicia, thanks for your help," she says quietly before hanging up.

Piper does the only thing she knows to do next. She calls her dad.

"Piper, I'm so glad you called," he says. "I was just about to call you. I spoke with the college. They wouldn't give me any information, but after explaining the situation, I asked them if Hoover lived in your building. They said they couldn't tell me that, but if I should be more concerned or less concerned, I should definitely be more concerned. I think that was their unhelpful way of telling me he lives in your building."

"Dad, he does. He lives in my building. He's lived there for the past eight months," she says, trying to keep her voice down despite wanting to scream at the top of her lungs. "I just called my building management, and they confirmed it. What am I supposed to do now?"

"This is just sick! That college...had they just handled this the right way, we'd never be here. I am so frustrated with them. All the money we paid to have you three kids go there, and you're not even safe years later."

"Dad, I hear you. I'm on the same page. What do you think I should do now?"

"I think you need to talk to someone. I think you need to file a police report. Why don't you call the non-emergency police line and get some direction?"

"Great idea. I'm going to do that now. I'll keep you posted," she says.

Piper immediately dials 3-1-1, and a woman answers the phone.

"Chicago Police Department, non-emergency line. How can I help you?" Her voice is kind and warm.

"Hi there, I'm actually hoping you can help me. I am in a very weird situation, and I think I need to file a police report, but I don't know what to do or where to start."

"No worries, ma'am. That's what I'm here for. Why don't you start by telling me your name and what's going on, and we can go from there," the woman says.

"Okay, thanks. My name is Piper Hawthorne. For background, a little over two years ago, one of my college professors wrote me a really disturbing email confessing his obsession with me. I've been seeing him around town where I live for the past two months. I was positive he never saw me...that is, until this morning. I saw him in my workout room in my apartment building. I've since confirmed he's been living in my building for the past eight months. So, I guess he's actually been stalking me all this time," Piper admits, feeling both relief and disgust getting it out there.

"Okay, ma'am, this is a very serious situation. This is what you need to do: you need to come down to the station and file a police report as soon as you can. You need to protect yourself. Do you have a place to stay?"

"Wait, what? Place to stay? As in, aside from my apartment?" Piper asks, confused.

"Listen," the woman says, sternly elevating her voice, "I don't think you understand the magnitude of what is happening. Do you have plans this weekend, sweets?"

Piper thinks of all the things she has planned: happy hour tonight, a long run with a girlfriend and some grocery shopping tomorrow, and a birthday party Saturday night. "Yeah, I have a pretty busy weekend. Tonight I'm meeting friends..."

She sharply cuts her off. "Piper, you're not understanding what's going on. This is *a very serious* situation. Listen, dear, you need to stay away from your apartment. Get out of the city. You need to hide out far away from this person. Forget the parties; you need to start thinking about protecting yourself. I've seen countless situations like this, and I'm going to just cut to the chase: they don't all end well. I'm sorry — I don't want to sugar-coat it for you."

Piper can feel the heat overtake her face, tears welling in her eyes. This situation has freaked her out, but she had never thought about it quite like that.

"Okay...I hear what you're saying," she says.

"This is what you need to do," the clerk says. "Write this down. You need to go to the police station. You need to file a report with one of the officers at the desk. You need to tell them everything — everything, Piper. We want details. The more, the merrier. Every time you've seen him, every encounter, what you know. You need to tell them you want to file an Emergency Order of Protection, effective immediately. Then you need to start the process for filing an Order of Protection. That should buy you a few weeks in case you see him while you wait for him to be served papers for your court case. Oh, and get yourself a lawyer."

Piper is writing as fast as she can, simultaneously trying to comprehend everything she's been told. She was immune to all of these things just yesterday. An order of protection? A lawyer? She feels overwhelmed at best.

"Thank you so much," Piper says, tears rolling down her cheeks. "I don't know how to thank you. Can you tell me your name again, in case I need to reach you? Will you be at the police station?"

"I can't share that with you. I have so many relatives in the force, and we like to keep things confidential."

That's a strange response.

Still confused after they hang up, it hits her — God sent her this woman on the phone. Some people cross your path only for a moment, placed there by His hand to guide you and help lead your course. Piper feels it deep in her spirit — this woman was exactly that.

And yet, as she sets her phone down, her hands won't stop trembling. If this was God's way of reassuring her, then why does her chest still ache? Why can't she stop feeling like the walls are closing in?

19

PROFESSOR HOOVER

Everything he's set in motion leads him here. Professor Hoover makes his way toward River North. In the distance, he spots the corner where Harmon Consulting sits and slows his pace, eyes narrowing as he catches sight of Piper leaning against the window. She does that often. He's certain it's when she's meeting with Kate, taking a brief moment to stretch her legs. He would do the same.

Hoover inhales deeply, a wave of satisfaction washing over him. His mission is officially underway.

The closer he gets, the more his nerves make themselves known, which catches him by surprise. Rarely does he get nervous, but he's realizing he doesn't have much to do once he gets to her office, aside from walking around the block. Which he can only do once, twice, maybe three times before someone might notice and think he's up to no good. Which, of course, he's not.

He's recently taken up photography as a new hobby of sorts. He has to be careful, though. Even he's aware enough to know it looks a little out of place when he snaps paparazzi-style photos of Piper from afar, especially when it's clear it's through her window.

He finds a bench a short distance from Harmon Consulting that not only offers shade but maintains a bullseye view. He snaps a few photos of her...her back leaning against the window, and a side-profile shot of her ever-so-delicately brushing her hair behind her ear. He's particularly fond of that one, so much so, that afterwards, he gives it a rest. She quickly leaves her perch. She's never there long. He pulls out his phone and starts drafting.

Dearest Piper,

It has been far too long since we last connected. And while I know those circumstances weren't ideal, I want to clear things up. I have nothing but good intentions ~~for us~~ for you. I wanted to see if, by chance, you would do me the honors and let me explain things to you in person, say over brunch at a quaint restaurant ~~in our neighborhood~~, or coffee, or even just a walk.

Point is, I would love to explain myself ~~and see you~~. It has been too long, and I have nothing but pure intentions...as a former professor to an amazing student.

Please do let me know what you think.

Wish you nothing but blessings on blessings on blessings.

~~Always yours,~~
Professor Hoover

Well, that was easy, he silently affirms himself. *Three trips around the block keep me in the clear. Three trips, then back home.*

I'll send this later this week, after a few more shared moments. After I'm sure she's seen me. She needs time to feel it, to wonder, to want it. To imagine how good it will feel when we're finally together.

Hoover slips his phone into his pocket and starts his roundabout trek.

20

GAME PLAN

Piper closes her eyes and inhales as much air as she possibly can, pining for clarity. *One thing at a time,* she tells herself as she frantically thinks through what needs to be done. Thank God it's Friday, in the most literal sense. She's suffocating and needs to get out of here.

Following the officer's warning, she's finally taking this seriously and feels an immediate need to go to the police station. Upon admitting the reality of her situation, work feels wildly unimportant. Piper suddenly feels like she's fighting for her life.

Is Hoover going to come and get me? Is he going to try to track me down if I leave town? What are his real intentions? What if he gets mad and tries to kill me? What if I had been alone in the gym? What if this all hasn't been a coincidence? Where else has he been watching me?

Piper exhales the breath she didn't realize she was holding in.

I can't go down this hole. Piper, stop.

The phone on Piper's desk rings, startling her out of her downward spiral. It's Kate.

"Hey, what's up?" Piper says, her tone muffled, for no other reason than whispering feels safe.

"Piper, I know your world is spiraling right now, and your biggest priority is keeping yourself safe, as it should be. Where are you going to stay while you sort this all out?"

Piper meets Kate with silence. She hasn't given much thought to anything beyond the fact that she needs to get out.

"I was going to suggest you stay with me and my family in Naperville. That way, you're far enough away from your apartment, this creep, and the whole situation that you can get some distance while still staying engaged with work and any commitments you have…to the extent you feel comfortable, of course."

A tinge of relief rises at the thought of staying with Kate, and she leans into that gut reaction.

"Yes, I would love to take you up on that. Being away but not alone sounds like what I need. Thank you. I can't thank you en—"

Kate cuts her off. "Don't thank me. Just know this is what I'm here for. This is what matters. If we can't be there for each other during the messy stuff of life, what are we even doing? Do your thing and call me when you're on the way to my house. I'll text you directions to let yourself in if I'm not home yet. The kids will probably be home with our nanny, so welcome to the chaos."

Click. Kate hangs up, and Piper feels a glimmer of relief, knowing that while this is her battle to fight, she's not fighting it alone.

Piper haphazardly packs up her work stuff, trying to think of anything she may need for the weekend, or for who knows how long. She feels a warm hand on her arm and looks up. Her colleague Kristen is watching her with concerned eyes and begins to whisper.

"Hey, I — well, first of all, I'm so sorry you're going through this, I really am. I just, ah, I couldn't help but overhear your conversation, and I connected with Bobby, and we'd love to go with you. I mean, it sounds like you're going to file a police report. Bobby's a lawyer and all, and while he practices divorce law, I still think...I guess what I'm trying to say is, please don't go alone. Let us come with you. Just for, you know, support and reinforcement if needed. Which I'm sure won't be needed, but you know what I mean."

"Thank you," Piper says, glancing away, fighting back the tears begging to be released. She didn't expect all of this support. She's felt so alone harboring this burden for so long. She takes another deep breath and closes her eyes, trying to stuff it all back down. "Yeah, that would be really nice, actually. Thanks so much. I'm going to leave...now, I guess. I have to get out of here. Kate offered for me to go to her place, so I need to go back to my apartment first and pack a bag quick before I head out."

"Yes, I think that's a great plan," Kristen says. "You do that, and let me figure out logistics on our end, and we'll meet you, say, in thirty at your place? We can go with you to the station, and then you can head out from there." Kristen's dark, swept-up messy bun matches her personality: relaxed, intentional, and effortlessly put together.

"Yes, that's great. See you soon."

Piper continues packing up her stuff. She grabs her computer, charger, and a few folders filled with who knows what. She can't even think, her hands seem to move on their own, grabbing things as if they know what to do.

She closes her bag, walks to Kate's office, and stands at the floor-to-ceiling window until Kate looks up. Kate motions that she's on a call and makes an empathetic face. Piper waves and mouths bye, and Kate blows a kiss in return.

Piper calls to arrange for a taxi. She's relieved when the dispatcher shares that it's only two minutes away.

When her driver pulls up to the office, Piper can feel the pit of fear growing inside her, radiating through every inch of her body on the drive home. Thank the Lord he looks nothing like Hoover.

God, help me, Piper whispers. *I am so scared. I don't understand why this is all happening. But I just need You. I need You to protect me, Lord. Please keep me safe. Please don't let me see Hoover.*

As she gets out of the cab, she's terrified she'll see him on the way up to her apartment. Instead of keeping her wits about her and looking around, Piper keeps her head hung low, eyes down. She can't handle any sort of contact, so she'd rather just not know. Her arms wobble like they've been lifting something too heavy for too long and are about to give out.

The elevator doors open, and Piper gasps as a tall, skinny man steps out. She nearly faints as he walks by, giving her a *what the hell was that?* look, but she steadies herself against the cold metal wall.

She fumbles with her keys and finally gets her apartment door open, barely holding it together. She's buzzing with anxiety as a million questions race through her mind. *Has Hoover been back here? Has he been here this morning? What if he's watching me right now?* She forces herself to push them aside, finds a suitcase, and starts frantically grabbing things...handfuls of underwear and socks, random clothes, a pair of tennis shoes.

Normally, she's a very methodical packer. She starts packing a week in advance for trips, planning outfits and laying out clothes. Her current reality of haphazard, panicked packing is throwing her into a full-blown tailspin. She knows she's going to forget a million things, but the feeling of needing to flee and get out is overbearing.

She rips shirts off hangers, breaking the plastic in two, aggressively grabs a sweatshirt, and shoves it in her bag as forcefully as she can. She doesn't even know what she has or hasn't packed because she's throwing clothes so fast. She grabs some leggings and a hat, tosses her makeup into a plastic baggie, and chucks it in the suitcase.

Piper feels the heat rising in her cheeks, red as the blood that drips from the index finger she just sliced on the broken hanger.

"Gaaaaah!" she screams at the top of her lungs, grabbing a paper towel and running cold water over her cut. *He's taken so much from me...and now he's taking even more.*

Piper zippers her bag shut. It feels far too light for not knowing how long she's going to be gone, but there's no time to turn back.

Right then, a knock hits her door, and she slaps a hand over her mouth, stifling a scream. She freezes in place, praying whoever is there will leave. *What if it's him?!* Piper forces herself to take deep breaths and begins to pray. *Lord Jesus, protect me. Be present in this moment. Help me, God. Help me,* she begs.

Piper tiptoes to the door and ever so slowly looks through the peephole. She breathes a sigh of relief when she sees a man from maintenance standing there. She opens the door a crack.

"Can I help you?" Piper says, just above a whisper.

"Are you okay, ma'am? You look a little...frazzled. I hope I didn't startle you." His name tag reads George. He's not overly tall, about 5'8", with a full head of short curly hair and a thick brown beard. By the grace of God, he has the face of a teddy bear.

"It's been a rough day, honestly," Piper says, her eyes welling with tears. "Is there a reason you're here? Is something wrong?"

"I'm just here to change your air filter, is all, ma'am. I can come back, no worries," he says with an empathetic, closed-mouth smile, holding up a rectangular filter as proof.

"That would be great, actually. I'm about to head out, so come back in ten or fifteen?"

"You got it. Thank you, miss. Sorry again to startle you," he says, turning down the hallway.

Piper closes the door and lets her weight fall against it, breath unsteady. Her heart is still on edge, pining for safety despite what just happened. She snaps back to the task at hand and takes one last look around her apartment, soaking it all in.

It's her first apartment living alone, an experience that feels shattered yet has molded her in so many ways. She's grown in her independence here and in her self-confidence. She's learned to love her own company. She's discovered what makes her tick: running along the lake, curling up with a good book and a glass of wine, having the freedom to choose what she does and when she does it, uninfluenced by anyone else. She became decisive here because she had to be. She learned she didn't need a boyfriend or a man to complete her, because for the first time, she was happy completely alone.

This apartment isn't the most glamorous, but it represents a once-beautiful period of her life. And he took it all from her.

The overwhelming anger that grips her soul is consuming, relentless. But another feeling begins to rise from underneath it. One that refuses to let this horrible man steal anything else from her: perseverance.

Her thoughts are broken by the ping of her phone. A text from Kristen.

> We just got dropped off by a taxi and are downstairs in the turnabout. No rush.

With that, Piper walks out of her apartment, letting the door close behind her, knowing she'll never step foot in this place again for as long as she lives.

She wheels her suitcase in and out of the elevator, jog-walking through her apartment complex. Her feet have a mind of their own, and she can hardly keep up with herself.

Piper exhales a deep breath as she exits the building. She spots Kristen and Bobby right away. Kristen embraces her in a hug.

"Hey, Bobby," she says in relief, giving him a quick squeeze. She takes one final look at her building and knows that this is it.

"My car's in the complex. Let's go this way." Piper leads them around the corner to the attached parking garage.

"I know you work out every day and could probably kick my butt, but let me carry your bag," Bobby says, attempting to lighten the mood.

"Here we are." Thankfully, Piper spots her white RAV4 right away, unlike her usual game of parking hide-and-seek.

The moment she gets in, she feels like she can breathe, a small step closer to feeling safe. *The more distance I have between me and this place, the better.*

She slips her water bottle into the cup holder out of habit, then starts the engine, but notices her water won't lay flat.

What the heck? she thinks to herself. She picks it up and pats the bottom of the cup holder, searching for whatever is in the way. Her fingernails graze something. She lifts it out and gasps.

"What is this?" she yells, without even realizing it, startling Kristen and Bobby.

"What the heck, Piper, what is it?" Bobby says, trying to remain the voice of reason.

"This! This heart is what it is!" Piper yells, her breath sharp. "What is this, a charm? Did you bring this into my car, Kristen? Where did this come from?" Piper holds up an inch-wide red heart charm with a shiny silver back.

He's been in my freaking car. Is there any area of my life he hasn't invaded? What a sick, delusional coward.

Taken aback, Kristen calmly says, "No, I didn't bring that. But, Piper, it could be from anywhere. I think you're on edge, reasonably so, but one thing at a time." She gently grabs Piper's arm to steady her.

Tears stream down Piper's face. "I've never put a heart thing in my car. I haven't driven in a week. This wasn't here last week. Someone put this here." Piper slams her fist on the center console, her words barely audible as she begins to sob.

Bobby gets out from the back seat and opens Piper's driver-side door. He pulls her out of the car and wraps her in a hug. "You're going to be okay, Piper. I promise you." He takes her arm and leads her to the back seat. "I'm going to drive," he says, helping her get settled.

"Deep breath," Kristen says. "I know it doesn't feel like it, but you're going to get through this. You'll get justice. Until then, you just need to lay low, like, super low."

Bobby starts the car and makes his way toward the exit of the barren parking structure.

Piper presses her palm to her chest, her body trembling. It isn't just fear anymore. It's the awful knowing that he's closer than she ever imagined.

"When you go in there, Piper, I want you to be confident and direct. No second-guessing. No using words like *'I think.'* This experience will mostly depend on who you speak with, but either way, it's your story and your truth that matters. Just tell them your story," Bobby says, catching her eye in the rearview mirror.

Piper closes her eyes, wiping the tears from her face. She steadies her breath and nods. Her mind is racing, trying to fact-check her own story. She feels like she should've prepared more for this, but like everything else in life, there's no time.

Bobby parks, and the three of them get out.

They walk up the steps to the Near North Chicago Police Department. Five squad cars line the front curb, and Piper is surprised by how quiet it is inside. You could hear a pin drop. She doesn't know what she expected, but it wasn't this.

"Can I help you, miss?" an officer asks, clearing his throat while chomping gum.

"Umm, yes, I would...um, I would like to file a police report," Piper says, her voice shaking.

"Yes, ma'am, that's my assumption. Let's start with the basics: name, date of birth, address, phone number."

Piper rattles off the details he needs. Bobby and Kristen stand a few feet behind her. The tension caused by Piper's fragility meeting the officer's insensitivity is almost physical.

"Okay, next. Let's hear it. What's your reason for being here?"

"I have a stalker. My former college professor. He's stalking me. It began two and a half years ago."

"Ma'am, I'm going to cut you off right there. I can't go back two and a half years ago. Why don't you tell me something that's happened *recently*?"

As if she's just been slapped in the face, Piper pauses to compose herself. *Don't cry. Don't cry. Don't cry*, she silently repeats, begging herself to be strong.

"I understand. Okay, well...a few months ago —"

"I said recent. What happened to you, let's say, today?" he says, his brow furrowing. His slicked-back black hair and rolled-up shirt sleeves are a perfect match for his personality.

Piper forces herself to swallow, though her mouth feels dry as sandpaper.

"This morning. He was in the workout room in my apartment building at five a.m. Before work."

"So you're telling me you're filing a stalking emergency order of protection against some guy for being in your workout room *today*?"

Piper can't fight back anymore. Hot tears stream down her face.

Bobby can't help it. He steps forward, interjecting, "Come on, man, she's trying to tell you her story. You won't let her give you any backstory, so you're giving her nothing to work with. She has a stalker. A former professor has been stalking her for the last two and a half years and is threatening her safety. Is there someone else we can speak with?"

"For starters, I am it. Lucky for you all, it's just me on the desk today." He leans back in his chair. "Sure, give me a little backstory, but make it quick. I don't have all day."

At a loss for words, Piper searches for something to say. She feels as confident as an ant on a busy restaurant patio.

"My college professor admitted his obsession with me two and a half years ago. In the last two months, I've seen him around my apartment complex a handful of times. He keeps popping up in places I frequent. He showed up at my work last month. And this morning, he was in the workout room in my building. I've confirmed he moved into my building eight months ago. I don't feel safe, and I would like to file an Emergency Order of Protection until I can get a restraining order approved."

"Hmmm. Okay, thanks for wrapping that up so quickly. Given the circumstances, and the fact that pretty much anyone who requests a Temporary Order of Protection for due reason is granted one, I can do that for you. If I can give you one piece of advice, it would be to brush up on your story before you talk to any other authorities and certainly before you go to court."

Talk about kicking someone when they're already down. Piper glares at Officer P. Brenner, as his name tag reads. *This guy is less respectable than the scum on my shoe*, she thinks, repeating his words in her head.

"This will take me a few minutes to write up. I'll be back in a flash," he says with a cheap smile.

Piper turns and is met with a steady, grounding hug from Kristen.

"Now, this is not what I was expecting," Bobby whispers. "I mean, it definitely comes down to the person, but this prick is next level. Not that you care what I think, but don't listen to a word of his belittling advice. He's trying to get in your head. Just block it out."

Officer Brenner whistles on his way back to Piper. "Here you go, miss, your Emergency Order of Protection. While this does protect you legally, you'll need to file for an actual Order of Protection, which —" he glances at his watch, "yeah, you'll have to do on Monday at the County Court. And then, this professor will need to be served papers, which can be quite the feat. Good luck!"

Piper imagines herself punching the smirk off his face as hard as she can. "Thank you," she mutters, turning to walk out with Kristen and Bobby.

"Well, that went about as bad as it could've gone," Piper admits, staring off into the distance, feeling utterly confused. She arrived confident in her story, but now…

"I have a good story, right? I mean, it's clear to you that Hoover is a wack job? I used to be the naïve one and walked in here thinking it was so obvious, but now I'm just confused. Do I even have a case?"

"Piper, yes," Kristen and Bobby say in unison.

"Let me reassure you, you have a case," Bobby adds. "I'd put money on it that this loser got demoted to the desk for doing something stupid and is taking out his own woes on easy targets like you. Do not let him get in your head. The important thing is you got what we came here for, and nothing else matters. Upward and onward, one thing at a time. On Monday, you'll take your next step. In the meantime, I'd recommend getting a lawyer, just so you're prepared for what's to come."

Bobby runs his fingers through his hair.

"I think you're right. We'll consider this a step in the right direction. I know my dad's working on the whole lawyer situation, and I'll connect with him on that. Listen, I can't thank you enough for being here. Can you imagine if I'd been here alone?

This situation actually could've been worse," Piper says with a half-hearted laugh, throwing her hair into a ponytail, revealing the dark circles framing her eyes.

"Piper, I'm proud of you," Kristen says softly. "This isn't easy. In fact, it totally sucks. But you're standing up for yourself, and you *will* come out of this on the other side soon. I know it's not soon enough, but it's in the near future. If you need anything — *anything* — you call us. Doesn't matter the day or time. We're here."

"Thanks, girl. I appreciate you. I'll keep you guys posted on how Monday goes."

Piper walks toward her car. After closing the door, she stares down at the flimsy yellow paper in her hand.

EMERGENCY ORDER OF PROTECTION

PETITIONER
Piper P. Hawthorne

RESPONDENT
Joseph R. Hoover

THE COURT FINDS:
That it has jurisdiction over the Petitioner and subject matter, and that the Respondent will be provided with reasonable notice and an opportunity to be heard within the time required by Illinois law.

THE COURT ORDERS:
That Respondent is ordered to stay away from Petitioner.

The terms of this order shall be effective until May 6, 2011, at 11:59 p.m.

Piper starts to whisper another quiet prayer, then stops herself.

What's the point anymore? she fumes.

Three weeks. I am safe for three weeks.

Or am I?

Something deep down tells her she's anything but.

21

PROFESSOR HOOVER

After developing the photos of Piper from his 35mm film in the bathroom and hanging them to dry, Professor Hoover picks up his phone and types *H-A-R-M-O-N C-O-N-S-U-L-T-I-N-G* into Google, pulling up their business page. He hovers over the Call button, thumb trembling, before finding enough self-control to stop himself.

To call or not to call and ask if Piper is there...that is the predicament.

He replays the day in his mind, like he's done dozens of times on repeat since watching her roll away a suitcase midday with a girl and some tall man who hugged her. *Why the hell would someone be hugging my Piper?*

She left this morning, as she does every morning. Nothing out of the norm — except today we had our shared workout encounter, which is notable. She did take a taxi instead of walking to the L, but that's not too crazy.

But why did she come back? Thank goodness I have the day off and was able to catch her. I was eating lunch right here, about to go on a midday walk, and I'm one hundred percent positive it was her I saw exiting our building with a black suitcase.

That's it. I can't take this.

He presses *Call*.

"Harmon Consulting, this is Cheryl speaking. How may I direct your call?"

"Hello there. I'm calling from the *Chicago Tribune*...just returning a call for a Miss Piper. Could you put me through?"

"One moment, please. I'll place you on hold."

Hmm. I must have gotten it wrong. But damn, those binoculars don't lie.

"Hi, this is Piper. Sorry, I can't come to the phone right now. Please leave your name and number, and I'll ring you back ASAP."

Click.

"Arrraaagh!" Hoover screams. "This is not part of my plan!" Sweat begins pooling in his armpits.

Breaking the silent promise he made to Piper, he opens the iSpy app on his phone. She is, in fact, driving west on I-90.

I wasn't planning to take a trip today. But I'll do anything for you.

Little Miss Piper, where are we headed, my sweet girl?

22

SINKING DEEP

Piper stares out the small basement window. It's 9 a.m., and she's struggling to peel herself out of bed, her new norm.

She knows Kate left for the office hours ago. She heard the garage door creak open, thought about getting up, then rolled over and pulled a pillow over her face, sleeping for another three hours.

When Piper first moved into Kate's basement two weeks ago, she and Kate made a pact: Piper wouldn't leave the house unless absolutely necessary.

At first, she thought adapting to suburban life might be fun — making morning Starbucks runs for her and Kate, wandering Target aisles, taking daily walks through the park. But reality set in. Kate has a family to protect. And while she's trying to keep Piper safe, she's also shielding everyone else, which means not letting Hoover find out where she lives. So, Piper stays hidden in what she half-jokingly calls the dungeon, only venturing out for approved outings.

Even surrounded by Kate's nanny and five kids, ages two through twelve, Piper can't shake the constant urge to look over her shoulder. She sometimes steps outside for air, but that only makes it worse. Any passing car, any stranger walking a dog, sends her into a tailspin. She keeps telling herself there's no threat, but her body doesn't believe her. Her heart races. Her chest tightens. Her breathing shallows. Her palms slick with sweat.

Eventually, she stops going outside all together.

She feels like she's losing her mind.

Today, Kate and Piper agreed it was time for her to go to AT&T and get a new phone and number. Not for any specific reason, just to be extra cautious.

After filing for an Order of Protection at the courthouse, Piper had her RAV4 checked for bugs. It came back clean. Kate had pushed her to do it, since the car sits in their driveway and everyone needed the peace of mind.

She's been logging into her computer every day but mostly finds herself staring blankly at the screen, like rereading the same line in a book three times and still not comprehending it. She sends a few emails here and there so her colleagues know she's alive and think she's working, but in truth, she's been removed as lead from all her projects for the foreseeable future.

Kate has been nothing but gracious, giving Piper a place to stay and endless understanding at work. Still, last night Piper broke down, insisting Kate let her go. Kate wouldn't hear it. She told her, *this too shall pass*, and promised her mind would settle with time.

A knock on Piper's door startles her, and she jumps from the bed.

"Piper, just checking in on you, sweetheart," says Sophia, Kate's nanny. "Can I make you breakfast? You name it. Pancakes, eggs, cinnamon toast, yogurt parfait..."

"Morning, Sophia. I'm okay, don't worry about me," Piper says, forcing a small smile. "Just waking up as we speak. I'm good on breakfast for now, but maybe in a little bit."

"Hmmm, okay. I'll leave a yogurt parfait in the fridge for you. Be sure to grab it. You need to eat, my dear. I'm going to walk to the park with Georgey, and we'll be back in about an hour."

"Sounds good," Piper calls through the door. "I'm going to run to the phone store to get a new one and will be back in a bit."

She cracks open her blinds, letting in just enough light to see what she's doing. Stretching her arms overhead, she slowly walks to the closet. She grabs a pair of black leggings and an oversized black T-shirt. A month ago, she wouldn't have been caught dead wearing this, but here she is.

Piper's space is surprisingly nice. Kate has given her everything she could hope for: an espresso machine, a small workout room, a bedroom with a kitchenette, and a cozy area to work. Her situation could be much worse.

Her eyes land on her running shoes. She hesitates, then looks away. Kate's workout room has everything she needs, including a treadmill, an elliptical, and free weights. But she hasn't touched it.

Instead, she walks to the small, connected bathroom. Catching her reflection, she studies her grease-laden hair and debates taking a shower. She really should. Instead, she grabs her dry shampoo, sprays a cloud of herbal-scented mist, and pulls on her plain black hat. She's been wearing a hat almost every day. It's comforting, like a disguise, a small way to feel invisible.

She grabs her phone. It's 9:35 a.m. *Right on time*, she thinks, heading toward the office Kate set up for her.

She looks like she's playing a game of hot lava, sidestepping over Legos, blocks, racetracks, and toy cars on her way to the desk. Tucked in the far corner of the basement, she's carved out a quaint little nook. Kate had an extra desk and outfitted it with a Sonos speaker, a vase of fresh flowers, and Piper's laptop.

The finishing touch is the watercolor print she found on Etsy, a verse from Isaiah written in soft brushstrokes —

> "When you pass through the waters, I will be with you; and through the rivers, they shall not overwhelm you; when you walk through fire you shall not be burned, and the flame shall not consume you." — *Isaiah 43:2*

It should be comforting. It should remind her to breathe, to trust. But lately, every time she looks at it, it only makes her fume.

Piper powers up her laptop and is greeted by an inbox of 102 emails, nearly all of them she's copied or blind-copied on. She does a quick scan and exhales. None require her to respond.

Her phone catches her attention when it pings with a text from Kate.

> Text me after you get your new number. I'll send it around the office. See if they can forward anything from your old one that's important. Oh, and good morning, sunshine! I have a work dinner tonight, so Sophia will be there late.

Piper holds down Kate's message until a heart appears, liking it, before responding.

> Sounds good. I'm headed there now.

She walks upstairs and is met by the quiet of an empty house, with four kids at school and Georgey at the park. Plates and bowls clutter the counter, remnants of a rushed Wednesday morning.

Outside, she hesitates on the porch, scanning the street for any sign of movement before hurrying toward her car. Her pulse spikes when she spots a long-stemmed white rose tucked inside the handle of the driver's door.

She freezes, eyes darting around. The air suddenly feels too still. Then her gaze lands on Kate's rose bushes near the front walk. She exhales a shaky breath. *One of the kids,* she thinks. *They probably meant it as a sweet surprise.*

Still, her hands tremble as she unlocks the door.

Piper pictures Kate's second-grade son sneaking out with scissors, crouching low, dodging razor-sharp thorns to pick this one flower. The image feels absurd the longer she entertains it, but who else would've done this? No one knows she's living here. *It can't be him.* She swallows hard. *I'm safe here,* she tells herself, downplaying the paranoia she can't seem to shake.

As she slides into the driver's seat, Ryan's face flashes in her mind. Not even he knows how far she's gone to hide. A knot forms in her stomach. *Guess neither of us will ever know what could've been.* There's been so much chaos lately, she hasn't even had time to think about their recent flirty exchange.

Right on cue, her phone pings.

Ryan.

> Hey there, beautiful. I'm so sorry it's taken me so long to reach out. Thanks for being patient with me. Work's been killing me. Which reminds me...we both need to ditch our late-night work antics and hang. When can I take you out?

What in the world, Piper thinks. For the first time since everything fell apart, a small smile breaks the rigidity of her face. *How do I even begin to explain my mess? I can't go out right now — not even for errands, let alone a date.*

> Ryan, it's so good to hear from you! My life is kind of a mess right now. It's such a long, crazy story, I can't even begin to explain it over text. I'm actually on my way to get a new phone and number, but I promise I'll text you after, and we can set something up.

He responds without haste.

> Ok, deal. I'll be waiting…

The twenty-minute drive to the mall feels like a small reprieve from the isolation she's grown used to. Yet at every stoplight, Piper's eyes dart around, searching for any sign of Hoover.

After parking, she pauses, scanning her surroundings in a full circle before crossing the street to AT&T.

"Hello, miss, welcome in!" chirps a plump, middle-aged woman behind the counter. "How can we help you today?"

"I'm here for a new phone. A new everything, really…a new phone and number, please."

"Okaaaay," the woman says, drawing it out. "Hmm, alright, I got you, girl. Is your plan up? We don't do new numbers often, but we certainly can."

"No, my plan's not up." Piper hesitates, her voice tightening as she fights back tears. Through clenched teeth she says, "I have a stalker, and I need a new phone. I don't care what it takes or costs. I need it done today — as in, now. Can you help me?"

Karen, as her name tag reads, clears her throat. "Ah, yes, ma'am. Yes, I can do that. I don't know what's going on, but I just want to say I'm so sorry. I didn't mean to pry…it's just an unusual request, that's all."

"Here's my current phone. I'd like a new iPhone. Whatever color, whatever size you have in stock is fine."

"Let me check what we've got in the back. Give me five."

Piper exhales and offers a silent prayer for help as she wanders through the aisle of phone cases.

"You're in luck, dear!" Karen calls out a few minutes later, her excitement bouncing off the walls. "We've got one white iPhone 4 – 32 gig. This one's been impossible to get. Someone ordered it and never picked it up, so it's yours if you want it. Well, yours for a price," she adds, laughing harder than necessary.

"I'll take it. Can we transfer everything over here?"

"Yes, no problem," Karen says. "Now, I do have something I want to ask. Not to dig…it's obviously none of my business, but before we transfer everything, would you like me to do a quick sweep of your phone? It's not a service we normally offer, but given what you mentioned…you might want to make sure nothing suspicious is running before you move your apps over."

This hadn't even crossed Piper's mind. "How long does a phone sweep take? What are you thinking you might find?" She waves a hand. "Actually, never mind, yeah, let's do it. No downside, right?"

I never leave my phone out of sight, so this feels like a total waste of time, Piper thinks. *But now if I don't do it, I'll drive myself crazy wondering what might've been on there. Thanks, Karen.*

"Okay, great," Karen says, rolling her chair closer. "Say, I can show you how to do this yourself next time. I'm not sure how tech-savvy you are."

From one woman to another, Karen seems like the least tech-savvy person Piper has ever met, but here goes nothing.

"I mean, I know the basics," Piper admits.

"Perfect. Let's start by reviewing your apps. The ones we're looking for are things like PhoneTracker or iSpy. They're not obvious, unfortunately. They usually disguise themselves or run in the background, but we'll comb through everything.

Let's see...wow, you do have quite the app collection! I have a lot of these too. So similar!"

Piper forces a polite smile, catching herself from rolling her eyes. *Get to the point already.*

Karen keeps scrolling. "Whoop — there it is! Would you look at that. You do have one. Did you install this?"

"Did I install what?" Piper asks, her pulse quickening.

"The iSpy tracker," Karen says carefully. "Do your parents track you? Or maybe...a boyfriend?"

Piper frantically rips the phone from Karen's hand. *There it is.* Who would have thought a tiny icon could be so terrifying? Her heart pounds so violently she can hear it in her ears.

"I don't know what this is. No boyfriend. No, I didn't install this. I don't know how this could've happened. How long has this been on here? Don't answer me — just get it off!" Piper's voice cracks, startling even herself with the force of her own panic.

"Okay, alright," Karen says gently, holding out a hand. "First, hand me the phone back."

"I'm sorry," Piper stammers, thrusting it toward her. "This is just...terrifying. I've done everything to keep myself safe. And this..." She lets out a bitter laugh through tears. "I had my car checked for bugs last week, for crying out loud. How did the most obvious thing, the one I take everywhere, not cross my mind?"

Tears streak down her face, and Karen steps forward, pulling her into an unexpected hug.

"It's okay, sweetheart," she murmurs. "It's a tricky one to find. It doesn't live with your main icons. You'd have to dig into the backend. Why would you ever do that? You've done nothing wrong. It's going to be okay. Let's clean this up."

Piper sniffles, nodding. "You know what? I just want to start over. Transfer only my contacts and photos. No messages, no emails, no apps. I'll re-download what I need later. I want a bare-bones phone. Nothing else."

"I hear you, honey. Easy peasy." Karen gives her a small smile. "I'll delete the app first, just for the satisfaction. Let's send this creep a message when he realizes he can't track you anymore."

Her tone softens. "And this might sound strange, but there's something about you. I can't explain it, but I know you're going to be okay. God's got big plans for you. I can feel it in my bones."

Piper meets her eyes. An unfamiliar calm trickles through her. She wipes her nose with the back of her hand. "Thank you, Karen. Truly. I needed that reminder. It's been hard to see God in any of this."

Karen grins and slides the new phone across the counter. "Here you go...new phone, who's this? Contacts, check. Photos, check. No apps, no messages, no emails. Clean as a whistle. Go pick out a fun case. New start, you know what I mean? On me, honey."

Piper scans the store and, for the first time in weeks, doesn't glance over her shoulder when the door pings open. "Really? Thank you so much. I appreciate everything."

She picks a clear case dusted with gold flecks. Karen rings her up and waves goodbye as Piper steps out into the parking lot.

The second she's in her car, the floodgates open. She cries so hard her breaths come in broken gasps, her chest heaving until her eyelids swell.

She cries for how much worse this is than she imagined. She cries for the stranger's kindness. For the loss of her freedom, her apartment, her work, her peace. For the life she used to know. She cries because she wants nothing more than to text Ryan, to go on a date, to feel normal again. She cries because she has never felt so alone.

Her life feels like a swirling black hole, sucking her under... quicksand she can't escape. She's clawing for light, but it refuses to show itself. And just when she thinks she's catching her breath, realization hits like a blow.

She has to drive back to *the dungeon*.

And now she knows the truth —

Hoover knows exactly where she's been hiding.

He's known all along.

23

PROFESSOR HOOVER

Professor Hoover is run-walking his way along the Lakeshore Path, hopeful that if he runs long enough, he'll find clarity. It's been exactly fourteen days since he last saw Piper wheeling away a suitcase, and he feels heartsick over it.

At first, he told himself it was a coincidence...that she'd simply gone on vacation. But his tracker shows she's been staying in the suburbs and hasn't left the house once since arriving. The place looks nice. He looked it up on Zillow, of course. He's particularly fond of the white rose bushes out front. Her boss, Kate, must have plenty of hired help to manage everything she does. He'd assumed Piper was visiting family or tied up with an extended work project.

But one can only hide from reality for so long.

He's lost in thought, running through his options — what he can still control, what he can execute from afar...when his phone pings. A surge of excitement hits. *Maybe she's finally come around. Maybe she's reaching out.*

He slows to a stop and glances at the screen. It's an alert from iSpy. His pulse quickens, then drops.

Contact deactivated: Piper has been removed from your favorites.

"No. No. NO!" he shouts, before realizing people around him are staring.

Without thinking, he dials her number.

"We're sorry. You have reached a number that has been disconnected or is no longer in service," says the monotone voice of a female operator.

"No. No! NO!" he screams again.

He throws the phone down. It hits the pavement and shatters.

"This is not part of my plan! Stop messing with what's meant to be and just let it happen!" he yells, oblivious to the eyes on him.

After a long beat, he straightens, forces a slow breath, and crouches to gather the broken pieces. Then he turns and starts the long walk home.

Game on, Piper.

You can run. You can hide. You can even deactivate.

But I am smarter.

And I will find you.

I always do.

We're meant to be, Piper. If you can't see that yourself...I'll have to make you.

24

NEW DIGS

The last week has been nothing short of a whirlwind. After discovering the tracker on her phone, Piper's parents immediately drove to Chicago with one mission in mind: to find her a new apartment. By the grace of God, on day one of searching, they did just that.

They worked with a kind man named Percy, who helped them find a place that felt safe — a studio apartment in the city's Streeterville neighborhood, just off the Chicago River. Piper will be able to live near the water, run along the path outside her door, and walk to work once things settle.

The best part: the building's management company allowed Piper to rent the unit under an alias, making her effectively untraceable. Her dad even connected with the head doorman to explain her situation.

Mike, the big, burly teddy bear her dad described him as, went straight into protector mode. He asked for a photo of Hoover to tape at the front desk so every doorman would recognize him and ensure he never steps foot in the building.

Piper has done her part, too. She deleted all her social

media accounts and opened a P.O. box to protect her privacy this time around.

Now, as she packs the last of her belongings at Kate's house, Ryan drifts into her mind. She still hasn't texted him like she promised, and now that she's heading back to the city, it finally feels right.

> Ryan…it's Piper. Remember me? Haha, sorry for the delay. I'm moving back to the city today (long story) and would love to see you sometime.

To her giddy surprise, her phone pings right away.

> I could never forget you, Piper. Sounds like an occasion we need to celebrate. Can I bring dinner and help you unpack?

Piper can't contain herself. She sends him a text right back.

> Dinner, yes! That sounds great. I promise I won't put you to work. I'm hoping I'll be settled by then. Fingers crossed. See you at 7?

Her phone pings with a response.

> 7 it is. Looking forward to it.

Piper's stomach twists with anticipation. She zips up her suitcase, hauls it upstairs, and exhales. For the first time in weeks, the day ahead doesn't feel suffocating. It feels like a new beginning.

"Is it that time already? Piper, these three weeks have flown by. We've loved having you here with us," Kate says, tears welling in her eyes. "You're like a daughter to me, you know that? Or maybe more like a sister, I'm not *that* old," she adds with a laugh as tears spill down her cheeks. "You are smart, strong, brave, and resilient, Piper. Don't you forget it. You're going to find redemption in this trial. I just know it. Hang in there, and don't let go. God's got you, girl. I had that watercolor made downstairs just for you. Take it with you, as a housewarming gift."

Piper embraces her, speechless. "It's hard to put into words how thankful I am for everything. You have a beautiful family, Kate. I mean that. I'm so grateful you let me be part of it. Thank you, truly. And thank you for the painting. You're too good to me."

Kate wipes her cheeks and smiles. "Now stop making me cry. Take the weekend, and however much time you need, to get settled and feel comfortable. We can't wait to have you back at work, but there's no rush. Alright, I'm off to the office. Catch you soon, Blondie!"

Piper heads back downstairs to straighten up the bedroom that's been her safety net. She strips the bed, grabs her towels, and starts the washer. She tidies up her makeshift basement office and leaves a note on Kate's desk, mentioning that something is coming in the mail as a small thank-you. She picks up the painted scripture verse to take with her, knowing she won't be able to hang it for a while.

Before leaving, Piper stops by the kitchen to drop off a note for Sophia and a baggie filled with treats and goodies for each of the kids.

She steps outside, breathes in the fresh morning air, and lets herself hope — really hope — that this will be the start of something safe and new.

On her drive to the city, she dials her parents.

"Hey, Piper! Are you on your way?" her mom answers. "I've got you on speaker. Your dad's here too. We're so sorry we can't be there today for the big reveal. We've got that charity event we committed to months ago, but it doesn't feel right not being there. Still, it's reassuring that we didn't see that creep even once while moving you out."

"You guys, please don't worry," Piper says. "You've done enough already. You spent the last three days moving me out of one place and into the next. I still can't believe you did that."

Her parents had spent two straight days boxing up all her belongings, then oversaw the movers who packed and delivered everything to her new apartment, and even stayed to help unpack. It was exhausting and emotional for everyone, but they did it without hesitation.

"Piper, someday you'll understand…you do these things for your kids without thinking twice about it. We love you, and all we care about is your safety and well-being. When we thought we couldn't do it, we came up with the mantra 'one shelf at a time,' and that made things manageable. You should try that too…one shelf, one day, one minute at a time. You'll get through this. We all will."

"I don't even know how to thank you," Piper says, her voice breaking.

"You don't need to," her dad replies gently. "Just stay safe. Be smart. Take cabs. I know you know all the things. And let's check in every day, okay? A call, a text, whatever. We just want to hear from you." He pauses. "Oh, and when you get there, make sure to connect with Mike. He wants to meet you. He's going to make sure you're safe, trust me."

"Mike, got it. Sounds good. I'll be there in ten. Love you guys," she says, hanging up.

Piper pulls up to the turnabout of her new apartment building, Riverside Place, and turns on her flashers. She steps out, unloads her suitcase, and heads toward the entrance.

"You must be Piper," calls a man with short gray coils, a raspy voice, and a warm smile.

"Yes, that's me. You must be Mike. My dad's a big fan already," she says, smiling back.

"Yes, ma'am. Good to finally meet you," he says, extending a fist for a friendly pound. "Now listen, I've got your back, you hear me? I've got a photo of this guy, and everyone on staff knows the situation. We won't let anybody in who shouldn't be here. You have my word."

"Thank you so much, Mike. That's really reassuring." She exhales, tension leaving her shoulders. "Alright, I'll get to it."

"Oh, and your car," he adds. "Give me your keys and I'll have it valeted. Ring the desk whenever you need it, okay? I got you, girl. And here are your two sets of keys. You know which apartment's yours?"

"Yes, I do. My parents filled me in after their entirely too long week." She grins. "This is all so great. Thank you for your help."

Mike opens the glass double doors to Riverside Place, and Piper wheels her suitcase through. She takes in her surroundings as she presses *four* on the elevator panel, her stomach fluttering with something that almost feels like excitement.

The building is clean and sophisticated. After walking past the doorman's desk, another set of glass doors opens for Piper as if on command. She steps through and finds herself in an expansive foyer with forest-green suede chairs opposite the elevator and a large glass entry table topped with a massive decorative vase. This place is already so much nicer than her last.

She enters the elevator and steps off on the fourth floor. Apartment 406. She unlocks the door and gasps, covering her mouth. Piper didn't expect this place to look so settled. Her bed is made, furniture arranged, closet organized. A bouquet of fresh tulips sits on the center island beside a wooden slab etched with *Welcome Home*.

Her studio apartment is everything she could have hoped for. The wood floors are an upgrade, complemented by linen-colored cupboards and a creamy white tiled backsplash. Her parents must have run out and bought the neutral patterned rug that warms the space and separates the bedroom area. *She is in love.*

She dials her mom. "Okay, you've outdone yourself. I'm literally speechless. Not only did you move me in, but it actually feels homey, which I didn't expect. I feel safe here, and I'm surprisingly excited to be back in the city," she says enthusiastically.

"Oh, Piper, we're thrilled to hear you say that. Your voice sounds happy, and that's exactly what we were going for. Relax, get settled, and enjoy your night, sweets. At some point, take a little tour of the building. The indoor lap pool and outdoor patio with grills and chaise lounges are quite spectacular. We love you."

"Gah, I can't wait. Thank you...thank you both so much!"

Piper cues up some country music on her Sonos and gets to work on the final step of moving in — unpacking her suitcase.

For the first time in a long time, she feels at home. In this moment, something unmistakable whispers to her heart, *you're going to be okay.* It feels like God's reaching out, like He's there. It feels good, familiar, like she wants to reach back, but right now, in the thick of her chaos, she just doesn't have the capacity.

Piper hangs the clothes that got her through her weeks at Kate's and gets lost organizing her bathroom. Her phone buzzes, and she can't help but smile when she sees that it's from Ryan.

> You still want to hang tonight? Don't forget to send me your address (assuming you're not having second thoughts ;).

She's lost track of time. It's 5 p.m. They agreed on 7. p.m. Piper desperately needs to shower.

> Yes, of course I'm down! Riverside Place, apartment 406. The doorman will ring me when you get here (I think). Otherwise, call me and I'll run down. See you soon.

Ryan replies right away.

> Can't wait.

Piper finishes organizing and hops in the shower. She rinses her hair with her best-smelling shampoo, takes extra time shaving all her parts for no particular reason, and pats herself dry. She takes her time getting ready. She hasn't blow-dried and styled her hair, or even worn makeup like this, in weeks. She doesn't want to look like she's trying too hard, so she opts for black leggings, a cropped T-shirt that shows a hint of her stomach, and an oversized chambray button-down. Comfortable. Sexy. Effortless.

She picks up the last of her things, straightens the bathroom, and lights the soy candle her mom left behind.

Her phone rings, and she immediately answers. "Piper girl, it's Mike. You all settled up there?"

"Yes, I am! Believe it or not, my parents did all the hard work. I just had to show up."

"Glad to hear it. You deserve it. Listen, I've got a visitor here. Some guy..." She hears muffled chatter on the other end. "He goes by the name of Ryan. You want me to let him up?"

"Yes, I'm expecting him. You can let him up. Thanks, Mike."

"You got it." He drops his voice to a whisper. "Hey, listen... you save this number. You need anything, and I mean *anything*, you call down and I'll be up faster than you can count to three. I got you, girl."

"Thanks, Mike. That's so reassuring. I'll definitely call if I need anything," she says with a chuckle.

The next thing she knows, there's a light knock at her door, and her heart jolts.

She casually opens the door and is met by Ryan, wearing a white henley and jeans, his dimpled smile exactly as she's remembered it the past few weeks. He's so handsome she can hardly stand it.

She breathes deep to slow the pace of her heart.

He steps inside and hands her a stunning bouquet of pastel-colored flowers before wrapping his arms around her waist. Even his scent, sandalwood and citrus, feels intoxicating.

"Piper, it's been way too long," he says softly into her ear. When he pulls back, he holds her gaze, and the air between them seems to hum.

She feels a flutter in her chest. She can't quite pinpoint what she's feeling, which is unfamiliar. She wants this, but her life is complicated. She doesn't want to get emotionally attached, not when everything around her feels so fragile. But it's been so long since she's felt this good. *Stop overthinking, Piper. Just let go for once.*

He glances around the apartment. "The place looks great! Here I thought I'd have to help you unpack, but you're already settled." He sets down a takeout bag.

"I can thank my parents for that. They did all the hard work. I pretty much just showed up."

"Sounds like a last-minute move. Crazy that your parents did it all for you." He studies her face. "Feels like I'm missing some pieces to the story. You said we had a lot to catch up on."

"Yeah, we sure do." She laughs nervously. "My life's... honestly, I don't even know where to start. But we don't have to get into it. I'm just happy for this distraction. My first night in my new place. Thanks for being here."

"I want to hear it all. Lay it on me." He pulls two glass bottles from the bag. "I brought us some pre-mixed cocktails, mules or margaritas. Take your pick. And I hope you like Thai food, because that's what we've got."

"This is perfect. Sounds delicious. I'll take a margarita. My favorite." She grabs two glasses and watches him pour.

He hands her one. "Cheers to new beginnings, Piper. Thanks for letting me be your first guest." He winks, and they clink glasses. "Alright, start from the beginning."

Piper motions to the loveseat in the main room. Technically it's across from her bed, but the way her parents arranged the rug and furniture makes the studio feel bigger than it is.

"Okay, well, first of all, judgment-free zone, please. This story's so wild you might not believe it's true. But it is." Heat rises to her cheeks. She takes a deep breath, pushing it down.

Ryan leans back and tucks a pillow under his arm, forearms flexed. "This is a safe zone. No judgment here. How bad can it be?"

"Okay, here goes." She inhales sharply.

"When I graduated college, two and a half years ago now, the night before my final exam, one of my communications professors sent me a long, disturbing email confessing his obsession with me.

"This wasn't someone I was ever close to. He was just a teacher...socially awkward, but harmless...or so I thought.

"I filed a police report and went to the school, but they did nothing. They kept him on staff, said he was getting counseling.

"Fast forward to a few months ago...I started seeing him around. Outside the Barnes & Noble by my train stop, at the commissary in my old apartment complex...he even showed up at my office pretending to be a potential client while I was away on a business trip. It was all strange, but I kept telling myself he never actually saw me.

"Clearly, I was naïve. A couple weeks ago, we had a run-in, at 5 a.m., in my apartment building's workout room. I completely freaked out.

"After some digging, I learned he'd moved into my building eight months earlier. I filed another police report, got an emergency order of protection, and moved out that day.

"I've been living with my boss for the past three weeks, until I found out he'd bugged my phone. Tracked me. I have no idea how.

"So, I got a new number, and my parents helped me find this apartment. They just moved me out of my old place and into this one this week.

"That's me in a nutshell. Take a moment to process the train wreck. Still want to hang out with me? I'm a mess, Ryan…a complete mess."

She exhales for the first time in minutes.

Ryan's jaw tightens, his lips pressed thin. "Piper, what the hell? I'm so sorry. I can't believe you've been going through that. Dang, now I'm really kicking myself for not calling sooner. Where does this guy live?"

"I don't need you to do anything. I've got it handled." She sighs. "Who knows where he's living now. Maybe he's still in my old building at Lake Shore and Banks, or maybe he's somewhere else. My parents never ran into him when they moved me out, so I have no idea."

"Promise me something," he says, voice low and steady. "Next time something happens, or you feel scared — call me. Promise me you'll call."

"Okay, sure. I can do that."

The thought of bringing Ryan into her chaos fills Piper with both comfort and dread. It would be such a relief to share the weight of it, but she can't let him get pulled in.

Ryan interlaces his fingers and leans closer. "I can't explain it, Piper. I care about you, and I don't even know you that well. But every time I see you, I want to know you more. Whatever you need, however I can help — I'm here."

Piper holds his gaze, unsure how to respond. Her teeth graze her bottom lip, and his eyes flicker downward.

He clears his throat, breaking the tension. "You hungry? Let's dig in." He stands and walks toward the bag of Thai food. "You okay if I make myself at home and find some plates? I figured we could share."

"You go right ahead. I haven't even gotten that far. I don't know where anything is yet, so we're in the same boat," she says with a laugh, her cheeks warm as she smiles with her eyes.

Ryan divides the chicken pad Thai, spicy broccoli cashew rice, and pork egg rolls between two plates.

"Okay, your turn," Piper says, tucking a strand of hair behind her ear as she lifts a bite of pad Thai. "What's going on in your world? Hopefully it's a little less dramatic than mine."

"My world's...chugging along," he says, shrugging.

"I mentioned this before, but I can't seem to find any balance. I'm on track to be a partner at my firm in the next few years, which, honestly, is kind of unheard of. It's great. I'm grateful.

"But it's coming at the expense of everything else. I don't have much time for anything social, or even for myself. I want to eat home-cooked meals, work out every day, live slower. But my reality and what I want are at odds.

"I'm trying to figure out what success is worth, and whether I actually want it."

"That's tough." Piper nods, chewing thoughtfully. "I was in a similar boat — well, not really. But I was a workaholic before all this happened. Everything that's gone on lately has put things into perspective. I'm not making any promises, but when I go back to the office, I hope the old me is gone. I'm going to make boundaries." She pauses, then smiles. "Can you try that? Easier said than done, I know."

"It's so cutthroat. I don't know if it's even possible. But I'm trying to figure that part out," he says, swirling his fork in the noodles.

"Where do you see yourself in five years, Ryan?" she asks lightly between bites, then instantly cringes at herself. *Why did I just ask that?*

He laughs. "Cutting right to it, huh?" His gaze locks on hers, that same easy smile that makes her insides melt.

"I'll be honest with you, Piper. I know most guys my age wouldn't say this, but — I want to settle down. Don't get me wrong, I still want to have fun. But I'm not looking to date around just to pass time. Being with someone doesn't scare me.

"I want a partner. Someone to navigate life with, travel with, laugh with. In five years, I hope I have that. And hopefully I'll have figured out this work-life balance thing by then."

Piper laughs softly. "You're already ahead of most."

"What about you, Piper?" he asks, his tone gentle. "What do you think your life will look like five years from now? A lifetime away…and yet just a blink."

Piper looks down at her plate. The question stings more than it should. *I've been living one day at a time*, she thinks. *How can I picture five years from now when I'm barely getting through today?*

"My life is complicated, as you now know. I've been living day to day for so long, not by choice or because I've mastered living in the present. I wish that were the case." She sighs, her gaze drifting toward the window. "Five years from now, I just hope I feel safe. I hope I'm not running anymore. I hope Hoover is out of my life once and for all. I hope I can sleep through the night without looking over my shoulder."

She exhales.

"To be totally honest, it's hard for me to share my life right now. I can't quite explain it, except to say it's messy…and I don't want to lean on someone emotionally because of that. I don't want to cling to someone for the wrong reasons."

She meets his eyes. "What I'm trying to say is — I like you, Ryan. I really do. And I want to spend more time with you. But the timing of my life is complicated. And while there's never a perfect time, this doesn't feel like it. Five years from now, I hope I'll be free and open...and ready for more."

Piper looks away, her pulse quickening. She knows this isn't what he expected. She hadn't expected it either; it just spilled out. She doesn't even realize until now that Ryan has taken her hand, his thumb tracing gentle circles across her palm.

"While I can't completely relate to what you're going through," he says quietly, "I can imagine why you feel that way. It makes sense, and it's okay." His voice softens. "Despite everything I just told you, I promise there's no pressure. We can take things slow. Be friends. Let things unfold however they're meant to."

He gives a small laugh. "Okay, time to lighten things up." But Piper can see the truth flicker in his eyes — he wants more.

"Where's your dream trip, Piper?" he asks after a pause. "If we could hop on a plane tonight, where would we go?" The way he speaks, intentional and unhurried, is something she admires. Despite everything she's said, all of her is wrapped up in this moment...in him.

Piper takes a sip of her drink, buying time. "If we were packing our bags tonight, I'd tell you to pack for somewhere warm." She grins, lost in the image unfolding in her mind. "We'd go to a beach somewhere secluded and impossibly beautiful, like Bora Bora. We'd swim, soak in the sun, and finally rest. Just rest."

"Let's do it someday," Ryan says, serious now. His eyes lock on hers, searching for a sliver of hope that she feels the same.

Her heart lurches. She wants to shout *yes, of course*. But she knows better than anyone that the future has a will of its own. Still, her hopeful heart betrays her. "Let's do it," she says softly, even as doubt whispers in the back of her mind.

"Pinky promise me." Ryan extends his pinky.

For some reason, the gesture feels more intimate than it should. "Pinky promise it is," she says, hooking her finger with his.

He lowers his voice to a whisper. "I think you're supposed to seal a pinky promise with a kiss."

"Oh, really?" Piper laughs, unable to hide her smile. He kisses his thumb first, slow and deliberate, and as he starts to lift his head, she follows. Their cheeks brush. She can feel the stubble on his jaw, the warmth of his breath. Then he tilts her chin, closing the gap between them. His lips are soft, his touch gentle.

As quickly as it begins, it's over. His touch lingers like a trace of sunlight on her skin, and she wishes it had lasted longer.

"The moment got the best of me," Ryan says, grinning as he steps back. "I respect you and everything you've shared tonight. I don't want you to feel any pressure from me, Piper. I mean that." He gathers their plates, rinsing them in the sink before loading the dishwasher.

"How are you feeling," he asks, glancing over his shoulder as he wipes the counter, "being in a new apartment on your own again?"

He's too good to be true, Piper thinks.

"So far, I feel pretty good. I'm trying to focus on the things I'm thankful for. The fact that my parents moved me in, the view of the lake, the doorman downstairs, how homey it feels here." She looks off toward the window before her voice drops. "I'm also scared, Ryan. I'm scared he's going to find me again. But I'm really trying to take it one day at a time."

Ryan rests his hand gently on her back, his thumb tracing small circles through her shirt. "Anytime you're scared, you should call me, Piper."

"I don't know...your phone would be ringing off the hook," she says with a laugh.

"I mean it. Call me," he says, his tone soft but steady. "I'll remind you how tough you are. How far you've come. That you've got this."

The next two hours disappear in a blink. Piper loses herself in the evening. Ryan is everything she could want — charming, handsome, funny, grounded. *If only I could just let go and let this happen.*

When they finish their second drink, Ryan glances at his watch. "Oh wow, I didn't even realize it's 10:30. You probably want to get some sleep. I've got a 6 a.m. call tomorrow that's already haunting me." He grabs his black canvas jacket, rugged yet perfectly fitted.

"I'd love to see you again sometime soon, if you're up for it," he says, slipping it on and holding her gaze.

"Yes, I'd love that."

She's torn. Every logical part of her says be careful, but her heart pulls closer. She takes a step toward him, and his hug lingers a beat longer than friendly. When she looks up, he leans down and kisses her — soft, hesitant, deliberate. It ends too soon.

He brushes a loose strand of hair behind her ear. "Thanks for having me tonight, and for trusting me with all that. You helped me forget about work, and maybe you forgot a few things too."

"I did," she says quietly. "You helped me forget everything, even if just for a few hours."

"Anytime, Piper. See you soon."

He lets himself out.

"Gah," Piper mutters, leaning against the closed door. Her heart aches for more. Ryan is the first man she's truly been drawn to in so long, but her head keeps whispering *protect yourself.*

———

The next morning, sunlight slips through her blinds, brushing her cheek. Piper reaches for her phone, half hoping for a text from Ryan, but the only notification is from her dad.

Disappointment gives way to guilt. She's the one who told Ryan to take things slow.

> Nothing urgent, just wanted to update you. Our lawyer, Jennifer, was able to have papers delivered to Hoover—amazing news! What a blessing. He was out of state, so this was a big undertaking. It means our court date will go on as planned. We'll see you for it next week. Call us when you're settled today. Love you!

The pit in her stomach returns. Last night, for a few precious hours, she'd managed to forget the chaos her life had become. But reality always catches up. You can only outrun it for so long before it finds you again.

What am I thinking? Trying to start something with a guy, some amazing guy she actually likes, when this is her reality. She can't let herself get attached just because she's drowning.

She takes a shaky breath and meets her own reflection in the mirror.

Alright. Here we go.
A promise to myself:
I will not see Ryan again until this is over.
I need to protect him.
I can't pull him into this. What if Hoover tries something?

Tears streak her cheeks as she whispers, "I've always kept my promises."

And this one, she knows, she can't afford to break.

25

PROFESSOR HOOVER

Professor Hoover sits on the frail twin bed in the tiny guest room of his sister's house in St. Louis, Missouri, tracing the faded green-and-blue paisley comforter. This is not how he pictured things unfolding. After being kicked out of his apartment for what he still calls "confusing reasons," he truly had nowhere else to go. And since he's now barred from contacting the one person he loves most in the world, leaving town until things "settle" seemed like the wisest move.

So he called the only person who came to mind — his sister, Myra.

Myra, three years his senior, skipped college and moved in with her high school sweetheart, Colton, the week after graduation. Their life, as far as Hoover is concerned, is painfully dull.

The two of them grew up *close enough*, bound by necessity more than affection. Their father was always working, and survival required teamwork. But once Myra left for small-town married life and Hoover headed to Chicago, their relationship withered. Not out of animosity, just disinterest. Hoover has never been one for small talk or family visits.

After ignoring repeated calls from his apartment management and being formally let go by Midland College, he finally packed up and left. He told himself he was doing it on his terms, even though breaking the lease came with a penalty fee.

Unemployed and essentially homeless, he realized he had no one to turn to. When he called, Myra answered on the first ring. She was thrilled to hear from her little brother after years of silence. She and Colton eagerly converted a downstairs storage closet into a makeshift bedroom. It's cramped and windowless, but Hoover told himself it was temporary.

Myra, a horticulturalist, knows better than anyone that most living things can't survive without light. And the sight of her brother hiding in the dark for days on end worries her deeply.

When the sound of paper sliding under his door breaks the silence, Hoover feels his chest tighten. He picks up the envelope and scans the pages, his pulse ticking faster with every line.

Page one: *Emergency Order of Protection — granted to Piper Hawthorne.*

For a long moment, he just stares. Shock ripples through him. In his mind, they were finally reconnecting. He was making progress, showing her he cared.

Piper's confused, he thinks. *She just doesn't get it...yet.*

Page two: *Notice of Hearing — One-Year Order of Protection Requested.*

A bitter laugh escapes his throat. "A year?" he mutters. "That seems unnecessary." He could choose not to appear, but that would be surrender. And Hoover doesn't surrender. "I'm not a loser," he says aloud. "And I'm sure as hell not letting her think this is over. I'll convince her otherwise."

"Someone just dropped that off," Myra calls from the other side of the door. "Didn't mean to pry, but is everything okay, Joseph?"

He doesn't respond.

After a few seconds pass, she tries again, voice tentative. "You know, I'm baking something real nice for dinner. Why don't you join Colton and me tonight? We can have that long-overdue catch-up."

"Mmhmm, yeah, Myra. Sure. Sounds good," Hoover replies absently, eyes still fixed on the court papers.

Her footsteps fade down the hall.

He exhales through his nose, the anger simmering just beneath the surface. *Fine, Piper. Do whatever you think you need to do.*

A slow smile curls his lips. *You'll see. I'm going to hire the best lawyer in the city. And when it's all over, you'll understand what I've been trying to show you all along.*

That we're meant to be together.

Hoover slams his laptop shut. The sound reverberates through the small, stuffy room.

26

COURT DATE

Piper rolls out of bed with a pit of both anticipation and dread building in her stomach.

What are you up to today? she imagines someone casually asking.

Oh, just going to court to try to get a restraining order against my college professor–turned–stalker. You know...just normal twenty-something-year-old stuff.

She often has to remind herself this is real.

After moving back to the city, she finally admitted she couldn't handle this alone. She'd started seeing both a psychiatrist and a therapist. It was time. When she tried to prepare for that first appointment, thinking about how to explain the hole she felt trapped in, she took pen to paper.

I feel like my world is dark, bleak, and black as a moonless midnight. I'm falling into a hole that never ends. And in the far distance, I can see the tiniest pinprick of light, the size of a pencil tip. But I keep spiraling, falling, never reaching it. The darkness consumes me...my mind, my heart, my body. It's all-encompassing. And I will never reach the light, no matter how desperately I want to break free.

It's heavy. There's no way around it.

Piper doesn't really care for her psychiatrist, Lynn. She's kind, but her personality is dry, clinical. She prescribed Effexor XR for anxiety, Wellbutrin for depression, and Naproxen for the migraines that have become relentless.

Now, Piper feels like a medicated shell of herself, going through the motions, chasing that distant light she still hopes exists. But she keeps her appointments every few weeks, if only to ensure the refills keep coming.

Piper looks in the mirror, drawing in a slow breath as she tries to muster confidence for the day ahead. Her hands smooth over her hips, plush and soft from the beloved pounds she's started to gain as a side effect of her medication. She pinches the back of her waist and exhales with a frustrated huff. Her self-worth seems to slip lower with every pound the scale climbs. She's never been one to obsess over weight, but there's no denying that none of her pants fit.

Still, she's hopeful that today will mark a turning point, that she can reclaim some peace of mind, and finally win her restraining order against Hoover. She doubts he'll even show up. Why would he travel all this way when he's so clearly guilty? Though she doesn't dare say it out loud, it feels like a sure thing.

She skims the clothes hanging in her closet, debating what to wear. Normally, she'd care about looking and feeling her best, but today she just wants to disappear. She settles on a black blazer, a crisp white T-shirt, and J.Crew pixie pants, no frills, no flash. She straightens the ends of her blonde hair and keeps her makeup minimal — concealer, mascara, a swipe of blush, and chapstick.

Piper studies her reflection again and wishes she had a softer edge. She's aware of her resting bitch face, and on a day like today, it's bound to betray her. She hopes she can conjure up tears on the stand, but the truth is, her anger burns too hot.

There are terrorists in the world, she thinks, *and then there are terrorists of individual people.* That's what Hoover is to her: a mental terrorist.

She slips on her black Tory Burch flats and grabs her black work tote just as her dad pulls up outside. Stepping into the morning air, she inhales deeply. There's something about fresh air that always seems to steady her. *It's like God made people that way,* she thinks. When nothing else works, deep breaths and sunlight do.

Piper climbs into her dad's car.

"Hi, Piper. How are you feeling?" he asks, concern etched in the lines of his brow.

"Hey, Dad. Thanks for picking me up. I'm okay," she says softly.

Seeing him unravels her composure. She tries to blink back tears, but they spill anyway, tracing slow, steady paths down her cheeks. She turns toward the window, watching the skyline blur as they cruise along Wacker Drive. The familiar rhythm of the city, buildings whizzing by, the hum of traffic, offers a strange kind of comfort.

Her dad places a hand over hers and gives it a gentle, reassuring squeeze. "Just remember, Piper, you're not alone. You've got so many people in your corner. I know this isn't easy, and I'd do anything to take it away. I mean that. I'd trade places with you in a heartbeat if I could. But here we are, and I'll be with you every step of the way today. When we get there, Jennifer, our attorney, will meet us and go over everything."

Piper wipes her cheeks, breathes deep to regain her composure and returns her gaze to the window, letting the quiet between them fill the car.

Her dad pulls up to the Cook County Courthouse on the city's north side and parks. They walk up the building's expansive steps, which only increases her anxiety. Her dad opens the door and Piper walks in first. Inside, it's buzzing with people milling about — heels tapping, papers shuffling, voices echoing. Piper is surprised by how busy it is.

They walk through the metal detector and are stopped by a woman whose tone is all business. Her hair is slicked into a low bun; the faint smell of cigarettes lingers as she speaks.

"Why are you here?" she asks, voice flat.

"We're here for the case of Piper Hawthorne versus Joseph Hoover," her dad says.

He looks nice — black jeans, a button-down shirt, and a Patagonia zip-up, his go-to uniform. He looks far less uptight than Piper but carries a weariness that runs deeper than lack of sleep, the kind that seeps into a parent's bones.

"Courtroom thirty-two," the woman replies. "Up the stairs, take a left, third door on your right."

Piper realizes this is just another day of work for everyone here. But for her, it feels like a crossroads, one that will catapult her life in one of two directions.

Before they reach the stairs, her dad stops and gently takes her elbow. "Piper, before we go up, I want to take a moment and pray with you."

Her throat tightens. "Yes, of course. We can do that."

Faith has always been her cornerstone, but lately it's felt distant, blurred by fear and exhaustion. She's angry, confused, unsure how to reconcile God's goodness with the chaos her life has become. More often than not, she's found herself putting Him on pause.

Her dad places a steady hand on her shoulder, and together they bow their heads in the corner of the courthouse stairwell, the hum of the crowd fading around them.

"Dear Heavenly Father," he begins. "We pray You meet us here today in this courtroom. We pray for Your justice. We pray for closure for Piper and for Your protection over her. We ask that You be with Piper as she takes the stand, that her memory may be crisp and her words clear. We pray for Your peace that surpasses all understanding. May we feel it wash over us. Ultimately, Lord, we pray for redemption. In Jesus' holy name, Amen."

"Amen," Piper says in unison.

With a shared look filled with hope, Piper and her dad follow the directions and enter Courtroom Thirty-Two. Jennifer is waiting for them.

"John, Piper," she says, sticking out her hand. "Jennifer Smith. Nice to officially meet you. Let's debrief outside."

They walk out to one of the worn wooden benches lining the hallway. Piper hadn't put much thought into what Jennifer would look like, but this isn't it. She pictured someone powerful, wearing a sharp suit and pointy pumps, commanding a room. Instead, Jennifer has lackluster brown, thin, straight hair that falls just past her shoulders. She's dressed in a dark gray skirt suit with a black tee underneath and round-toe pumps with a kitten heel. Honestly, none of this is what Piper expected. Thanks to the movies for creating false expectations.

Jennifer is off to the races, talking so fast it's hard to keep up. "So, I didn't expect Professor Hoover to show up today, and he is in fact here. And he has a very high-powered lawyer with him. Really, really was not expecting this," she says as she gathers her paperwork together. *Dear Lord, please tell me she's not...nervous.*

"So, let's just stick to our original plan, which is, um..." Long pause. Deep breath. She closes her eyes. "Okay, Piper, you'll take the stand first. Professor Hoover's wildly high-profile lawyer will question you, and then I will question you. Then Professor Hoover will take the stand. I'll question him, and then his lawyer, the defense, will question him. Hopefully, at that point we can wrap things up. We'll just have to see how this plays out. Okay, that should do it. Actually, just a reminder: less is more. We're talking one-word answers. We want this story to speak for itself, the facts, that is. It's so clear he's guilty; we don't need you to say more than you have to."

"Understood," Piper says, her mouth dry. Moisture gathers in her palms, and she wipes them on her pants.

"Okay, let's go," Jennifer says, standing and leading them back into the courtroom. "Your case is about halfway down the list," she whispers, "so it'll be a little bit before it's our turn."

Piper had always pictured it being just them in a courtroom before a judge. She didn't realize that, in civil cases, it's a whole room of people waiting their turn, listening as other people's baggage is laid bare for all to hear.

Piper and her dad find a seat in one of the pews on the left side, toward the back. She glances around the room, and her heart comes to a dead stop when she sees him. She could pick out his profile at any distance, in any room. She looks up at her dad, and he meets her eyes.

"There he is," she whispers, nodding toward Hoover. He's sitting in the right row of pews near the front. Piper can't, with all that's in her, believe he had the nerve to show up. Her dad puts his arm around her and rubs her shoulder. She buries her face against him, stifling the tears that burn her eyes.

It's 9:00 a.m., and for the next hour and a half they listen to case after case: child custody, domestic abuse, drug possession, each one sadder and more depressing than the last.

Finally, Piper hears her name called. She stands and walks to the stand. Her stomach somersaults.

"Piper Hawthorne, you may take a seat," the judge coldly proclaims.

Piper shakily walks up the handful of steps and turns when she reaches her resting spot, to the right of the judge. The bailiff stands in front of her and swears her in. She has never been more aware of what blacking out feels like, but this must be it, as the room seems to close in around her.

Hoover's attorney rises from the front row, and Piper screams inside when she sees Hoover seated nearby.

"Nice to meet you, Piper. My name is Ford Mitchell. I'm going to ask you a series of questions to gather information about your relationship with Professor Hoover," his lawyer begins.

He's suave-looking in a navy suit pulled together with a caramel-brown belt, matching shoes, and a coordinated checked pocket square. He reeks of success.

Piper is so nervous she finds herself staring out at the abyss of strangers, like a deer in headlights, listening to herself relive her worst nightmare.

"Piper, approximately how many classes did you take from Professor Hoover during your time at Midland College?" he asks.

"Umm...let me think." Her soft voice quivers, and Piper cringes inside. You never really know how you'll appear in a situation like this. She pictured herself strong and fearless, but in reality, she's terrified, and knows it shows.

"I believe four classes," she answers, looking down at her hands, picking at her red polish, something she normally wouldn't dare do.

"Did you elect to take classes where Professor Hoover was your teacher, or were you placed in those classes?" Ford asks.

"Following my first class, I chose those classes." She sees what he's doing here but can't find a way out. Jennifer's warning from earlier, "less is more," rings in her ears.

"And is it correct that you chose to start a public relations club with Professor Hoover as the advising teacher, when you could have approached any professor about overseeing this club?"

"Yes, but..." she answers, feeling her dignity die on the bench.

"Is it also correct that you had Professor Hoover oversee your internship credit?" he asks.

"Yes," she answers.

"So it's safe to say that you welcomed opportunities in which you had more interactions with Professor Hoover?"

"No, it's not safe to say that," she replies, unintentionally raising her voice. "He was an easy grader, and I wanted to succeed in school."

"Can you confirm if you wrote this email, and then read it aloud, please?" he asks pointedly.

Piper glances at the paper Ford hands her, and her heart sinks. She can feel warmth slowly invading her entire face. Her mind flashes back.

From: Piper.Hawthorne@Midland.edu
To: Joseph.Hoover@Midland.edu
Date: November 1, 2008, 12:15 p.m.
Subject: Thanks

Professor Hoover,

I just wanted to say thanks so much for overseeing my internship and your help kicking off our public-relations club. I baked you some cookies as a token of my appreciation and left them by your office. Enjoy!

All my best,
Piper

"Yes, I wrote this email, but not to be taken any other way than what's stated. I was saying thank you, and that's that," she admits, disgust audible in her tone.

"Do you see how Professor Hoover might have read into this?" his lawyer asks, raising his perfectly coiffed eyebrows.

"Objection. Speculation," Jennifer says, rising.

"Objection sustained," the judge replies.

"Ms. Hawthorne, did you regularly interact with Professor Hoover outside of class?"

"No, sir. No, I did not. In fact, once he asked me out to lunch to discuss something, and I said no because —"

Piper is cut off. "Objection, Ms. Hawthorne. Please answer only the question I ask."

Piper feels her cheeks flush hot.

"Ms. Hawthorne, did you share personal information with Professor Hoover, for example that you struggle with anxiety?"

How her kind interactions are being twisted because this deranged, socially awkward professor tried sharing personal information with her, and she simply felt bad for him, is unimaginable.

Her mind flashes back to what they must be referring to. She remembers the email he sent her...

From: Joseph.Hoover@Midland.edu
To: Piper.Hawthorne@Midland.edu; Joanie@midland.edu; Cmcally@midland.edu; Profcharles@midland.edu
Date: March 31, 2008, 4:58 p.m.
Subject: Prayers for a Friend

Hello there,

Hope this email finds you well. I apologize for the presumption in approaching this core group with an unusual prayer request. Before you read on, could you please keep this confidential? I wouldn't want the world to know the deepest and most painful parts of my life. Instinctively, I feel a deep sense of trust and comfort when I think of each of you.

Recently, I've suffered major panic attacks, what felt like actual heart attacks, dealing with a situation involving my family. I love my dad deeply, and I know he means well, but lately I've been under tremendous pressure to move back home and take over his business.

Every part of me resists it. It feels like he's trying to rewrite my life for me, and it goes against how I believe God has called me to live. It feels too forced, too rational, too cold...completely at odds with who I am as a person. This has been going on for months now, to the point that I've been experiencing panic attacks and feeling a deep sense of abandonment by God Himself. I've prayed about it, but I only seem to sink deeper into a bottomless pit of anxiety and guilt.

Would you please pray for me? I've made up my mind not to do what my dad is asking, but I also feel heartbroken about disappointing him. I care for him deeply, yet I fear I've alienated him so much that our relationship may never be the same.

I'm asking for prayer that our relationship would be mended and that he'd respect my individuality and the path I believe God has set for me.

If I've overstepped by sharing this, I promise not to burden you with personal matters again. I just need prayer. I've never needed Jesus more than I do right now.

By the same token, please feel free to count on me to do the same for you.

Yours in Christ,
Hoover

Bile rises in her throat, and she swallows, remembering the note she wrote in reply.

From: Piper.Hawthorne@Midland.edu
To: Joseph.Hoover@Midland.edu
Date: April 1, 2008, 11:20 a.m.
Subject: Re: Prayers for a Friend

Professor Hoover,

Wow, I am truly so deeply sorry you've been feeling this way for the past nine months. However, I'm glad you feel you can trust me. And don't ever apologize for coming to people with such a request as this. I don't see it as a burden by any means.

I will, of course, be praying for you — praying for your relationship with your dad and your relationship with God. I personally think you're making the right decision, and it seems as though you're sure of it too, so I hope you can rest assured your choice is right for you.

I've actually suffered from panic attacks myself and have dealt with that for some time, so I can relate to you. I do pray the Lord will help you with the anxiety and depression causing them. In my own struggles, I've found it very helpful to seek counseling, and I actually have a great Christian woman in the area I've seen. If you're ever interested, let me know and I can give you her information.

I just want you to know you're a really great, genuine, and sincere person, and I'm so sorry you're dealing with this. You are in my thoughts and prayers, and I do hope this situation gets better.

My favorite Bible verse that has always helped me is Jeremiah 29:11 — "For I know the plans I have for you," says the Lord. "They are plans for good and not for disaster, to give you a future and a hope." I hope this brings you comfort. Even though it may not feel like it, He's there for you and wants what's good.

Hang in there, and please let me know if there's anything at all I can do.

I'm praying for you.

In Him,
Piper

He sounded genuinely desperate. I still don't know why he included me, a student, on that email. If I could go back in time, I'd change so many things. With all of me, I believe we're on this earth to love people the way Jesus loved the world. He loved, and loves, the outcasts, the weird, the ones who don't fit in. My response was simply me trying to show grace and kindness to a struggling human. If only I'd known what was really going on in his mind.

Piper snaps back to the courtroom and says a silent prayer she doesn't have to read the email aloud. She doesn't want this man flattered or her words misconstrued any more than they already have been. She'd sent her lawyer every single email between them, so she's sure Hoover has done the same.

"In my opinion, Professor Hoover shared details with me that should never have been shared with a student, like how his dad is trying to force him to take over the family business, how he's struggling with anxiety and depression, and how he feels like the Lord has forsaken him. What did I do to bring that upon myself?"

Her own voice rises before she catches Jennifer's wide eyes and quick, subtle shake of the head — *no*. Piper takes a deep breath and steadies herself.

"Professor Hoover shared his struggles, and I was worried about his mental health, like I would have been for anyone who shared such things with me. So I said I would pray for him and shared that I, too, have struggled with anxiety. That's it. There's nothing to read into. If anything, he was extremely inappropriate by sharing these things with me. I never did anything to make it seem like he should share that burden."

"Ms. Hawthorne, last question. When was the last time you exchanged words with Mr. Hoover?"

Piper's heart sinks. She knows what he's doing and why he's asking.

"The last time was...December of 2008, I think." *That was two and a half years ago. Ugh.* "But listen, I've seen him countless times since then...in my apartment complex, near where I get off the—"

"No further questions, Your Honor," he says abruptly, cutting her off before walking back to his seat.

27

PROFESSOR HOOVER

Despite being in a courtroom defending his own case, Professor Hoover can't wipe the grin off his face. He couldn't help but go all out for the attorney he hired. Sure, it cost him all his savings, but it will be worth it. He expects to, after all, win this case without a doubt and prove to Piper that they belong together. When he wins, she'll see how right he is about them.

Not to get ahead of himself, but he already feels empowered, like this is the next step in the right direction for the rest of his life. There are some moments that shape you, that change your trajectory, and this is one of them. He can feel it in his soul, and it makes him quite giddy.

He came prepared today. Not only did he hire Ford Mitchell, but he's also wearing a brand-new black velvet jacket with coordinating black pants. He finally splurged on shiny new leather loafers to match. A day like today calls for setting aside his typically strapped budget.

He has two clear goals for the day:

1. Prove his innocence, and prove that Piper did express a mutual interest in him and still does.
2. Set the record straight in Piper's eyes so they can bring their relationship back on course.

Just seeing her on the stand, poised and confident, a little flustered, full of life and emotion, gets under his skin in the best possible way.

Thus far, Piper has admitted to all the right things: the cookies, the emails, the vulnerability they shared, how she prayed for him and revealed her struggles. He rubs his hands together in anticipation. He can't wait to share his side of things...

28

HOLDING BREATH

Jennifer stands and takes a swig of water. The dryness in her mouth is tangible.

"Ms. Hawthorne," she begins, clearing her throat. "Describe your relationship with Professor Hoover in a few words."

Few means two or three, she reminds herself. But despite her conscious thought, her tongue takes over...

"It was strictly school. He was my professor for a few communications classes. I took classes from him because they were easy. He was the faculty lead for the PR Club my friend and I started. However, that was really just a formality. It was our club and required little interaction or oversight from him. He also oversaw my PR internship, again a formality. I had to do a few assignments, and that was that. He was an easy grader. There was no relationship beyond this. That word isn't even an appropriate descriptor," Piper blurts out in a rush.

Jennifer's eyes start to bug out again, signaling Piper to *shut her mouth*, whether she realizes she's doing it or not.

"What did you do after you received the email in December

2008, when Professor Hoover made his feelings for you known?"

Piper's mind immediately flies to the moment that changed everything. *My first instinct was to throw up. My second was to run outside and scream bloody murder at the top of my lungs, hoping I could wake myself up from the nightmare that was becoming my reality.*

She snaps back. "I didn't know what to do. I was utterly blindsided and completely disgusted by that email. I called my dad to tell him about it and to ask for help on what to do next," she says, her face stoic and emotionless.

Piper has envisioned and rehearsed this very moment countless times, playing it over and over in her head: the questions, her responses, the reactions. She pictured herself being charismatic, compelling, emotional. In reality, it's an out-of-body experience watching herself up here, knowing she's coming across dry, maybe even a little cold. The truth is, she doesn't know what to do with the anger raging through her body.

"I understand that after receiving that email, you did not see or hear from Professor Hoover for two years. Is that correct?" Jennifer asks, her tone sharp and precise.

Piper takes a deep breath. She knew this gap in time would come up. "Yes, that is correct," she says after swallowing. "The school gave us little to no direction on their course of action with him. I understand he remained employed at the college. I lived in Midland for a short while after graduation, then moved to Chicago. I didn't start seeing Professor Hoover again until February of 2011, just over two years after I received the letter."

"Can you go through and document the times you've seen Professor Hoover since receiving that email?" Jennifer asks.

Thankfully, Jennifer had sent Piper a prep email detailing some of the questions she planned to ask, so she could prepare. Lord knows this one is a doozy to remember.

"Yes. I saw him three times. The first was when he was sitting in the window of the Barnes & Noble bookstore, reading a newspaper. I walk past that corner every single workday when I take the L to and from work. The second time, I saw him shopping in the small market in the lobby of my apartment building. The third time, I saw him on the treadmill in the workout room of my building. I work out every single weekday at 5:30 a.m. He was in there before me one morning."

"What unfolded after you saw Professor Hoover in your apartment building's workout room?"

I knew there were two possible scenarios. The first was that he'd had a fling with someone in my complex and spent the night there after hooking up. But the more I thought about it, the more I knew there was a zero percent chance that was the case. I mean, look at him. So by default, I knew he had moved into my building like a sick freak.

"Ahem." Piper clears her throat. "I immediately knew something wasn't right. As I thought about why he could be in my building at such an early hour of the day, in a workout room that requires a key for entry, I just knew he had moved in. I went through the motions of my morning and called my parents and my apartment building shortly after that. They, along with Midland College, confirmed what I had suspected: Hoover did, in fact, live in my building, and had for eight months."

Piper's heart thuds in her chest, partly because her nerves are shot and partly because saying her story out loud, even to a room full of strangers, feels like she's being seen and heard for the first time.

"When you went to work that day, did you share this news with your colleagues?" Jennifer asks, eyes wide, a sheen of sweat forming on her upper lip.

Piper suddenly remembers the biggest detail of all, the one she nearly left out.

"I did. I met with my boss, Kate, and shared the news because, one, I was terrified, and two, I thought she should know since all boundaries had been crossed by Hoover. Which reminds me, Hoover had also previously stopped by my work."

"Where do you work, Ms. Hawthorne?"

"I work at Harmon Consulting, a public relations firm located in River North."

"When did Professor Hoover show up at Harmon Consulting?"

"I was on a work trip in California when he showed up early one morning. My colleague Chloe called me right after he left because it was such a bizarre encounter. He said he was opening a new nightclub business venture and was looking for a PR agency to represent him, but he had no details to share about the concept, its location, or opening timeframe. Chloe said he was panning my desk area like he was looking for clues or something. It's almost like he knew I was out of town."

"Objection! Speculation," Ford says sternly from his seat.

"Overruled," the judge replies, his voice steady and monotone.

"So to recap, you saw Professor Hoover near your home and inside your building on three separate occasions, and he showed up at your workplace once. Is that correct?" Jennifer asks, visibly hitting her stride.

"Yes, that is correct," Piper confirms.

"Your Honor, no further questions."

"Thank you, Ms. Smith. Ms. Hawthorne, you may now leave the stand," the judge announces. "Mr. Hoover, please rise."

Piper walks down from the stand, her legs as wobbly as a bowl of Jell-O, and makes her way to the third row to join her dad.

After he's sworn in, Hoover takes a seat at the stand, lengthening his arms and pulling at his sleeves to straighten his ink-black velvet jacket. Jennifer questions him first.

"Professor Hoover, do you know my client, Piper Hawthorne?" She stretches out her arm, pointing at Piper.

"Yes, ma'am, I sure do."

"How do you know her?" Jennifer probes further.

"I had the pleasure of teaching her in a handful of college communications classes. I also oversaw a public relations club she and her friends created, as well as her internship," Hoover says with a smirk.

"Did you, Professor Hoover, write Piper this email professing your obsession with her, dated December 16, 2008, the night before her last final exam as a college student?" Jennifer hands him a thin stack of papers.

"Yes, ma'am," he says. "I did write her that email, but may I humbly admit that I was not professing an obsession, but asking her to take a chance on me? I had become fond of her through all of our interactions, and as I thought she was done with her exams, I felt compelled to admit that admiration to her in hopes she might feel the same."

Piper squeezes her eyes shut. This is so hard to listen to it pains every ounce of her body. *Why would he in a million years think I was interested? He's deranged and delusional. I can't even believe we're still going through this. It could not be more clear he is a guilty creep and I have zero interest ever.*

"Professor Hoover, in addition, did you write this letter to my client, Piper Hawthorne, dated December 2, 2007? If so, can you please read it aloud?"

"Yes, ma'am." Hoover begins to read.

From: Joseph.Hoover@Midland.edu
To: Piper.Hawthorne@Midland.edu; Bill.Rodriguez@Midland.edu; Laura.Clancy@Midland.edu
Date: December 2, 2007, 8:17 a.m.
Subject: Christmas Celebration

Bill, Alice, Piper, and Laura,

Hope this email finds all of you well. Please forgive me for my shoddy planning in inviting all of you so late.

I was thinking along these lines. I live in a small studio apartment in the city and have a Christmas tree lit up in a post-modern sort of way. Wouldn't it be nice to have people over who mean the most to me from the Midland community in my small abode? Since space is limited in my apartment, I have extended this invitation only to the best of the best.

- *Bill – you've been my spiritual mentor and favorite colleague at Midland, hence my invitation for you and Alice.*
- *Piper – you've taught me more than you know about the meaning of grace.*
- *Laura – you are one of the funniest people I know.*
- *Hoover (of course) – is your humble host.*

Proposed date: Tuesday, December 18, anytime after 6:30. I can cook for all of you (seafood).

Blessings,
Hoover

"Did you think it was appropriate to invite your students to your home in downtown Chicago for an intimate gathering?" Jennifer asks.

"Yes, ma'am. I had no ill intent. I simply love a good party and thought it would be fun."

"Did anyone show up for said Christmas gathering?"

"No, ma'am. If memory serves me right, no one showed up to my dismay." He hangs his head low.

"Professor Hoover, did you also write my client this email, dated November 5, 2008? If so, please read it aloud."

From: Joseph.Hoover@Midland.edu
To: Piper.Hawthorne@Midland.edu
Date: November 5, 2008, 5:15 p.m.
Subject: Apologies

Piper,

I want to apologize profusely because you were sharing something important about school and I just bolted like a barbarian for the train. Only now do I realize that I think you were sharing something about difficulty in classwork.

You should know you have already passed the internship, and I am just waiting for them to make the grade sheet available online. Similarly, I have no doubts in my mind that you will do well in your other Comm classes.

Are the English classes not going so well? Could you please let me know what's going on? Is there anything I can do to help you? Please let me know. God has blessed you with an amazing mind, and I have no doubt that you will ace your classes.

If you need a sympathetic ear, you should know that I am your well-wisher and will go to bat for you to the ends of the earth.

Always at your service,
Hoover

"Yes, ma'am," Hoover admits, staring off into the distance as if picturing the incident in real time. He reads the email aloud and pauses before continuing. "Piper took many classes from me, and I grew to care for her immensely and thought, as such, that she should know."

"Did you find it appropriate to tell her, one of your students, that you, quote, 'are her well-wisher and will go to bat for her to the ends of the earth'?" Jennifer asks tensely, making air quotes with her fingers.

"At the time, I didn't see anything wrong with it, no ma'am. I realize I'm a professor and she was my student, but I had no ill intent. I'm just a wordsmith, and that's merely how I express myself."

"In your time knowing Piper as a student of yours, is it true you did each of the following: sent her a Starbucks gift card in the mail over fall break when she was at her parents' house, invited her to lunch to discuss a 'project,' and invited her to come pick up a couch you were getting rid of?"

"I sent her a gift card, yes, ma'am. I was her internship coordinator, so inviting her to lunch to discuss her project is quite normal. And yes, I didn't want to throw the couch away, so I offered it to her for free if she would come pick it up."

"And do you find these to be normal professor-student interactions?" Jennifer asks, her brow furrowing.

"Yes, ma'am. For me, yes," Hoover answers.

"Professor Hoover, when did you move into the Lake Shore Drive Residences?" Jennifer asks, fire in her eyes.

The space between Piper's shoulders is so tight it hurts. Her heart aches reliving these situations. Listening to Hoover play the naïve-professor card and pretend he didn't orchestrate this whole fake, messed-up reality is enough to drive her mad.

"I moved in August of 2010. The rent was affordable and overlooked the Lakeshore Path. What more could I ask for?" he replies, smiling.

"And when you signed your lease, were you aware that Piper already lived at Lake Shore Drive Residences?"

"No, ma'am, not exactly. I had seen her walking in the area, but I wasn't one hundred percent certain she lived there," he answers.

Liar. You are a liar! Piper screams inside her head. She balls her hands into fists and squeezes until the pressure from her nails digging into her palms hurts too much.

"At what point were you certain that Piper lived in the same apartment building as you?" Jennifer asks.

"Umm, hmm, let's see here..." he pauses in thought.

Piper glances at the bailiff, a stocky woman with long black braids, who gives her a quick wink. It feels like something you're probably not supposed to do in a courtroom, but Piper appreciates the gesture nonetheless. Even she seems to know he's guilty. The woman strikes Piper as the jovial type, despite her occupation. Piper can't imagine listening to stories like these all day, every day. Maybe you just grow immune to it all, like everything else that can weigh you down.

"You know, I saw her in passing a time or two...or three...or four, perhaps," Hoover continues. "And then, you know, it wasn't until I saw her working out early one morning when I made a promise to myself to get back in shape, that I thought it might be a real possibility," he says, with a smirk that makes everyone question the validity of his words.

There's something about that smirk that makes Piper's mind wander. It jumps between snapshots: the heart charm she found in her car on the way to the police station, the single white long-stemmed rose hanging on her car door at Kate's house, the time she came home from a night out and her apartment was spotless when she had left it a disaster. Piper throws her hands over her mouth, stifling the scream that begs to escape. She startles her dad sitting next to her. Piper buries her face against him as he wraps his arm around her. It's all so clear now, yet how can she go back and tell the court that it was all him, all along?

The questioning continues.

"Professor Hoover, you were Piper's internship coordinator, correct?"

"Yes, ma'am. Public relations internship coordinator," he says matter-of-factly.

"Can you tell me what company she was working for when you oversaw her internship?" Jennifer asks.

"She was working for...she was working for...yes, that's right, Harmon Consulting," he answers.

"And were you aware she took a full-time position at Harmon Consulting when she graduated?"

"Yes, ma'am, I was. Since I oversaw her internship, it was natural I knew she took a job there. I don't remember if she mentioned it, or if Kate mentioned it, or maybe Chloe when we chatted...something of the sort. But yes, I was very happy for her," he says.

"You mention Chloe. Can you explain who she is and how you know her?"

"I mentioned who? That must be an oversight on my part. I have no clue who you're referring to, ma'am," Hoover says, shifting uneasily in his chair.

"Professor Hoover, did you ever visit the offices of Harmon Consulting when Piper was working there?"

"No, ma'am," he replies.

Wait — what?! He's lying! Piper thinks.

He clears his throat and continues, "I stopped by Harmon Consulting one time, actually, but Miss Piper wasn't present. So technically, no, she wasn't working there."

"Professor Hoover, that's a somewhat misleading answer. Please answer this question yes or no. Did you set foot in the office where Piper holds a position, Harmon Consulting, in March of this year?" Jennifer asks, voice steady and firm.

"Yes, ma'am," he answers.

"Your Honor, I have no further questions."

Hoover remains on the stand as his lawyer rises, exuding confidence.

"Professor Hoover," Ford begins, "can you please describe your relationship with Miss Hawthorne?"

"Of course. Piper was a student of mine at Midland College. She transferred to the college her junior year, which happened to be the same year I began teaching. She took a handful of classes from me. She also started a public relations club with a friend of hers, which I oversaw, and I also supervised her senior internship," he answers.

"So you could say, from a professor-student perspective, you spent a lot of time together?"

"Yes, sir. I saw Piper quite regularly through all of the aforementioned classes and clubs," Hoover replies.

"Did Miss Hawthorne ever do anything to make you feel as though she might be interested in a relationship with you beyond a professional manner?" his lawyer asks, confidently gesturing with his hands.

"This is what I'll say about Piper. She's kind, one of the kindest people I know. We share commonalities, like our love for running, writing, and reading. We both love a spotless apartment. We both struggle with things like anxiety. I felt like she opened up to me in such a way that we might hit it off, yes."

Piper feels a single tear roll down her cheek. She's never felt *used* like this before. Used for simply being herself. Not for making horrible decisions, or being promiscuous, or forgoing her self-respect. Just for being honest, vulnerable, transparent in her class assignments and speeches and writing projects.

And this deranged professor is using it against her. Twisting her words, making it sound as if she'd confided in him. *How is he getting away with this? How is he bending my reality?* She's never felt this much shame in her life, and she hasn't even done anything to deserve it.

"Did Miss Hawthorne ever pursue spending one-on-one time with you?" his lawyer asks.

"I feel like she did, but I can't pinpoint a specific time right now," Hoover answers.

Piper's eyes narrow in disgust, her mouth slightly open in disbelief. She is one hundred percent certain she never tried to spend an ounce of time with that creep unless she absolutely had to for class.

"Can you provide insight into the times Miss Hawthorne claims you were following her around town and in her apartment complex?" Ford asks.

"Yes, sir. Those instances are a true coincidence. I have no explanation for you. Did I notice her a few of those times? Yes, I did. Did I talk to her? No, sir. I kept my respectful distance and left her alone," Hoover says.

"And when you moved into Lake Shore Drive Residences, did you know she lived there?"

"No, sir," Hoover answers. "I had seen her from afar a few times in the general area, as has been stated. When I signed that lease, it was a true cosmic coincidence that we both happened to reside in the same building. No explanation other than that."

"Thank you," his lawyer replies, pausing as he considers his next question.

"Did you show up at Piper's place of employment in March of this year? And if so, can you share more insight with us?"

"Yes, sir, I did go to Harmon Consulting one day. I know it may seem odd, since I oversaw her internship when she worked there with Kate in college. However, I'd like to say it was another cosmic coincidence. I knew Miss Piper took a job there when she graduated, but when I went there that day in March, I was actually unsure if she still worked there. Yes, sir, that's the truth. I was, in my dream life, thinking of opening a nightclub and knew that agency was the very best. So I thought, why not just stop by to see what they'd recommend, should I end up pursuing this thing?"

"No further questions, Your Honor," Ford says, as Hoover remains on the stand with a confident smirk across his face.

The judge nods. "Mr. Hoover, you may step down."

Hoover rises slowly, adjusting his blazer before returning to his seat.

Jennifer stands. "Your Honor, I'd like to call our last witness to the stand: Chloe Hart."

The next thing Piper knows, Chloe is walking gracefully down the aisle of the small courtroom. She exudes exactly what Piper had hoped to project: someone chic and composed, wearing a green shift dress and loose, glossy curls. Even before she speaks, her pursed lips give off a no-nonsense energy.

After Chloe is sworn in, the painstakingly longest day of Piper's life resumes.

"Miss Hart, can you share with us your relationship with Piper Hawthorne?" Jennifer asks.

"Of course. Piper and I work together at Harmon Consulting, a public relations agency in River North. We both handle our hospitality accounts."

Piper exhales a deep breath of relief.

"Do you know who Professor Joseph Hoover is, Miss Hart?" Jennifer asks.

"I don't know him, but I know of him," Chloe answers.

"Can you share with the courtroom what you know, please?" Jennifer's voice is filled with hope.

"Yes, I can do that. Hoover is Piper's former college communications professor. He sent her a very long, disturbing and unwanted, might I add, email confessing his creepy obsession with her," Chloe says matter-of-factly.

"Objection! Outside the scope," Ford shouts, his voice heated.

"Sustained. Miss Hart, please do your best to answer questions without any outside opinions added. Thank you," the judge says flatly.

"Have you ever met Professor Hoover before?" Jennifer asks.

Piper's fingers tap against her crossed arms like she's playing a piano melody. The anticipation is killing her. *Come on, Chloe, you've got this.*

"Yes…" Chloe pauses so long it's hard to breathe. "I have met him. Once."

"Can you please clarify that with details for the courtroom, Miss Hart?" Jennifer asks.

"Professor Hoover came to our office one day. Piper and our boss, Kate, were out of town on a work trip. It was a Friday morning. He didn't have a meeting or appointment with anyone. He just buzzed, and we let him up, thinking it was a package delivery or something," Chloe explains confidently.

"Was this a typical encounter?" Jennifer asks.

"It wasn't, really. It was memorable because it was off. Our office has an open floor plan with desks in a wide area, newsroom-style. He was talking to a few of us who sit near the entrance, but all the while frantically looking around our office, like he was trying to find something…or someone. He stumbled through what he said he needed help with, mentioning something about possibly opening a nightclub. It was all so vague, like he didn't even know what kind of business he was opening or why he was there. When he left, my colleagues and I talked about how strange the whole thing was. It was so weird, I immediately called Piper to report what happened."

"How did you know the man who showed up that day was Professor Joseph Hoover?" Jennifer asks.

Chloe exhales deeply. "Well, for one, he used his name when he introduced himself, Joseph Hoover. And for two, to be totally honest, he's a pretty quirky, recognizable person. Always wearing crushed velvet, you know? I knew who he was even before he introduced himself, just based on the conversations I'd already had with Piper."

"Can you point out Professor Joseph Hoover, the man who came to your office that day, in this courtroom?" Jennifer asks.

Chloe raises her hand without hesitation and points directly to where Hoover sits.

"Your Honor, no further questions," Jennifer says.

Ford Mitchell stands briefly. "No questions, Your Honor," he says before sitting back down.

Piper is still in shock. She wants to look toward Chloe but can't even force herself to turn that way.

The judge, encased in a hard exterior shell, looks out across the courtroom. He's middle-aged, with a thick head of short hair making its slow transition to gray. The wrinkles on his forehead are etched deep. After today, Piper can imagine that years of listening to people's messy, painful stories have worn him down. You can hear the fatigue and lack of empathy in his tone.

"This is a very difficult decision for me to make." He pauses for what feels like an eternity. He doesn't look at Hoover or Piper. He just skims his papers and examines what appear to be notes.

Finally, he looks up. "I'm going to be honest with you. I am very torn on this case."

Piper's heart drops.

He continues, "My decision ultimately relies on one sole fact. Because Mr. Hoover showed up at Miss Hawthorne's place of employment, I believe he's fifty-one percent guilty of stalking. Therefore, I am going to grant Miss Hawthorne a one-year order of protection. Miss Hawthorne, Mr. Hoover, this case is adjourned. Miss Hawthorne, the bailiff will escort you out."

Piper feels like a weight she's carried for years has finally been lifted. And yet, she's confused by the judge's parting words. Fifty-one percent guilty? As in, one measly percentage point above half-guilty? After all the fear, mental terror, and personal destruction he's caused her...that's where this officially stands.

What she's realizing about the legal system is that "innocent until proven guilty" isn't just a saying; it's the ground everything stands on. And it means that, at the same time, the plaintiff is, in some capacity, doubted or considered wrong until proven right. In Piper's case, as with so many women making claims against men in positions of power, you should be utterly blameless but you're not.

Piper looks at her dad, tears in both of their eyes, as they embrace in a long, joy-filled hug. Her dad whispers, "God is good, Piper. Praise Jesus for this victory and for protecting you. I love you, my girl."

"Thanks for being here, Dad," Piper whispers, burying her face in his chest.

As she lets go, Piper once again locks eyes with the bailiff, who gives her a warm smile before escorting them from the courtroom.

All Piper knows is that she's never been more grateful that, by the slimmest margin, the truth finally landed where it needed to.

For the first time in a long time, she feels like she can breathe again, even if the relief comes with an expiration date.

29

PROFESSOR HOOVER

Back in St. Louis, Hoover paces three steps back and forth, the full extent Myra's guest room allows. The single lamp casts the space in dim light, mirroring how he feels inside: bleak.

He's trying to process everything. On the one hand, he's furious about the court outcome and being legally shut out of Piper's life for a full year. On the other, knowing the judge found him fifty-one percent responsible gives him a perverse sense of vindication. *Even the judge thinks I have a chance,* he tells himself. Now he just has to convince Piper.

He taps his slippered foot on the shaggy brown carpet beneath his desk. The thing he misses most is his sense of purpose. It feels as though everyone important in his life and the mission he was given have been stripped away all at once. He can't think rationally. A tiny voice inside tells him to move on...to get a new job, find someone new, settle down. But his heart won't let him.

"I can't take this," he mutters, pressing his face into his palms and letting out an audible moan. "The writing's on the wall — she's not interested in me. Who do I blame for this? It isn't my fault. It's Midland College. I blame Midland for shutting me out of Piper's life for two years when I had momentum with her. That's when this fell apart. If they hadn't kept me from her...if I could've explained my confession in person...this would've worked out. I'm sure of it.

"Instead, they threatened my career if I contacted her, and now here we are. They will pay for stealing my life with Piper. And I will still come out on top. I will convince her that I. Am. The. Love. Of. Her. Life."

He taps his knuckle against the wall with each enunciation.

He glances at the running countdown on his desk: 357 days. He knows he can't wait that out without doing something... without getting revenge for the shell of a human he's becoming.

30

CHAMPAGNE GLASSES

Life is funny, Piper thinks as she gets ready to go out for the night. She dips her makeup brush into a shimmery charcoal shadow and sweeps it across her eyelids, blending a soft, smoky haze. She thought she'd feel immediate relief after getting the restraining order against Hoover. But she doesn't. She still looks over her shoulder everywhere she goes.

Maybe it's because, in some twisted way, she attracted him. Or because he thought she might actually be interested. Or because he followed her for what felt like forever before she finally caught on to the truth of what was happening.

Did I somehow lead him on? The question loops through her mind, and the shame that comes with it makes her stomach twist. She's stuck in a spiral of reflection, feeling dumb, naïve, and dirty.

She runs her fingers through her spiral-curled hair, trying to coax both her curls and her nerves to relax. It feels like she's living inside a ticking time bomb — one that will explode in exactly 357 days, filled with fear, paranoia, and everything she's been holding in.

Her phone buzzes. It's Chloe.

> You ready? Coming to pick you up in 5.

Piper types and presses send.

> Ready.

Piper slips into her black bandage dress and nude platform heels. She grabs her Chanel bag, the one Kate gave her for her bonus last year, and steps out of her studio apartment just as Chloe pulls up in a yellow taxi.

"Hey, girl! You look so cute," Piper says as she slides into the back of the cab. Piper always pushes the edge of what's appropriate when she goes out, but with her smaller chest and narrow frame, it never crosses the line. Chloe always nails effortless sophistication — tight black jeans, a sleeveless bodysuit, pointy tan pumps.

"You wanna do the usual? Club Five?" Chloe asks. It's where they end up most weekends. It's only 10:30 p.m., the night's still young.

"Yes, of course. But let's grab a drink and something to eat at Georgette's first so we're not the first ones there?"

"Perfection," Chloe agrees.

They walk into Georgette's, the American bistro near their office, and are greeted by a cute new hostess.

"Table for two?" she asks.

"Yes, please. A high-top in the bar, if possible," Chloe says with practiced confidence, exuding regular status.

They settle into a table near the back and order their usual: a bottle of house cabernet, steak tartare, grilled oysters, and hand-cut fries to share.

"So," Chloe says once their wine is poured, concern softening her tone, "How are you doing, Piper? Now that the dust has settled from everything. Seriously, how are you?"

The genuine warmth in her voice makes tears burn behind Piper's eyes. She blinks them away.

"I'm okay." She pauses. "Actually...no, I'm not. I don't even know how to find myself again. I'm filled with so much anger, I don't know what to do with it. I hate myself for what I'm living through. It feels like somehow I brought this on myself, even though I know I didn't. I feel so dirty. And I'm constantly paranoid, looking over my shoulder everywhere I go, feeling like at any moment I need to be ready to run."

She exhales slowly.

"All I want is to feel normal again. To feel alive. I'm tired of being the girl who prays and hopes and still ends up hurt. I want to stop thinking so much, stop caring so much, stop feeling so much. I want to be carefree. To have fun. To feel wanted by someone, anyone, and forget this all-consuming burden for a while."

Her voice trembles. "Maybe that makes me reckless. But maybe reckless is the only thing that makes sense right now."

"Piper, first of all, it's fair to feel all of that," Chloe says gently. "This isn't the course you expected your life to take. You've been in survival mode. It's normal to be scared about stepping back into something lighthearted after everything you've been through. But you need to give yourself some grace, girl. You deserve fun, free from worry. And where better to start than right here, tonight?" She smiles and lifts her glass.

Piper clinks hers against it, managing a small smile. "Thanks, Chloe. You're right. I need to embrace the protection I have and try to let loose a little." She pauses, then adds with a smirk, "It's just so hard sometimes. I wish I weren't doing this alone. You know what I mean? I know I have you and Kate and the girls, but I wish I felt ready to date again."

She takes a sip of wine. "Speaking of which, life's been so

crazy with the trial and everything, I don't think I ever told you about Ryan."

Chloe perks up. "No, you most definitely have not! Spill it!"

"A few weeks before our day in court, he came over. It was my first night in the new apartment. He brought Thai food and drinks, and it was honestly the most amazing night. We stayed up late talking about life. It was so natural and easy. I don't think I've ever been more drawn to someone."

She can picture the way he looked at her, the way he listened, really listened, and she feels that familiar flutter in her stomach just talking about him.

"Part of me wants to dive in headfirst," she admits quietly. "To let myself fall. But the other part, the rational part, knows I'm not ready. I'm still angry and paranoid and trying to heal. And honestly, I don't want to drag Ryan into my chaos. He doesn't deserve that. He's such a good guy. I need to figure myself out before I even think about something real. I just..." She sighs. "I don't know. Maybe that's why I'm craving something that isn't real right now. Something easy. Something temporary. Is that awful of me?"

"Well, first off, I'm so happy you two hung out and had such a great night together," Chloe says. "I can totally see you two together, and I love it. But I hear you. Your perspective makes sense. What if you dedicate the next six months or so to working on yourself? Then, when the time feels right, you reach out to him, or we finagle a way to let him know you're still interested."

Piper laughs softly. "I love that plan. I actually feel good about it...but what if he lands a girlfriend between now and then? I'd be heartbroken."

"I think we can both agree that if it's meant to be, it will be," Chloe says, taking another sip. "Trust that." She grins. "Speaking of men, I went out on another date with James last night.

Piper brightens. "Oh really? Tell me everything."

"He's actually great. Picked me up at my place with flowers. Real ones, not gas station ones. I thought it was too good to be true, but the conversation was so easy. He's funny, has a great job, and he's taller than me. He's checking all the boxes. It almost makes me nervous. Timing is everything, Piper. A year ago, or heck, even two months ago, I wouldn't have been ready for this."

"Well, cheers to that," Piper says, raising her glass. "To new beginnings, hopeful relationships, and much-deserved happiness for us both."

They clink glasses and finish what's left of the wine.

After dinner, they pay the bill and are escorted next door to Club Five through a back hallway, a perk of having the owners as clients. It's 11:45 p.m.; the perfect arrival time.

As they step inside, they're met by smoky air, dim light, and a DJ they don't recognize but instantly approve of.

"Want to make a lap?" Chloe shouts over the music.

Piper nods, a flicker of adrenaline stirring. For the first time in a long time, she lets herself lean into the feeling, not thinking about safety or consequences, just the pulse of the night ahead.

They weave toward the stage, hands linked, pushing through clusters of people hovering around small square tables, sipping vodka sodas and shouting over the music. Four bottle service girls parade by in miniature black crop tops and ruffled skirts, holding a magnum of Grey Goose and three bottles of Veuve, each with a sparkler raised high. The crowd erupts as they pass.

As Piper watches the spectacle, she feels a warm hand on her lower back. She turns and finds herself looking up at a chiseled jawline and a body that's unmistakably built.

"You ladies want something to drink?" Mr. Mysterious asks

with a wink. "We've got plenty to go around, as you can see." He laughs, flashing perfect, white teeth.

Piper glances at Chloe, who gives her a nod of approval before drifting toward his friend. Within moments, they're all dancing.

"What's your name?" he shouts over the bass.

"Piper!" she calls back. "You?"

"Chase!" he yells, grinning. "You come here often?"

"Yeah, actually, I do," she admits, shouting over the noise. "You?"

"Nah," he says. "I'm more of a bar guy. But my buddy had a big week at work and dragged us out to celebrate, so here we are." A strand of dark blond hair falls into his eyes; he runs his fingers through it, brushing it away.

He pulls Piper closer, resting his hands lightly on her hips. They start to sway together, the rhythm pulling them in. Piper can feel the solid warmth of his body against hers. It excites her and terrifies her all at once.

He leans in, his cheek brushing hers, his stubble grazing her skin. *Is this really how I'm going to meet someone? No, probably not. But it sure is fun.*

"I completely forgot...you need a drink," he says, glancing at her empty hands.

"Sure, I'd love one!" Piper answers, maybe a little too eagerly, flipping her hair off her dewy shoulder.

"What kind of girl are you — vodka soda, champagne, gin and tonic? We've got it all tonight," he says, flashing another smile.

"Hmm." She grins. "I'll go with bubbles. Make that two; my friend needs one."

He returns with champagne and hands her a glass, pulling her close again. For a moment, something about it feels right. Not necessarily him, or this place, but the simple feeling of being wanted.

She feels light, untethered. Free. And she doesn't want to let go of it, not yet. Even if it's just the wine and the bubbles doing the convincing.

"You live near here?" he asks.

"Kind of — in Streeterville. You?"

"Lincoln Park," he says, his eyes flicking down to her lips.

"What do you do for work?" she shouts over the music, trying to keep the conversation going.

"I own a web design company," he says, still watching her closely.

Normally, she'd look away. She'd retreat. She wouldn't linger or invite it. But not tonight. *Not tonight.*

Before she realizes it, Chase's lips are on hers. She kisses him back. The music fades into a blur. Just lips, warmth, breath.

When they part, he smiles, his fingers grazing her cheek. "Sorry," he says softly. "You're beautiful, and I've admittedly had a few drinks."

Piper smiles, her pulse steadying. "You don't need to apologize." She slides her arms around his neck. *I'm having fun. That's all this is. Just fun.*

Chase pulls her closer. Their hands interlock as their bodies press together, warm and slick with sweat. He leans down and kisses her shoulder. Piper finishes her champagne before meeting his eyes again.

"Refill, please?" she says, glancing around for Chloe before spotting her nearby, dancing with Chase's friend.

Chase tops off Piper's glass and mixes himself another drink. Before she knows it, someone's pressing a shot glass into her hand.

"On three!" a muscular guy in a tight white T-shirt shouts. "One, two, three!"

Without thinking, Piper clinks glasses with Chase and

downs the shot. It burns, and she giggles as the heat rises to her cheeks.

"I'm not usually one for shots," he says in her ear.

"Clearly neither am I," she laughs, feeling warmth flood her chest and blur her vision.

Chase traces his fingers down her arm before leaning in for another kiss. They find a rhythm, moving together as the music pulses around them.

It feels like they've been dancing forever, long enough that the lights finally start to come up.

"Want to come to my place?" Chase asks, voice tentative.

Now that the lights are on, Piper sees how flushed they both are. A pang in her chest urges her to say no, but she doesn't want to. *You always say no. Not this time.*

"Sure," she says.

She spots Chloe nearby, still laughing with Chase's friend. Maybe they're hitting it off too.

"One sec, let me tell Chloe real quick." Piper takes Chase's hand and weaves through the crowd until she's within reach.

"Hey, Chloe!" she shouts above the music. "We're going to head out. You good?"

"Yes, I'm so good! What a fun, random night. I'm grabbing a cab soon. What are you two up to?" Chloe smirks.

"We're heading out. Together," Piper says with a wink.

"Mmm-hmm. Okay, have fun. Don't do anything I wouldn't do. Text me if you need anything. Let's chat tomorrow."

"Okay. Love you, girl."

Piper turns to Chase. "We're good now."

They take a cab back to his place. He fumbles with his keys, finally unlocking the door. Inside, they stumble through the dark, laughing, until Chase pulls her close and kisses her with urgency.

A flash of Ryan cuts through her mind: his eyes, his steadiness, the safety she felt. *Don't think about him. Not now.* She forces the image away and lets herself fall back into the moment.

Their lips meet again, softer this time, as they move through the apartment, tripping over shoes in the dark until they reach what must be his bedroom.

Chase lies back on the bed and pulls her on top of him.

"There's no pressure," he whispers. "I'm a great cuddler. We can just skip to that part."

"No, I want to," she says, though something inside her whispers, *this is your perfect out*. In this moment, Piper just doesn't care.

He tugs at the hem of her tight dress until it finally gives. She sits back, undoing his belt and tugging at his jeans. The next thing she knows, he's pulling off her panties and drawing her down against him. He kisses her slow and deep, and she only wants more.

His hand brushes her cheek, then drifts lower. Everything blurs — the warmth, the rhythm, the wanting. She cranes her head back and lets herself follow his lead until they both finish. Then silence. For a few minutes, neither of them speaks. Chase wraps an arm around her, and she feels herself slipping away.

Piper wakes hours later with a pounding headache and a mouth parched and aching. Her watch reads 7:30 a.m. She glances over. Chase is asleep on his stomach, one arm draped across her. Moving carefully, she eases out from under him and scans the room for her black dress. It's crumpled on the floor.

She slips it on, grabs her purse, and checks her phone. She has ten missed texts from Chloe asking where she is, if she's okay. Piper tries to replay the end of the night, but it's too foggy.

She calls to arrange a taxi and breathes a small sigh of relief when the dispatcher says a driver is only a few minutes away.

She looks back at Chase, sleeping peacefully, and feels a faint pang of *what if*. They never exchanged numbers. She considers leaving hers on a note, something simple and cutesy, but decides against it. *This isn't how things that last begin.*

She slips quietly out the front door, praying she won't run into anyone. Her cab is already waiting. She slides into the backseat.

Then it hits her. It's Sunday.

A pit forms in her stomach. *Before my life fell apart, I'd be getting ready for church right now.*

She stares out the window as the city blurs past. Her cheeks flush, burning with shame *I'm done with God...at least until I can make sense of any of this. I don't deserve to feel like this.* She swallows hard. *Maybe I'll come back at some point. But not now. Not like this. Right now, He feels a million miles away.*

31

PROFESSOR HOOVER

Professor Hoover rereads the draft of his email for what feels like the hundredth time. He's been perfecting it for days. It must be flawless before he presses send. After all, he's demanding a hefty sum from Midland College, and they need to understand just how serious he is about being paid.

He's halfway through his tenth, and hopefully final, revision when a knock interrupts him.

"Joseph," Myra says softly. "Come out for a bit. Why don't you get some fresh air and eat something warm? You can't keep doing this. It's been two weeks, and we've barely seen you."

She pauses. "Joseph? Say something. Anything."

"Aaah, okay, Myra. I hear you. I'm almost done with something I've been really wrapped up in. I'll come up when it's complete. Give me an hour," he says, monotone.

Myra presses her hand against the door. "Okay, Joseph. I'll give you one hour."

He rolls his eyes before returning to the top of his email. If she only knew what, or who, was at stake.

He reads on:

Dear Provost Bryce Jones,

You must understand, I am not pleading for help. I am demanding restitution for the damage inflicted upon me. Bryce, this is an extremely serious matter. Both you and the Midland community are complicit in the destruction of my life.

32

GOING CRAZY

Piper takes a deep breath and closes her eyes. Her first week back in the office has been uneventful, yet for some reason, this morning she woke up on edge. She pauses, inhaling once more before buzzing herself into the offices of Harmon Consulting. She wasn't ready to be back, not really. But her team has a media event today. For the sake of staying present, she came. There probably never would be an ideal time to jump back in. Being here feels both comforting and unsettling.

As she steps off the elevator, she glances over her shoulder to make sure no one's following her, even though she knows Hoover showing up here is near impossible. But still.

She steps into the main office floor where she spots Chloe firing up her laptop.

"Hey, can we take five this morning to review all the press attendees for lunch at Bohemian House?" Chloe asks.

"Yes, of course. Let me set my stuff down."

Piper catches the stress in her friend's voice. *I used to sound like that too,* she thinks, *before my life unraveled and the things I worried about completely changed.*

Piper wheels her desk chair over to Chloe's and opens the press RSVP list. Their Central European restaurant client, Bohemian House, is launching its lunch service to the press today before opening to the public tomorrow. Over the past few weeks, she, Chloe, and the team have invited every top-tier local outlet they could think of. Lately, though, so many people cancel last minute that hosting events has become a gamble.

"Okay," Chloe says, scanning the spreadsheet. "We've got forty press confirmed, most bringing guests, which puts us at two seatings, at eleven and one. Can you reach out to the client to make sure they're feeling good about everything and send over the RSVP list?"

"Yes, I'm on it," Piper says, fingers flying over the keyboard.

"Perfect. I'll head to the restaurant early to oversee setup and handle table assignments. Cool?"

"Cool. I'll be there at ten-thirty. See you soon."

The morning slips by, and Piper has to give herself a mental pep talk just to walk the three blocks to the restaurant. Even with the restraining order in place, her body doesn't trust it. Her head stays on a swivel, scanning faces, doorways, reflections in windows.

She forces herself to breathe in rhythm. The warm wind lifts the hem of her navy pleated skirt, and for a fleeting moment, the breeze feels grounding.

Her phone buzzes in her hand.

Ryan.

> Can I see you tonight? Take you out for dinner?

Her heart lurches. *Not after what I did the other night. I can't think about this right now.* She slips the phone into her bag, trying to push the thought, and the guilt from it, aside. She needs her head in the game.

Piper climbs the short flight of stairs to Bohemian House and is surprised to find Kate already there.

"Hello, beautiful," Kate greets, effortlessly polished in a Diane von Fürstenberg wrap dress and tan pumps.

"Hey," Piper says, setting her bag on a brown leather banquette. Together, they start prepping for the event, laying out final place cards, setting gift bags, and making last-minute seating adjustments.

The first guest, a food writer from *Eater Chicago*, arrives five minutes early. Instinct takes over. Piper smiles, escorts them to their seat, and gushes about the to-die-for new menu. It's automatic, like slipping into a familiar routine. For a while she forgets everything, until the bell over the door chimes.

A tall, lanky man in a black blazer walks in, his hat pulled low.

The calm inside her chest shatters.

Chloe seats him, unbothered. He appears to be someone's guest, maybe from *The Chicago Tribune*.

Adrenaline floods Piper's body. Her vision narrows. *No. It can't be him. It can't.*

Her pulse pounds in her ears as instinct takes over. She's no longer frozen, but ready to run or fight. Her eyes dart across the room until they find Kate.

Kate reads her instantly. She stills, scanning the crowd.

Where is he? Kate mouths.

Piper's heart hammers so violently it feels audible. She can't speak. Her throat locks. She simply lifts a trembling hand and points to the man in the hat.

Kate takes off in a sprint, phone already in hand. Before Piper can even process what's happening, Kate is snapping photo after photo of the man in the hat.

Yes. Yes, thank you, yes. Relief floods Piper. *I knew Kate would know what to do. This is what we need — proof. Proof that this creep is back. So I can lock him up for coming near me again.*

Kate crouches low, angling her phone to catch his face beneath the brim. The shutter clicks again and again.

Across the room, the dining editor from *The Chicago Tribune*, Sierra Smith, walks in, scanning the space for her guest.

Kate is oblivious to the stares around her. Guests whisper, their eyes darting between one another and the woman behaving like paparazzi. But Kate's deep in protective overdrive. She'll do anything — *anything* — to keep Piper safe.

Chloe crosses the floor in record time and raises her voice, her tone bright and controlled. "Looks like the paparazzi have made their debut," she says with a light laugh, cutting through the tension. "Kate, have you two not met?" She gives Kate a pointed elbow.

Kate blinks, as if coming to. The room is silent, all eyes on her. She lowers her phone, clears her throat, and forces a smile. "Sierra! How are you, darling? Thank you so much for coming. Lovely to see you."

"Hello, Kate." Sierra's brow furrows. "Thanks for having me, but what in the world are you doing?"

Her guest turns, removing his hat in greeting.

Kate stiffens. The man across from her has a strong jaw, his hair pulled back into a tight man bun. Definitely not Hoover. He looks up, clearly irritated. "Can I help you with something?"

Kate's face drains of color. "No, I'm all good. Sorry…just got a little carried away capturing guests." She forces a brittle laugh. "Let me get one of the two of you!" She raises her phone again, desperate to recover the moment.

Chloe sweeps in, smiling wide. "Sierra! So great to see you. We're thrilled you could make it. Please, make yourself comfortable." She gestures toward the table, her movements calm and deliberate. Then, under her breath, she hisses at Kate, "Knock it off."

Piper stands frozen, watching the disaster unfold in slow

motion. *How could I have let this happen? How could I have caused this?*

Heat rushes to her cheeks. The embarrassment is unbearable. Without another thought, she turns and bolts. She runs out the door, across the street, heels clattering against the pavement. She runs up the steps to the overpass, across the NBC Plaza, down a narrow staircase to Riverside Place.

By the time she stops, she's panting, sweat dampening her back. Her feet ache. She finds a bench along the riverfront and sinks onto it.

Tears spill before she can stop them. *How could I have mistaken him for Hoover?* she thinks, gutted. *How am I supposed to move on when this is what happens in public? When I can't trust my own mind?*

She lets herself cry until the storm passes, then slowly walks home.

Inside her apartment, she kicks off her shoes and dials her mom.

"Hey, Piper! How did your lunch event go?" her mom answers brightly.

"Awful," Piper says, her voice breaking. "It was awful. I'm a paranoid mess. I freaked out thinking one of our guests was Hoover, and it turned into this whole thing. I'm so embarrassed."

"Listen to me," her mom says gently. "You need to give yourself some grace. Think of what you've been through. Cut yourself some slack. This is your reality, Piper, and you have to love yourself while you work through it."

"You're right," Piper says quietly, changing into sweats. "I felt so good being back at work, like maybe I could finally move on, and then it just...snuck back in. It ruins everything. I can't escape it."

"It's normal, sweetheart," her mom says. "You're going to have moments like this for a while. Let them happen. Don't fight them." She pauses. "Hang on, I'm putting you on speaker. Your dad's here."

"Hey, Piper," her dad says, his voice steady, serious.

"Hi, Dad. Is everything okay?" The question slips out. The one she always asks now.

"Everything's fine, Piper." He exhales. "I heard about your day. I'm so sorry. I wish I could take this away from you. Truly. I actually was about to call you anyway." He hesitates. "And I'm sorry to say it's not going to get better...not right now. There's something I need to tell you."

"Oh my gosh, what's happened?" Piper asks, her voice fragile as she looks out the window at the riverfront below, the water as still as glass.

"I just received an email from Bryce Jones, the provost. It's, uh...there's no way around it...it's disturbing. I promised you from day one that I'd never hide anything from you, so I'm not going to. You deserve to be kept in the loop." His voice wavers. "Hoover emailed the provost. It's concerning, to say the least. I'm forwarding it to you now. Read it, and then call me back."

"Umm...okay. I'll call you back in a few." Her voice shakes in unison with her hands.

She opens her laptop, her fingers trembling as she clicks into her inbox. A new message flashes: *FWD: Compensation*. The subject line alone makes her stomach drop. She clicks.

From: Hoover.Joseph@Midlandcollege.edu
To: Jones.Bryce@Midlandcollege.edu
Sent: Sunday, July 17, 2011 4:49 PM
Subject: Compensation

Dear Provost Bryce Jones,

You must understand, I am not pleading for help. I am demanding restitution for the damage inflicted upon me. Bryce, this is an extremely serious matter. Both you and the Midland community are complicit in the destruction of my life.

What I am asking is that you come clean about your involvement in stripping Piper Hawthorne from my life. You and the administration bullied me into submission, forbidding me from having contact with her for two years, thereby destroying my future with the love of my life, my soulmate. I am giving you a chance to make restitution in a Christian fashion.

Please do not evade your moral responsibility or attempt to turn this into a psychiatric issue, as though I were delusional. Even if I were (which I am not), there would still be no justification for the torture you have inflicted upon me. By the grace of God, I am at least able to argue coherently, and that is what I am putting forward.

You know what you did, and it is IMMORAL. YOU HAVE TO COMPENSATE ME FOR WHAT YOU'VE DONE. IF NOT, I WILL FIGHT FOR MY RIGHTS. YOU AND THE BOARD HAVE BEHAVED IN AN UNETHICAL AND MORALLY REPREHENSIBLE MANNER. DO YOU UNDERSTAND ME? YOU HAVE TO COMPENSATE ME.

HOW DARE YOU CALL YOURSELF ADMINISTRATORS OF A CHRISTIAN COLLEGE? THIS BEHAVIOR IS MORALLY DEBASED, PERVERSE, AND MACHIAVELLIAN TO DIABOLIC DIMENSIONS. YOU HAVE NO RIGHT TO CALL YOURSELF A CHRISTIAN.

I EXPECT TO HEAR FROM YOU SOON. IF YOU CONTINUE WITH YOUR USUAL BULLYING TACTIC OF "I AM GOING TO CONTACT LAW ENFORCEMENT," PLEASE BELIEVE ME THAT I WILL DO THE SAME. YOU SHOULD BE GRATEFUL THAT

THE TONE OF THIS EMAIL IS UNUSUALLY POLITE AND RESTRAINED.

YOU PRESUMED THAT I WAS STUPID BECAUSE I AM A COMMUNICATION PROFESSOR AND THEREFORE YOU AND YOUR COHORTS COULD GET AWAY WITH YOUR BULLYING ABOUT MY LOVE FOR PIPER. YOU SHOULD HAVE BEEN TRANSPARENT ABOUT YOUR ROLE BEFORE AND DURING MY EMPLOYMENT AT MIDLAND COLLEGE.

INSTEAD, YOU CHOSE TO DAMAGE IT. WHAT I WANT FROM YOU IS A TEARFUL APOLOGY. AN ADMISSION THAT YOU ARE ASHAMED OF YOURSELF FOR RUINING MY LIFE AND FUTURE WITH HER, THAT YOUR BEHAVIOR IS UTTERLY DIABOLICAL, AND THAT YOU ARE SEEKING GENUINE REPENTANCE. THE DEMONSTRATION OF THAT REPENTANCE MUST BE MANIFEST IN YOUR WILLINGNESS TO PAY REPARATIONS.

I DEMAND WHAT IS RIGHTFULLY MINE RIGHT NOW. YOU WILL COMPENSATE ME WITH THE SUM OF $1,000,000, AND THEN I WILL DECIDE WHETHER I NEED THERAPY TO DEAL WITH THE INDIGNITIES INFLICTED UPON ME DURING YOUR ADMINISTRATION.

Courteously,
Hoover

Her body shudders as she finishes the final line. Her hands go numb.

She dials her dad, barely able to breathe. "Dad?" she manages, gasping between hyperventilating breaths.

"Piper, I'm really sorry," he says softly. "He's clearly gone off the deep end over all of this. On the bright side, he didn't contact you directly. I know that doesn't change how you feel, but at least he hasn't reached out."

Piper tries to steady her breathing.

"I just spoke with the provost," her dad continues. "Here's what we're going to do. He's alerting campus security and filing another police report. And I'm hiring a private investigator to track Hoover down. Once we confirm he's not in Chicago, you'll have some peace of mind."

"Dad, the college security is basically a bunch of mall cops. What good is that going to do?"

"I know," he says patiently. "That may not help much, but did you hear the rest? There's going to be a formal police report, and I'm already working with a private detective. We'll find him, Piper. I'll do anything — I mean it — to keep you safe. I'll call you the second I hear something new. Hopefully within a week."

"Okay, that's...good, I guess." She exhales, her body still trembling. "But wait...I don't understand. This email. What does it even mean? It's like he's unraveling, but I can't make sense of what he's saying other than demanding some ridiculous amount of money."

"Piper, I'm as confused as you are, and so is Provost Jones. It doesn't make sense. When I say Hoover's gone off the deep end, I mean that literally. He needs help. Serious psychological help. His words are unhinged." He pauses. "I love you, Piper. So much. Remember that. God's got you. He's your protector. And I'll do everything in my power to keep you safe."

Piper lets out a breath that feels heavier than air. "Well, I'm glad we're all dumbfounded together. I just...I can't believe this is my life. Thank you for hiring a private detective. I was already on edge today, and now this?" She presses a hand to the cold glass, letting the chill steady her.

"I know, sweetheart. It's beyond messed up. There are no words. Just hold tight. We'll get some clarity soon. I promise."

"Okay. I love you." Piper ends the call.

She walks to the kitchen, opens a bottle of Cabernet, and fills her glass to the brim.

I can't even comprehend that this is my life. She takes a sip, her throat burning. *It's starting to feel like I'll never move past this. Hoover's going to haunt me forever.*

33

PROFESSOR HOOVER

Professor Hoover meticulously folds his clothes and gently lays them inside his worn mahogany leather duffel bag, the one imprinted with his monogram: JHR.

Much to Myra's dismay, he's packing up all his belongings, what few he has, and taking a road trip with only one destination in mind: Chicago. His mental stability is fragile at best, and he's convinced the only thing that will help is finding her and, eventually, getting back to the place they were. He won't reveal himself, of course. Not yet. Just seeing her from a distance will be enough. And if he can't find her, he'll fall back on his old research techniques. He just needs to make sure she's okay and reassure himself that she's still within reach.

He zips up his bag, folds back the sheets on his bed, opens his black buckle briefcase, and slides in his laptop. He takes one last look around the room before heading upstairs.

Myra and Colton are still asleep. He prefers it this way. Goodbyes have never suited him. Besides, this isn't really goodbye, more of a *see you later*, though he's not sure when.

He starts the engine of his white 2007 Buick and drums his

bony fingers against the center console in steady rhythm. He places his GPS unit on the dashboard and punches in the address. St. Louis to Chicago: approximately 297 miles. It should take him five hours. One stop for gas and a restroom break, and he'll arrive by early lunchtime.

He hasn't decided where he'll stay. *Too soon for that.* He needs facts first...proof of her location and confirmation she's all right. The plan, like all good plans, is fluid.

He scrolls through his playlists, searching for something to calm his mind. Finally, he lands on the mix he made back in 2006, "Piper: Love of My Life." The first song, "Walking on Sunshine," bursts through the speakers as he reverses out of Myra's short driveway, the sunrise flashing across the windshield.

He grips the steering wheel tight, voice low and steady.

"I'm coming for you, Piper. Now be a good girl and get ready for me."

34

BAR NASH

Piper rolls over in bed and opens her eyes with a jolt upon feeling something warm next to her. She abruptly sits up and is met with a pounding in her head so fierce it forces her right back to her pillow. A chill comes over her body as she realizes she's completely naked.

Confused, she pulls the bedsheet up to her chin before taking in her surroundings. She's in a bedroom that's not her own. The walls are a light shade of gray, the sheets black. There's a worn wood dresser, a nightstand with a crooked lampshade, and books strewn about. Posters of girls clad in tiny bikinis in provocative positions hang on the wall. Piper cringes, nervous to find out more.

She sits up again and peers over at the guy next to her. *What did I do last night?* she thinks, racking her brain. She remembers the nightmare of a day she had...the work event gone wrong, Hoover's email.

She remembers downing a glass of wine after she got off the phone with her dad and texting with Chloe. *Texting with Chloe*, she thinks to herself, and frantically searches for her phone.

Thankfully, she finds it under her pillow. She opens her

messages and scrolls up to where their texts begin, hoping to trigger any memory of the events of last night.

9:28 p.m. PIPER:

> Chloe, SOS. While hard to believe, today has gotten even worse since the fiasco at work. Can you meet up? Any interest in going out tonight?

CHLOE:

> Going out? On a Thursday? It's already 9:30 and I'm in my pjs…

> But like you said, you only live once. Let's do it. Where do you want to meet? I need ten to get myself to a presentable place.

PIPER:

> You're the best! Let's meet at Bar Nash?

CHLOE:

> The country bar? Say no more. See you there soon.

12:40 a.m.
CHLOE:

> Did you make it back to that guy's place okay? Piper, you need to text me when you do these things… or else I worry like I'm your mom… which I am not.

> hello????
>
> Text me as soon as you see this. Don't do anything I wouldn't do!

The texts trigger a flashback: Piper pictures Chloe and her on stage singing. She closes her eyes tight. Her mouth is so parched it's hard to swallow the regret invading every corner of her body. Karaoke is not her cup of tea. Not unless she's in the right mindset, which she clearly was, based on her blank-slate memory.

Piper tries to picture what she drank last night. She remembers having the wine at home and can visualize herself and Chloe ordering drinks at Bar Nash. Sure, they're strong, but not strong enough to make her black out from two drinks. It dawns on her — *the meds*. They seem to be amplifying the effects of alcohol. *Which is a shame, because now is not the time to abstain from drinking.*

I don't even know what we did last night, Piper thinks, guilt closing in on her. *What's his name? Bryan? No, Billy. Something with a B. Bobby? Who am I that I don't even know this guy's name? Did I just sleep with a random? Gosh, I hope not.*

Desperate for water to quench her thirst and soothe her pounding head, Piper quietly slips out of bed. She looks around for her clothes and sees a torn foil wrapper on the floor, the kind that makes her stomach drop.

The guilt, disappointment, and raging headache become too much at once. Piper covers her mouth with her hands and sprints through the door in front of her. Much to her relief, she makes it to the toilet just in time to empty the contents of her stomach, of which were few. After heaving a handful of times, she regains her composure.

She splashes cold water on her face and sips water from the faucet, rinsing her mouth. She grabs a nearby towel and wraps herself in it before tiptoeing her way back to the bedroom.

It comes as no surprise that she's now woken up the mystery man. He peeks his eyes open and offers a sympathetic, "Hey, come here. You okay?"

Piper is relieved to find the mystery man is at least somewhat attractive. His brown hair is buzzed tight, a little longer on top. His right arm is covered in tattoos from shoulder to wrist. He looks fit, but not like Ryan. He's skinnier and has more of a bad-boy appeal.

"Ah, well, I'm definitely not one hundred percent, as I'm sure you heard," Piper says with a laugh, because if she can't laugh in this moment, she might cry.

"All good, don't even worry about it. Do you know what time it is?" he asks, rolling over to hug his pillow and close his eyes.

"It's 7:23 a.m. I...uh...yeah, I need to sort myself out. Shoot, work. I need to work today. It's Friday, isn't it?" It dawns on Piper.

"I don't have to be back at the bar until two, so I'm going to catch a few more hours of sleep," he says.

I slept with a Bar Nash bartender?! Piper's taken aback. She scrambles around the room until she finds her underwear, bra, jeans, tank, and shoes, then hurries to get dressed in his bathroom.

She feels the overwhelming urge to get out immediately. She needs fresh air. She tiptoes over to the bed and whispers, "Bye, uh, thanks for last night," unsure why she even said those words.

"Your number...I need to get your number, Penelope," he says, eyes still closed.

Did he just call me Penelope? Piper cringes.

"Yeah, sure. I'll just write it down right here." Piper pretends to jot down her number and jets out of the apartment as fast as she can.

Note to self: avoid Bar Nash, she thinks.

Piper walks aimlessly down the hallway until she finally finds an elevator and notices that she's on the twelfth floor. She presses down and opens her maps. Upon realizing she's in Lincoln Park, her heart pangs. *Ryan. I never texted him back yesterday. What is wrong with me?*

Piper exits the apartment building and starts to walk. She breathes in the fresh air and slowly tries to gather her thoughts.

She opens her phone and starts to compose a new text to Kate and Chloe.

7:50 a.m.
PIPER:

> Hi ladies! I'm going to work from home today. Don't worry…nothing's wrong. I'm fine and safe, just not feeling 100. I'll be signed on though, rest assured.

CHLOE:

> Are you sure you're okay…??

PIPER:

> Yes, positive. Just think I ate something off. I'm good, I promise!

KATE:

> No worries, take care of yourself, Piper. The only thing I really need from you is that new restaurant opening proposal. Can you get me that draft today?

PIPER:

> Yes, of course! On it as we speak. Have it to you soon.

"Coffee," Piper says aloud to herself. "I need coffee."

Chloe calls her a minute later.

"Piper, are you okay?! What happened last night?" she asks, concern coloring her tone.

"I'm good, I promise. I'm so hungover I puked…at that guy's house this morning. So that was mortifying." Piper pauses to catch up with her thoughts. "This isn't me, Chloe. These late-night antics on work nights…horrible hangovers…making stupid decisions I regret. I feel so stuck right now. My life is a mess. This isn't me. But I don't even know who I am anymore."

"Ugh, Piper. I'm sorry. You're being so hard on yourself. You need to sleep this off, and you'll think more clearly." Chloe sips her coffee. "You'll find your way back to you. You just need time. You're still processing everything. You need time and space where life is chill to figure out who you are. You don't have to have it all together right now, and that's okay.

"Side note, are you really okay to work on that proposal today?" she asks, half-laughing. "If you're in a bind, I can totally help you."

"No, it's on my plate. I'm not having you do that. I'll be signed on in 30, realistically, and will start cranking. I'm sure I'll be reaching out soon with questions."

"Call me if you need anything. Seriously."

"Thanks, Chloe. I owe you." *Click.*

Piper keeps walking, trying to get her stomach under control before she hails a taxi home.

Ryan…I need to get back to him, she thinks. *What better time than now…doing a walk of shame probably somewhere near his house? What do I even text him?*

> Ryan! It's so good to hear from you. Sorry I didn't get back to you in time… yesterday got away from me. Maybe we can meet up sometime soon?

Five minutes go by. Much to Piper's relief, her phone pings and it's Ryan.

> Don't sweat it. I got stuck at work, so it would've made for a late night.

Ugh, I'd rather have had a late night doing nothing with Ryan than a night I have no recollection of, she thinks.

Realizing what time it is, Piper finally hails a cab back to her apartment.

She doesn't love taking taxis by herself, but she's gotten more comfortable with it lately. A wave of relief hits when her driver shows up in a silver Honda Odyssey minivan and appears to be around sixty. She climbs in, lost in thought.

As they round the final turn to her apartment off Lower Wacker Drive, the driver reaches his hand back toward her, waving some sort of card. She takes it and reads:

> *Proverbs 3:5–6* — "Trust in the Lord with all your heart and lean not on your own understanding; in all your ways acknowledge Him, and He will direct your paths."

He meets her eyes in the rearview mirror and smiles. "A message for you," he says.

Piper loses her breath for a moment, taken aback. She reads the card again, her heart aching with yearning and remorse.

This isn't who I am. Someone who goes out on a Thursday, blacks out, and doesn't respect herself.

Or is it? Is this who I'm becoming?

No. No, this isn't me, she thinks. *It's just my life...this wasn't how things were supposed to go.*

Why did such a good and gracious God let this all happen to me? Why didn't He stop Hoover or change his course? Why me?

How can I be so consumed by fear and anger and still have the peace Jesus promises?

Piper's heart thuds with confusion. *Maybe God's trying to tell me this is part of a larger plan,* she thinks. *But how could something this awful possibly be turned to good?*

She remembers what her mother always used to say, *He makes beauty from ashes.*

Is God trying to get my attention now, of all times?

"Thank you," she says quietly, before climbing out of the van.

She walks into her apartment building with urgency, relieved to finally be home.

"Piper, there you are, girl!" Mike says, cheerful as ever. "You didn't answer when I rang up this morning...I was hoping to see you."

"Hi, Mike. Rest assured, I'm fine and well. Just a late night and stayed at a friend's house," she says, feeling bad about not telling the full truth.

"I got you, girl. I was just trying to track you down because something was delivered to you first thing this morning."

"A delivery? What was it?" she asks, perplexed.

"I don't want to ruin the surprise," he says, grinning.

Piper racks her brain, trying to think what could possibly have been delivered that would make Mike this excited. She hasn't placed any thrilling online orders lately.

He finally walks out from the package room carrying a ridiculously stunning bouquet of flowers — white and pink roses, pastel ranunculus, and pale green and blush dahlias. Piper's breath catches. *He found me again,* she thinks, panic flashing through her.

"Who on earth sent this?" she asks, her voice thinning, tears threatening.

"That's what I want to know," Mike says with a hearty laugh.

A cold wave washes over her. *Oh no. It can't be. He can't be back already*, she thinks, her stomach twisting into a knot.

Just then, her phone pings. *Ryan.*

> Not sure if you got what I sent you, but just want you to know you were on my mind...as friends, of course.

Piper exhales the breath she was holding, and a smile overtakes her face.

"They're from...a friend. My friend, Ryan," she says to Mike, beaming.

"I would not have guessed those flowers were sent from just a friend," he says with a chuckle from deep in his belly. "Whatever you say, Miss Piper. This Ryan guy sounds like a keeper to me." Mike grins and returns to his post at the front desk.

Piper texts Ryan back as she walks toward the elevator.

PIPER:

> Ryan! These are the most stunning flowers I've seen in my entire life. Thank you...you made my day.

RYAN:

> You deserve them, Piper. I hope your life is slowing down and you've been met with some peace.

PIPER:

> It is…I think. Slowly but surely, I'm starting to get my head above water.

RYAN:

> When you're ready, I'll be here…to talk or hang or whatever you need. No pressure. Just reach out when you're ready.

PIPER:

> Thanks, Ryan. It's a deal.

Piper walks into her apartment, throws her purse down, and just sits for a minute, processing everything that's happened in the last hour of her life. She woke up in some random guy's apartment, then had a convicting cab ride, and came home to the most beautiful flowers she's ever seen…from Ryan.

The Bible verse echoes in her mind:

> "Trust in the Lord with all your heart and lean
> not on your own understanding; in all your
> ways acknowledge Him, and He will direct
> your paths."

Where in the heck did that come from? she thinks.

The question she can't keep avoiding pricks at her mind.

Knowing this is her current reality, *what does she really want out of life?*

35

PROFESSOR HOOVER

Professor Hoover pulls into a dingy motel just outside the city limits. He doesn't know what he was thinking. This wasn't part of the plan, but he's spent the entire day circling the city, searching for her face and finding nothing. He doesn't know where she lives, can't find her online, and her office is closed for the weekend.

"No, no, NO!" he screams.

He parks and slams his fist on the steering wheel until the horn blares and the sound snaps him back.

"I can't," he says aloud, arguing with the small, sensible voice in his head.

Or can I? he thinks.

He pulls out his phone and opens a browser. More out of curiosity than any real plan, he types search phrases, clicks through threads and news stories, and lets the pages feed the dark idea already forming in his mind. His pulse quickens. *This can't be this easy,* he tells himself, and yet the words on-screen make the possibility feel suddenly, dangerously possible.

If he can't find Piper...if he can't have Piper...and the college won't answer his emails or take him seriously, what choice have they left him? They've boxed him in, stripped him of his purpose and the life he imagined. The louder part of him, the part that's been wounded and furious for years, begins to drown out the doubt.

A plan forms in broad strokes, not yet a method but an intent: something public enough to make them all look up and remember his name. He doesn't know what the act will be yet, only that it must be seen.

It will make them take me seriously, he tells himself. *And it will make her look.*

It will show Piper that I am not small.

It will prove how far I'll go for us...how much I care.

The thought is wild and electric. In his mind, the act becomes less about punishment and more about drawing her back into the life he insists they share.

He reaches into his jacket for his monogrammed leather notebook and, with an unsteady hand, scribbles a list of steps that are vague, focused on purpose and timing, not specific details. He isn't creative; he's desperate.

He opens Maps, finds the closest store that might carry whatever he thinks he'll need, and slowly backs the car out of the motel lot. He just needs to find the right place. Somewhere crowded. Somewhere that will make them remember his name.

A strange, renewed purpose hums through him. *He is on to something.*

36

RAIN CHECK

The following week, Chloe, Kate, and Piper hop in a cab en route to The Husky Inn. They've just wrapped a work event, the opening party for Dolce Vida, a hot new Italian restaurant, and to say they're ready to let loose is an understatement. Piper's feet ache from being in heels all day, but nothing will slow her down.

"Who is ready to get after it tonight?" Kate squeals in the backseat. The funny thing is, she never really *gets after it*, but still manages to exude this level of energy, and it's contagious.

Piper and Chloe look at one another. "Meeeee," they say in unison, cracking up.

"But seriously," Chloe says, "can we, for a second, just talk about how much we crushed that event? There were so many good people there. Not to mention we had press from every local magazine and newspaper, plus a ridiculous number of influencers. Crushed it. I will sleep well tonight knowing that's off my plate."

"Same, girl. I've been stressing about that event for days. If we could start a new trend where people RSVP more than two days in advance, it would save me from the wrinkles starting to take over my face," Piper admits.

"Wrinkles, where?" Chloe jokes. "Forget wrinkles, you look amazing."

Piper's feeling pretty good about herself, but only because she splurged on a new outfit for the restaurant's opening. It's been a while since she's bought a specific outfit for an occasion; living in Chicago on a publicist's salary isn't cheap. But she's desperate to gain her confidence back. The second she laid eyes on the lacy black minidress, she knew she needed it. Her stick-straight blonde hair adds the perfect polish.

The trio struts into The Husky Inn and heads upstairs to the lounge, which is packed.

"What do you girls want?" Piper yells, hoping Kate and Chloe can hear her over the music.

"Vodka soda!" they say in unison.

Piper turns around, trying to get the bartender's attention on her tiptoes, when she feels a hand brush her back. Ryan immediately pops into her mind, and she quickly turns, hoping to finally see him again.

"Chase!" she exclaims, surprised. Her heart skips a beat with excitement while her stomach simultaneously drops with disappointment.

"Not so fast...this round's on me," Chase says in her ear. "What are you doing here? I was so bummed you disappeared the other morning. I've been hoping to run into you. I never got the chance to get your number, and I'm not making that mistake twice," he says with a grin.

"I know, I shouldn't have run like that. I just, you know, woke up with a pounding headache and needed to get myself back together," she says, laughing. She takes in his stunning golden-brown almond eyes. She hadn't noticed them last time because it was too dark. The faint wrinkles framing them and the freckles dotting his face are so attractive.

"So what are you doing in this part of town?" Chase asks, drawing her in with his eye contact.

"We had a work event tonight. To say I'm relieved it's over is an understatement," Piper says, her stomach twisting into a jumbled mess as she remembers all the questionable decisions she's made lately.

"You look beautiful tonight, Piper," he says while flagging down the bartender. Piper tries to hide the smile overtaking her face.

"I'm ordering drinks for my friends too. You don't need to do this," she says, scanning the crowd for Chloe and Kate.

"This is my pleasure. I can't believe we're running into each other again. Feels meant to be," he says with a wink.

"Three vodka sodas, please. Very original," Piper laughs, tucking her hair behind her ear.

When the drinks arrive, Chase hands her two vodka sodas for the girls and holds the others. Piper spots Kate with Chloe and walks over.

"Here!" she shouts, trying not to spill. "These are on my friend, Chase!"

"Oh my gosh," Chloe says, eyes widening. "The guy you met from Club Five? Dang, girl, what are the odds?"

"Well, what are you doing, Blondie? Introduce me," Kate yells. Wearing a silk leopard skirt with a black tank top and black cardigan, she's a vision of sophistication.

"Chase, this is my boss, Kate, and you may remember my friend and colleague, Chloe," Piper says, introducing the group.

"Cheers, ladies," Chase says, clinking glasses. "Cheers, Piper," he adds, looking at her with a side grin and a sparkle in his eyes.

Even though she doesn't want to date Chase, she can't resist the attention he's giving her. Feeling wanted feels so good. With each sip, she can feel her nerves loosen like a snapped rubber band, and she stops overthinking.

"So, how's your week been? And what are you doing here?" Piper asks, leaning into his space.

"Week's been kind of rough," Chase says. "Work has been stressful. We had a huge corporate design deal go sideways, and I can't talk to one more person about how we're going to try to save it. I had a work dinner in this part of town, and a few colleagues and I wanted to blow off some steam after."

"Well, I'm glad you came here," Piper says genuinely.

"Forget all this work stuff," he says. "What's new with you?"

"Outside of this? Not much," she chuckles. "Just surviving another week."

The crazy thing is, Piper wishes Chase knew she means it in the most literal sense. She's surviving — trying to make sure no one follows her, always looking over her shoulder, and drinking more than she should because she feels like her life is, in so many ways, still in shambles. She still feels the pull every day between wanting to find her faith again and wanting to quit partying, but at the same time, she keeps going out and distracting herself with anything and anyone. She succumbs easily to numbing the pain she feels inside that's all-consuming.

She smiles and, deep down, wishes Chase were Ryan. *He would know what she meant.* He genuinely cares about what she's going through. He asks all the right questions and seems to understand Piper, and she doesn't even know him that well.

"Hey, would you ever, you know..." he pauses, and suddenly Piper feels her stomach drop as a million things race through her mind. "Would you ever want to come over and just hang out? Like tonight or another time?"

"Yes," she says, not knowing where her confidence is coming from. "I would like that. Tonight, I'm honestly so wiped, I think I'm just going to call it early, but rain check?"

Half of her wants to say the hell with it and go. Chase is

attractive, fun, and kind. But she also knows it's not going anywhere. From that perspective, why even start?

The next thing Piper knows, Chase is pressing a quick kiss to her cheek. "I've got to run, but I'm taking you up on that rain check," he says, placing a folded piece of paper in her hand.

And just like that, he's gone. Piper feels a pang of disappointment and thinks she should've taken him up on his offer. Even though she completely regretted the last time she went home with the guy from Bar Nash, it feels nice to feel wanted, even if it's a dead end.

She unfolds the note and smiles as she reads: *Call me when you want to hang,* with his number scrawled underneath.

She tucks it in her purse with a smirk and sets off to find Kate and Chloe.

She walks through the coastal-inspired bar and finds the girls nestled into a rich brown leather banquette in the far corner of the room. Piper excuses her way through the crowded space and slides in.

Kate and Chloe stop talking with anticipation. "Need we even ask? Who was that cutie?" Kate says, sipping the last of her vodka soda.

"Oh, you know...a guy Chloe and I met out recently. His name's Chase. He's sweet and smooth, and obviously hot, but I know it's not going to go anywhere," she says, looking down.

"But you could've had fun tonight!" Kate laughs, shaking her glass and debating whether she should have another.

"I could've...and maybe I should've. I may or may not have gone home with him the night we met. If I'm being totally honest, I find myself wishing he was Ryan, a friend of Chloe's I met this summer," Piper admits with a sigh, lost in thought.

"Well, you should rekindle things with Ryan then, obviously!" Chloe says with excitement.

"Yeah...maybe I should. He sent me flowers last Friday. The most ridiculous display of flowers. Let me show you."

Piper gets out her phone and pulls up a photo of the stunning bouquet Ryan sent her.

"Girl, what?! I cannot believe you haven't mentioned this until now!" Chloe says.

"Okay, he is a keeper," Kate says. "I see why he holds a special spot for you right now. What's holding you back from Ryan?"

"I still feel like I need to get my life together. I am a disaster, Kate," Piper admits, tears pulling at her eyes. "I've been partying too much and making decisions I wake up and regret. Part of me wants to stop and grow up, but part of me just doesn't care about anything, because the truth is, my soul is crushed by the weight of my life. I still haven't processed everything. I still spend most of my time scared as shit Hoover is going to find me. I don't want to start a good relationship feeling like this. I want to put my best self into it, and I'm just not there yet."

"Okay, I can empathize with that. You've been through a lot, Piper. Just don't be too hard on yourself. You don't need to always be living in this black-and-white box. Give yourself some grace to not be perfect or have the perfect beginning to a new relationship. Let yourself live a little, and when the timing's right to pursue things with Ryan, you'll know. I'm sure of it," Kate says, wholeheartedly hoping Piper will take her advice.

"Thanks, Kate. I appreciate that," she admits. "Enough about me...I'm always stealing the show. Chloe, dating update, go!"

"We love you, Piper. You've got a lot to navigate and work through, and you're doing it so well. Counseling would be so good for you too, when you're ready for it," Chloe says. "Life update, let's see...I'm going out on a third date tomorrow night with that guy, James. Kate, he's in wealth management, from the East Coast, and he's very sweet, down-to-earth, and funny," Chloe says, a grin overtaking her face.

"Yes, girl, that's what I'm talking about," Kate exclaims. "Alright, girls, while I'd love to stay and be fun and young, I have five kids at home and a soccer game I have to be up bright and early for." Kate gives the girls hugs as she slides out of the booth.

Chloe and Piper look at each other.

"Let's call it. I do not want to be hungover tomorrow," Piper admits.

"You read my mind," Chloe says, leading the way out of the bar.

The following evening, Piper pours herself a glass of wine and starts boiling a pot of water as she preps to make pasta. She's successfully slept in, run six miles on the lakefront, gone grocery shopping, and done her laundry. Knowing she still has a full day of respite ahead tomorrow, she's feeling bored, but there is literally nothing going on. Chloe has that date tonight, and Kate has family stuff.

As she thinks about who else she can text, her mind jumps back to last night. *Chase*. She runs to her closet, finds her purse hanging on a hook, and searches until she sees the little square paper tucked in the back pocket of her black leather bag. She puts it on her counter — just in case.

A few glasses of wine and a bowl of pesto pasta later, against better judgment, she decides to go for it and reaches for her phone. Because, why not?

> Hey Chase, it's me. Piper. What are you up to tonight?

She rereads her words before pressing send and frowns, thinking it sounds too formal. She updates it.

> Hey Chase, it's me. Piper. Plans tonight?

It still feels a little formal for her liking, but she presses send. Much to her relief, she gets a bing in response a minute later.

> Piper, I wasn't sure if you'd reach out. I'm so happy to hear from you. I have a work event I have to go to at 9. :(

A work event? Lame, Piper thinks. *Who says we can't hang out before, though, right?*

She thinks about her night and the nothingness that lies ahead as she contemplates her next move.

> What are you doing before that? ;)

She stares down the wink face, unsure how lame or desperate it may come across, but hits send before letting herself overthink it. She receives a reply.

> You're welcome to come over for a little bit. You're always welcome over here :). Just know I'm going to have to jet.

Without thinking, her fingers take over, like they have a mind of their own.

> I'm coming over. What's your address?

She presses send.

She quickly freshens up, feeling a little buzzed and surprisingly lighthearted. She changes into a pair of high French-cut briefs, light-wash jeans with ripped knees, and a V-cut white T-shirt. She throws on some Nike tennis shoes and grabs her purse.

Just as she's ready, Chase sends her his address.

> I'm warning you…I want to spend time with you, but I really will have to jet a little bit after you get here.

Piper rolls her eyes as she hops in her taxi. On the ride there, she busies herself thinking about the week ahead. As the car comes to a stop, a flicker of *what the hell am I doing?* flashes through her mind, but she pushes it away.

She walks up the five steps to the three-flat building where Chase lives, reminding herself she's been here before, yet not recognizing anything at all.

Chase comes to the door with a smile, wearing baggy gray sweatpants and a plain black T-shirt, clearly not ready for a party. Piper can't help but notice the veins popping out of his biceps, which brings heat to her already flushed cheeks.

A football game is on, and a beer sits on the table beside him. The apartment is quiet except for the sound of the broadcast.

"Come sit," he says, motioning for Piper to join him. She does and suddenly feels both awkward and excited, like she's thirteen again, waiting for the guy next to her to put his arm around her.

"How did you feel after last night? You hungover today?"

"Me? No, I was fine…I didn't drink enough for that," she laughs. "I left pretty much after you did." She keeps her eyes on the game, feeling like there's an elephant in the room.

"I wasn't sure this rain check was ever going to happen," Chase says, giving her a playful elbow nudge. "I'm glad you texted me," he adds, taking a swig of his beer.

"Me too," Piper admits. "It's nice to see you outside of a bar environment," she says with a laugh. She takes in the living room: a massive TV spans the wall in front of her, flanked by bookshelves filled with an assortment of literature and man-knickknacks like a signed baseball, an antique clock, and a globe.

"I don't know exactly what you had in mind for tonight, but I know what I'd like to do," he says, turning fully toward her.

"Yeah, same," she whispers back, not recognizing the girl who spoke.

He pulls her onto his lap, and suddenly they're kissing, hard and desperate. The kind of kiss that dares her to let go, and for a moment, she does. She moves closer, pressing her body into his, her breath unsteady.

He stands, lifting her effortlessly as her legs wrap around his waist. They move toward the bedroom, familiar yet blurred, as if she's watching herself from somewhere far off.

"Now this is impressive," she says with a laugh, trying to mask how much she's mentally unraveling.

"You have no idea how bad I've wanted to see you again," he whispers against her neck.

He lays her gently on the bed and stretches out beside her. Their shirts come off, and she traces the lines of his arms, clinging to the illusion of connection. The voice in her head urges her to stop, to pull back, but it's drowned out by the louder one whispering how good it feels not to be alone.

"You're stunning, Piper," he murmurs, trailing soft kisses down her skin.

She notices him glance at his watch again before unbuttoning his jeans. He moves over her, closing the gap, the warmth of his body bringing her a momentary spark of life.

"I wish I had more time with you," he says, his voice soft, almost apologetic.

She yearns for this moment to last...to feel wanted, liked, not alone.

I'm done feeling paranoid everywhere I go. I'm done overthinking plans with friends...where we're going and who I might run into. I'm tired of the guilt invading my mind from every corner of my life...

Why am I thinking about this right now?

But as he quickens his pace, her mind disconnects. The room spins, past fear, past longing, until suddenly, it's over. He's catching his breath beside her; she's staring at the ceiling, numb.

He lies on her for a moment, breathing into her hair, then quickly gets up. "I'm so sorry...I have that work party I have to get to. I don't mean to run after doing that, I just...gah, I just have to."

Dumbfounded, Piper lies on the bed, pulling the sheet up around her. She watches as Chase throws on jeans and a T-shirt, then brushes his teeth in the other room.

She knew he had a party to get to, but this wasn't what she envisioned. A heavy rock settles in her chest. She thinks she might have to run to the bathroom to hurl up the guilt sitting there again.

She feels it happening deep within her soul, a breaking point she hadn't meant to reach.

Chase walks back in and plants a quick peck on her cheek. "Let's do this again soon," he says.

Piper stays silent, the pang wrecking her stomach.

"Take your time. When you leave, no need to do anything... the door automatically locks. Just let yourself out. See you soon, Piper."

She just lies there, feeling empty and utterly alone, wondering what the hell she just did.

I did this, she thinks, disgusted.

Her phone pings. She assumes it's Chase.

To her shock, it's Ryan.

> Piper, how are you holding up? Plans tonight? When can I see you?

Piper throws her phone. Tears spill as a wave of nausea rises up her throat. After what feels like an eternity, she gets up, uses the bathroom, and pulls on her clothes, trying to process everything that just happened.

Why am I doing this to myself? Why am I pushing Ryan away? Chase means nothing to me...so why did I just give myself to him? Is this rock bottom? Is that where I am right now?

Her stomach twists.

I did this. This is all me. I instigated this mess, and the regret feels unbearable.

She searches desperately for any justification to make peace with herself, but all she can find is emptiness: a void in her heart, loneliness in her soul, fear in her being.

The tears keep falling down her face, and she lets them as she walks out his front door.

37

PROFESSOR HOOVER

Professor Hoover finds himself lollygagging his way through the Midland campus. This is his fifth lap around the perimeter. He's forgone his typical crushed velvet blazer for an army-green and charcoal plaid dress coat. The collar is popped, and he's wearing a navy-and-tan plaid newsboy cap pulled low. While this isn't his typical style, he can't risk being recognized. Given that it's a Saturday, the chance of running into one of his few former faculty friends is slim.

He keeps getting distracted from the task at hand — when and where, precisely, he'll make his mark. He's spent the last week in and out of a Chicago Motel 6, toying with various makeshift devices. He's been tinkering, testing triggers, timers, and materials he barely understands. The time is near; he can feel it in his being. He doesn't actually want to go through with this. He really doesn't. But the school isn't taking him seriously. He's still gotten no response to his email, and his phone calls have gone unreturned. He's convinced Piper would have been interested in him, that they'd be together, had the school not shut him out of her life for two years. *They did this to him.* They ruined his life, and now it's time to make himself known.

Hoover stops himself from thinking about what happens after the explosion detonates. He can't go there. There will be no frills to this mission. All it will take is a simple, old-school briefcase, to be dropped in the middle of Belvedere Chapel during the very first gathering of the new semester. And by dropped, he means attached to the underside of one of the pews the night before. The entire student body under one roof...it doesn't get any easier than that.

Perhaps after this happens, she'll reach out, he thinks to himself, confidence building. *I mean, it only makes sense. When things like this happen, they're a community wake-up call, to cling tight to those you care about the most. To tell those who need to hear it how you feel.* He pictures Piper calling him as soon as she hears the news. *It's about time,* he tells himself. *After all these years.*

He tells himself this isn't about causing harm; it's about being heard. But deep down, he knows the truth. It's about control and making them all remember his name.

After his tenth lap, Hoover feels a sense of finality. Tomorrow, he plans to take a nice long road trip to the middle of nowhere, Illinois, to test his creation and see its effectiveness with his own eyes, which will allow him a few hours to make any necessary tweaks.

Two sleeps until go-time. He can hardly stand it.

38

HOLY PURSUIT

Piper wakes in a fog, cracking one eye open to the sun blazing into her apartment. Relief washes over her when she realizes she's here — at home, alone. She exhales a silent, *Thank God it's still the weekend.* She desperately needs one more day to collect herself.

She lies there, sweating in the sunlight that spills across her body, and starts to mentally retrace her evening. The solo wine. The desperation. Pursuing Chase...knowing exactly where it would lead and going along anyway. How quickly things started, how abruptly they stopped. The text from Ryan. And, of course, the flood of guilt that followed.

A quasi–one-night stand. Again, she admits, a lump forming in her throat.

She stops herself.

Today is a new day.

A bead of sweat forms in the nook behind her knees as the light grows warmer and presses in. In the chaos of last night, she'd left her shades cracked open. She welcomes the light; it feels cleansing.

Instead of spiraling into her usual cycle of self-loathing and pity, justifying her actions by the magnitude of her circumstances, she makes a decision. She's done letting Hoover hold power over her. Done letting fear dictate her choices. Done numbing herself with hangovers, regret, and a lack of self-respect.

As her thoughts steady, she feels something different inside her, lighter somehow. Last night was her self-proclaimed last straw. She's ready to reintroduce herself to *self-respect, grace, and love*. Feelings that have felt like distant friends she's finally ready to pursue again.

With that, Piper throws off her covers, a smile spreading across her face despite everything. She yanks her blinds open, inviting the light to spill into every corner of her apartment and fall fresh across her face.

When she turns to her closet, she's met face-to-face with the poster Kate gave her:

> "When you pass through the waters, I will be with you; and through the rivers, they shall not overwhelm you; when you walk through fire you shall not be burned, and the flame shall not consume you." — *Isaiah 43:2*

Her heart pangs.

As she carries on to the bathroom, she feels an unmistakable nudge on her heart. She presses her hand against her chest. It's subtle but undeniable, a gentle tap from something she can't quite explain.

She refocuses as she spreads a glob of toothpaste on her toothbrush, and suddenly thinks, *Hey God, it's me*. The thought catches her off guard. She meets her reflection in the mirror and whispers under her breath, "Why did I just do that?"

Because I've missed this, she admits silently. *This is the hole in my heart that's grown so big and so desperate for help.*

Her breath catches. She was raised in a Christian home. Faith was always part of her life, until recently. Until her anger became too much. Too heavy to process, too painful to face. She realizes she's been *angry with God.*

Angry that this happened to her.

Angry for how small and broken it's made her feel.

Angry that she still lives in fear.

That she panics at the sight of anyone who remotely resembles Hoover.

That this — *this* — is her life in her twenties.

God, where are You in all of this? Why did You let this happen to me?

And yet...she's here. Breathing. Healthy. Stronger today than yesterday. Stronger than she was a year ago. She has a good career, independence, a life that, despite everything, still holds blessings. Gratitude, she realizes, is the opposite of anger. And it's been foreign to her for far too long.

She can feel her heart beginning to soften at the edges. Looking in the mirror, she studies her reflection: the faint lines near her eyes, the shadows beneath them from too little sleep, the toll of simply surviving. She brushes her hair back and, for once, sees beauty in her imperfections.

Moving through her apartment with an unfamiliar lightness, she straightens her bed, pulling her tan-striped comforter tight, fluffing her pillows, and exhales a small, satisfied breath.

Without thinking twice, she grabs her laptop and settles onto her dark cotton-colored couch. Something inside her wants to make sense of what she's feeling, but she can't quite name it. She sits there, still, thinking.

How many others feel this way? she wonders. *Like life is spinning out of control? Like God is silent? Like suffering is endless and* undeserved? How many others are quietly drowning under something they didn't choose?

Another nudge, this time clearer. *Job.*

She doesn't know much about him, only that he suffered and somehow stayed faithful. She leans forward and types: *sermon series on Job and suffering* into Google.

The first link catches her eye: *Job: Five Sermons on Suffering* by Desiring God. It's a message series by John Piper, preached in 1985, the year before she was born. And the preacher even shares her dad's name.

Something about that feels like a whisper.

She clicks the first video: *Job: Reverent in Suffering.*

And it begins.

"One of the duties I believe I have as your pastor is to preach and to pray in such a way that when your calamity comes, you won't curse God," John Piper says. "And even more, I think, to preach and to pray in such a way that when your calamity comes, you will, in fact, worship God and bless Him in it."

Piper feels as though he's speaking directly to her. She's guilty of exactly what he describes, cursing God, and the conviction hits her like a punch to the stomach.

He continues, "Virtually everybody in this room will sooner or later experience a bitter calamity. And you can mark it down ahead of time. When it comes, it will seem absurd and undeserved and meaningless. And you will cry out *why* a hundred times. That's why the book of Job is so relevant: Job's suffering seems to come out of nowhere and have no connection to his character."

Like me. That's me, Piper thinks. *I've never done anything to deserve this. I know you can't earn your way to heaven, but I've certainly never sinned big enough to warrant this kind of suffering. That's the part I can't reconcile. I understand that Jesus died for me, that grace bridges the gap of sin, yet it's still hard to grasp why this happened to me.*

Piper pauses the message only long enough to grab a notebook and pen before returning to the couch. It feels like a Netflix series she can't stop binging, except she's scribbling furious notes instead of dropping popcorn crumbs.

John Piper goes on to explain what kind of man Job was. The Lord was good to the righteous, and Job was extraordinarily blessed, with seven sons and three daughters, vast herds, and many servants. Job loved his family and revered God. Yet behind the scenes, God and Satan had a meeting in which Satan argued that Job's devotion was rooted in his prosperity. If given permission to test Job, Satan claimed, he would turn against God.

God allowed the testing, but set the limits. Job could be struck, but not destroyed.

Is that like me? Piper wonders. *Am I being tested? Because if I am, I've failed miserably.*

Job's calamity came, and it came hard. Enemies raided his land, stole his oxen, and killed his servants. Fire fell from heaven, consuming his sheep and more servants. Raiders captured his camels and slaughtered the rest. And worst of all, his ten children were killed when a storm collapsed the house they were in. In one afternoon, Job lost everything.

Piper's heart aches. She can't fathom that kind of pain. And yet, when Job was stripped of everything, he still worshiped God. *How?* she thinks. *How could anyone praise God after something like that?* She remembers how quickly she turned on Him — how easily she blamed Him.

She lies on her back and closes her eyes, letting the message settle deep into her bones.

She's reminded that those who trust in God already have their sins covered by the blood of Jesus. He carried the punishment every person deserves. And in that truth, she begins to understand suffering differently: it isn't random cruelty, it's refinement. A kind of divine therapy from a gracious, all-knowing, all-loving God, shaping her faith, deepening her holiness, and pulling her soul closer to the One who saves.

Suffering, she realizes, is an opportunity for God to be glorified.

The first video ends, and she immediately starts the next. She can't stop. She needs to understand why all this has happened to her. She yearns for her heart to change, for her faith to come alive again.

Eventually, Job reaches his breaking point and curses the day he was born. He questions God, desperate for answers. God sends three friends who try to reason with him, insisting his suffering must be punishment for sin.

That, Piper relates to. She's wondered the same thing about herself.

Yet the message becomes clear: there's no direct link between righteousness and prosperity, or between sin and suffering.

By the end of the fifth sermon, Piper's cheeks are blotchy and her eyes are swollen, but her heart feels lighter. After so much wrestling, with fear, paranoia, depression, and doubt, she finally understands something profound: she can experience a closeness to God that people who coast through life may never know.

For the first time in years, she feels free.

She breathes deeply and wipes her tears with both palms. Her college professor became a stalker, and yes, he may haunt the corners of her mind for years to come, but she can finally accept that this is her life. She can stop running from it. Stop numbing it. Stop trying to control it.

God hadn't abandoned her. He had allowed her story to unfold in a way that would one day draw her back to Him. Even in her silence and rebellion, He was near.

Before all of this, she considered herself a Christian, but she had coasted through life and through faith. Now she can see the thread of His protection running through her story.

Her mind races through the moments where He was present: the police officer who told her exactly how to file for an Emergency Order of Protection, the clerk who walked her through every step, Bobby and Kristen helping at the station, Kate offering her a safe place to stay. Even the woman at the AT&T store, Karen, who uncovered how Hoover had been tracking her.

Her parents found her a new apartment, and Mike, her fierce new doorman, became an unexpected blessing. Her colleagues gave her grace when she couldn't give it to herself. Even Hoover showing up at work forced legal protection that wouldn't have existed otherwise.

When she steps back, she can see it now: God's fingerprints on every part of her story.

Yes, she's made choices she regrets, but that doesn't have to be her story. Her faith is returning stronger, purer, and more alive than before.

She doesn't have it all figured out, not even close, but for the first time in a long time, she feels steady, anchored by something real.

A sudden urge stirs in her chest to share this, to tell someone. The first person who comes to mind is Ryan. She longs for that connection again, for the comfort she felt in his presence. She can see it play out in her mind: running into him on the street, the familiar hug that lingers, the dinner invitation, the laughter, the possibility. She smiles at the thought but reins herself in.

Not yet, she thinks. *I'll let myself try again once I figure out this new me.*

Soon.

Piper brushes a loose strand of blonde hair from her face

and looks out toward the river. The sky glows pale blue, the skyscrapers gilded in light. A cloud has been lifted from her eyes.

God's been there all along, she had just stopped looking.

Like beauty from ashes, He's got her full attention now.

Piper Hawthorne is back.

39

PROFESSOR HOOVER

Professor Hoover finds himself in Bambrock, Illinois, the definition of nowhere. With a population of about five hundred, it feels like the safest place to test his "experiment," as he calls it. He hasn't seen a person, a car, or even a house in more than twenty minutes.

This is it, he thinks. *The pre-moment of truth.*

He's crafted two devices, each tucked inside a brown box: one for practice, one for the real thing. They're small enough to hide under a chapel pew, yet powerful enough to make his mark. He's assembled them himself from scratch, playing with parts and timing until the mechanisms hummed the way he wanted. A week ago, he had no idea how to create such things, but the internet taught him enough. He's spent days in his hotel room obsessing over weight and balance, until everything settled perfectly into place. He's managed to fit them inside six-by-four cardboard boxes and wired them so that, with a single press, they'll do what he intends.

His first test is anticlimactic. He sets everything up. Everything meaning a rickety chair he picked up from Goodwill with one of the boxes attached underneath. Once he's certain it's ready, he walks five hundred feet away and, with trepidation, presses the button he synced earlier. Much to his dismay, nothing happens.

Now he sits on the very chair he plans to blow to pieces, adjusting the wiring one last time. When he's confident every connection has been checked and tightened, he reattaches the box, walks three hundred feet away, and casually presses the detonator. He shuts his eyes and drops to the ground, covering his face with his arms. The boom is the largest, most magnificent thing he's ever witnessed.

When he's sure it's over, he walks back to assess the damage. The chair no longer exists. The wood has shattered into hundreds of fragments. Shrapnel has flown farther in every direction than he anticipated. The sight stirs a flicker of unease in him, but there's no turning back now.

Reminding himself he's accomplished what he came for, he packs up his things quickly. He tosses any fragments large enough to handle into an industrial trash bag and loads everything into his trunk. His hands won't stop shaking. Maybe he's more nervous about all this than he realizes.

Against better judgment, he does the only thing that ever brings him clarity and peace — he goes for a walk. He drives five miles to put distance between himself and the blast site, parks on the shoulder, and steps out into the stillness.

He walks the outskirts of Bambrock in long, deliberate strides, searching for clarity. The air hangs warm. The fields are empty. And as the dust settles with each step, one truth takes hold inside him bigger and bolder than ever before: he needs Piper back in his life and nothing will stop him from getting her.

40

THE INCIDENT

Ever since Sunday, Piper has felt an inexplicable peace, more secure than she can remember. She hasn't been looking over her shoulder as much. Her new understanding of God has lifted the weight of the unknown, the all-encompassing fear, and the anxiety off her shoulders. She keeps reminding herself that she's not in control, and while her situation is far bigger than she is, God's got this.

Piper is at The Eiffel, waiting for her clients to arrive for their final walkthrough. Tonight, the restaurant will host its soft opening, a private media and VIP cocktail dinner, and tomorrow, its doors will open to the public.

She feels her watch vibrate before she even sees who's calling. *Dad*, her phone screen reads. Her stomach drops, the way it always does when he calls. *Whatever this is about, it's going to be okay*, she tells herself, stepping out onto Hubbard Street.

"Piper?" her dad says, urgency in his voice before she even has the chance to respond.

"Dad, what's going on?" Piper plugs one ear to block out the city noise.

"Piper, I need to tell you something. I think you should sit down."

"You're scaring me." Her nerves jitter as she walks back inside and sinks into the first plush banquette she sees. Thankfully, the only other person in the space is Chloe, busy tapping away at her laptop. "Okay, I'm sitting. What's going on?"

"Hoover." Her dad pauses for just a few seconds, but it feels like forever. "Hoover was killed in a hit-and-run car accident, Piper."

Tears slide down Piper's cheeks before she can speak. "What did you just say?" she whispers, breathless, as time seems to stop.

"Hoover, Piper. Hoover is dead. He was walking along a two-lane road in the middle of nowhere, Illinois, last night when someone struck him. They didn't find him until this morning. It sounds like they're still trying to locate the car or figure out how he ended up out there alone."

Piper gasps, torn between relief and dread. *How could this be? There's no way he's dead. But if it's true...I can finally live free.*

"How do you know? How do you know this isn't some fake story someone's trying to sell?"

"I thought the same thing. Detective Smith called me early this morning. You know he's been keeping a lookout for you and tracking Hoover's movements. I don't know how he does it, but he does. He called at 5 a.m. I was as shocked as you are. I asked how he knew for sure, and he sent me a link to the morning news. I'm going to forward it to you. It's real, Piper. His photo and everything."

"Oh my gosh." Piper presses the phone to her ear with one hand and buries her face in the other. *Hoover is dead. Hoover is dead,* she repeats under her breath, as if saying it aloud will make it real.

"This can't be, Dad. I mean, I just came to terms with everything...with my life, with this mess. I finally sorted it out. This can't be." Her voice rises without her realizing.

"That's the thing about life. It just happens. We don't know why, and it rarely makes sense. But the older I get, the more I see that God is in control, weaving a plan far beyond what we can imagine. His timing, no matter how confusing or painful or even amazing, is always perfect. It may not be what we want, but it's for good. This is your story, Piper. It's messy and confusing, but try to see that you've been given a second chance. You can live without looking over your shoulder, without fearing what's around every corner. This is redemption, Piper."

Can it really be over, just like that? she wonders, her mind struggling to catch up.

"I feel guilty. I'm happy. I'm so relieved that my nightmare's over, but I'm happy because someone died. That's messed up."

"It's not," he says gently. "You have such a tender heart. It's strange, yes, but you deserve to feel relief and peace and freedom. Your nightmare is over. I know this will take time to process. Detective Smith said the same thing. It often takes victims a while to accept that their perpetrator is truly gone. But he said the news coverage helps. When you start to question it, just play that story and remember that it's over. I just sent you the link. Watch it. I need to make a few more calls, but we'll talk again soon, okay?"

Piper sniffles and wipes her face, trying to regain composure as she notices a few restaurant employees beginning to arrive.

"Sounds good. Thank you. I love you."

"I love you, Piper. More than you know. I'm so grateful for this peace you've been given. I hope you can grasp it soon."

Piper hangs up and sits for a moment. Her black peplum dress has bunched at her thighs, and she pulls it down, regaining awareness of where she is and why she's there. She glances around. The room hums with quiet movement, but her clients still haven't arrived. Looking down at her phone, she sees her dad has sent the link. She clicks it.

A young woman with dark skin and thick, shoulder-length black hair begins: "A fatal hit-and-run accident that happened late last night in Bambrock has local police searching for a driver who struck a man and drove away. The victim has been identified as forty-three-year-old former Midland College professor Joseph Hoover."

A photo of Hoover flashes on the screen. Piper gasps as her throat tightens into a hard knot.

"Authorities are asking for the public's help in determining exactly when Mr. Hoover was struck by a driver who failed to stop. His body was discovered shortly before four a.m. in a grassy area. The accident occurred in the 1400 block of Prelude Street, west of I-90. Police are hopeful someone will come forward with information that will help locate the hit-and-run driver. They have yet to release any additional details about the victim or what he may have been doing in the remote area. This story is developing. Viewers are encouraged to call the number below with any information they might have."

Piper keeps staring at her phone as the video ends. Her eyes stay open and unfocused, her mind struggling to process what she's just heard.

Noticing something is wrong, Chloe walks over and nudges her arm.

"Gah!" Piper startles, looking up.

"Whoa, girl. What on earth were you watching? Are you okay?" Chloe asks, looking effortlessly put together in ripped black jeans, patent pumps, a white blouse, and a leather jacket.

"He's dead, Chlo." Piper pauses before continuing, "Hoover. He's dead."

"He's what?" Chloe blurts. "Sorry," she whispers quickly. "That's just...the last thing I expected you to say." Tears well in her eyes.

"I don't even know where to start. I'm hanging on by a thread right now," Piper says, taking a shaky breath to steady herself. "I just found out." She swallows hard. "Hoover...Hoover was killed in a hit-and-run car accident."

"Oh my gosh, Piper." Chloe's hand flies to her chest. "You're free. I mean...I'm sorry he died...wait, no, I'm not actually sorry he died. Gosh, this is so crazy. But you, my friend, are free from the nightmare that's taken years of your life."

"I know. I just don't know how to process it. I feel relief, but also guilt, and I hate it. Why do I feel this way? I'm straddling two worlds. I'm relieved he's gone, yet guilty because I'm happy a human being was killed. Even though he's destroyed my life, obliterated my mind, haunted my dreams, and made me afraid to live."

She exhales shakily. "I just need time and space to think. My mental capacity is beyond its max. And now I have to put on a smile and pull it together, because no one wants to hear another woe-is-me story."

"Stop, girl. Give yourself some credit," Chloe says firmly. "You've been living a real-life nightmare for years. Cut yourself some slack. These feelings can coexist: relief and pain, clarity and confusion. You have to let yourself feel it all so you can finally let it go."

Tears spill down Piper's cheeks, and she wipes them away.

"Here, let me help." Chloe pulls a compact from her bag and gently powders Piper's face. She opens a tube of lip gloss and swipes it across her lips.

"We're going to pull it together. And as Kate always says, *act like you can*. We've got this, sister. One quick meeting, and then you can take a minute."

"Thank you, truly, Chloe. What would I do without you?"

Just then, her clients walk in.

41

PROFESSOR HOOVER

Inside the drafts folder on Professor Hoover's computer lies one final letter.

Dearest Piper,

If you're reading this, it means my plan didn't go according to plan. You must understand that all I've ever wanted in life is you.

From the moment I laid eyes on you, I felt it in my heart — a desire stronger than anything I could have hoped or wished for myself. You were made for me, and I for you. I wish it had been as clear to you as it was to me.

I can't leave this life without getting a few things off my chest. Please be my audience for this final confession.

My intention with the bomb was never to hurt anyone. It was only to prove my love and adoration for you. You are my first thought when I wake and the final image in my mind when I go to sleep. You were, and always will be, my why.

I need to clarify something. My email confessing my feelings for you, way back then, should have been done in person, properly. I wanted to ask you out, but since you were in the middle of finals, I wanted the timing to be perfect. I wish you could have seen from the start that my intentions have always been to bring you happiness all the days of my life. But Midland entered the picture and ruined everything...our entire future...over one email. The two years they forbade me from contacting you, that's where I lost you, Piper. I'm convinced of it.

They deserved a wake-up call. Poor decisions must not go unpunished. My attempts to communicate with Midland went completely unanswered, and they left me no choice.

If you take away one thing, let it be this: my love for you is unconditional, pure, and fierce. Unfortunately, I don't think you'll ever find this in another, hence my determination for you to see it in me.

As you've likely discovered by now, my research techniques and determination to keep you safe have made themselves known. Please understand, it was only because my life's mission was to protect you. I had no choice but to follow you and stay informed of your whereabouts. I was made to do this, Piper. Someday you'll discover your own life's mission, and when you do, I pray you cling to it as tightly as I have mine.

Lastly, I hope you'll cherish this box of items that belong to you as I have all these years. To know you mean so much to someone is a blessing I pray you'll one day recognize. These items will show you that. They are yours, and rightfully need to be returned.

Never forget the eternal place you hold as queen of my heart. As you look back on our time together, may you hold a similar space for what could have been between us.

Until we meet again one day in Heaven,

Yours always,
Hoover

42

MOVING ON

Piper wakes naturally as the sun peeks into her apartment. As she stretches, her first thought is gratitude — for rest, for peace. Then it hits her again: *Hoover is dead.*

She feels emotionally hungover in every inch of her body, stuck in that in-between space where joy and grief, happiness and anger, relief and overwhelm, confusion and clarity all coexist.

Her soft gray jersey-cotton pant legs bunch around her knees like an accordion. She rolls over and looks at the clock, 6:56 a.m. She thinks through her day and realizes how refreshing it is to have no plans. All she wants is to lie in bed.

But the feelings churning inside her are too heavy. A distraction would be nice, something to stop the endless replay in her mind.

Church, she thinks instinctively. Her first impulse is to push the thought away, as she's done out of habit for who knows how long.

She can't remember the last time she stepped foot in a sanctuary, but given everything that's happened, it feels like she owes it to God.

Piper brushes the sleep from her eyes and heads to the bathroom. She showers, brushes her teeth, and makes coffee with steamed vanilla creamer while letting her hair air-dry. She slips into light-blue jeans and a chunky cream-colored knit sweater, a few shades lighter than her hair. She applies makeup to enhance her features, curls her hair, and heats a frozen egg sandwich before heading out.

On the ten-minute drive to Northside Community Church, her mind spins, trying to make sense of what she's doing. She still can't grasp why God would give her a second chance, or how that chance came at the cost of Hoover's death. The truth is, she's thankful he's gone. His death has brought her freedom. *Just go with it. Don't overthink it,* she tells herself.

She parks in a *Visitor* spot, because today, that's exactly what she is.

Walking through the large double doors of the industrial-style church, her stomach turns with nerves. It feels like she's about to have a come-to-Jesus conversation with a friend she's fallen out with, and that friend is God Himself.

Piper keeps to herself as she enters, greeting the ushers warmly but not inviting more conversation. She slips into the end of a pew halfway up the middle aisle. Just as she sits, the band takes the stage. She didn't realize how much she'd missed this until now. Tears rise, and despite her best effort to hold them back, a few spill over. She wipes her cheeks and closes her eyes, swaying gently to the music, surrendering her soul back into God's grace.

When the song changes to another favorite, loneliness hits her. She silently acknowledges it. It feels good to be here, but she yearns for someone to share it with. Her life has been the equivalent of a *Lifetime* movie, and now that her situation is behind her, she doesn't want to face life alone anymore.

As the worship band wraps and a pastor she doesn't recognize steps onto the stage, she takes out her phone on a whim and decides to send a quick text.

She types *Ryan* into the search bar. Her heart races, and she takes a deep breath to calm herself. It's been a bit since they last texted.

Feeling like a student sneaking her phone during an exam, she quickly types:

> Ryan, sorry it's taken me so long to reach out. Life has been...messy, but things have recently sorted themselves out. Kind of. Anyways, I wanted to see if you'd be up for catching up sometime soon. I have so much I want to tell you. If your life circumstances have changed, just say the word.

Piper presses *send* before she can think twice, then tucks her phone beneath her thigh and turns her focus back to the stage.

Wearing dark jeans, white sneakers, and a black button-down, Pastor Mark begins:

"There are some of you here today who need to remind yourselves that, just as Jesus forgave Peter for denying Him three times, He forgives you too. Forgiveness isn't earned or deserved; it's freely given. Jesus Christ, God's only Son, walked this earth and lived a pure, perfect, blameless life. And yet He gave it up — for me, for you, for all of us — so we could have redemption.

"The story doesn't stop in the garden when sin entered the world. It doesn't stop for Peter when he denies Jesus, one of his closest friends. And it doesn't stop in your life, no matter what sin you're facing or what sin has been committed against you. God's got you, and He loves you. He loves you more than the person you love most on this earth. Think about that. He extends forgiveness without thinking twice, regardless of what you've done. Sometimes we need to remind ourselves that we're worthy to be called His, and, in turn, that we're called to extend that same forgiveness to those who cause us strife."

It feels like every word is aimed at Piper. Her hand moves to her chest; it physically aches. It aches because her life isn't what she pictured. Because she's made mistakes and been careless with herself and her heart. Because she can't fathom how God still loves her after everything. Because someone stole years of her life, and though she's not ready yet, she knows that someday she'll have to forgive him. Her heart aches because she knows God's been there all along, even when she walked away, and that He will take her back, no questions asked. The feeling is overwhelming in the best possible way.

"If this resonates with you," Pastor Mark continues, "I want you to say this verse aloud with me."

> *1 John 1:9* — If we confess our sins, He is faithful and just to forgive us our sins and to cleanse us from all unrighteousness.

Piper repeats the verse, then closes her eyes and prays silently: *Lord, forgive me. Continue to soften my heart that's been hardened for so long. Forgive me for deserting You when You remained faithful. Forgive me for my mistakes, for not respecting myself. I'm so sorry.*

Just as she opens her eyes, a soft buzz vibrates beneath her leg. She glances at her phone.

Ryan.

> Piper, no need to apologize. I've been hoping to hear from you. I can't wait to hear everything. What are you doing after this… want to grab lunch?

Piper's heart skips a beat as her pulse quickens. *The best response*, she thinks, *though also a little odd*. She debates whether to text him back right away or make him wait. But she's done playing games.

> Yes, I'd love to. You mean today…are you free to grab lunch today?

Her phone vibrates.

> Turn around, Piper.

Overcome with anticipation, she turns to the right and peers behind her. It takes a moment, but three rows back she finally sees him — Ryan, staring at her with a warm smile. Beaming with happiness, Piper turns back around and types:

> What are you doing here?

Her pulse quickens again.

She feels a gentle nudge on her shoulder. She looks up, and there he is — right beside her.

"Is this seat taken?" he whispers, pointing to the empty spot next to hers.

"It's all yours," she says, smiling.

He looks effortlessly handsome in a charcoal knit blazer, a textured white T-shirt, jeans, and brown dress boots. She's smitten. She reminds herself that she deserves happiness, and welcomes it.

Ryan slides into the seat beside her and mouths, "It's about time you reached out, Piper." He brushes his hand against hers, and she beams up at him.

A short while later, the service ends. Piper and Ryan stand, and by all appearances, it looks as though they'd come together.

As she starts to walk, Ryan reaches for her hand and interlaces his fingers with hers.

"I can't wait to catch up with you," he says, brushing his thumb over the back of her hand. "Where do we begin?"

Piper looks up into his brown eyes. "How much time do you have?" she says with a laugh.

43
BEGINNING ANEW

Piper drives herself and Ryan to a quaint lunch spot nearby, Pearl Street Market. After ordering, they find a quiet two-person booth in the back. The restaurant is fast-casual but upscale, with fresh flowers on every table and knickknacks that look as though they were sourced from antique shops around the world. The space hums with conversation.

Once they've settled in with silverware and napkins and their food has arrived, Piper looks at Ryan across the table, unsure where to start. She's waited for this moment for so long, she can hardly believe it's happening on such a whim.

"I wasn't expecting to hear from you today," Ryan says, breaking the silence. "I'm glad you reached out. It's about time," he adds with a laugh. "How long have you been going to Northside?"

"Today was my first time there," Piper admits between bites of her southwest salad. "My faith has been important to me for as long as I can remember. I grew up in a Christian home and transferred to Midland hoping to find like-minded friends and grow in my faith. And then, as you know, my world fell apart. I was so thrown by how my life turned out that I put my faith on hold. I was honestly mad at God and had a hard time understanding how He could let it all happen to me."

"I'm glad you ended up there today." Ryan smiles at her. "A colleague has been inviting me to Northside for what feels like forever. I kept coming up with excuses and finally ran out of them. About a month ago, I said yes, and I've been going ever since." He pauses, taking a sip of water. "I was raised in a Christian family too, but we only went to church on holidays. From the first time I went to Northside, I was hooked. Everything just...clicked. It felt like something had been missing all this time, and I finally figured out what." He pauses again, softening his tone. "When you texted me today, I couldn't believe it. I've wanted to see you, but I respected what you said last time we hung out. I don't want you to feel any pressure. There still isn't any. I've just really wanted to catch up and hear how you've been."

Piper blushes. "Me too. I kept feeling like I needed to get my life in order before I could see you again. But lately, God finally got my attention. I'm learning I don't control the minutiae of my life, no matter how hard I try. I still can't believe we both ended up there today."

"Guess it was meant to be," Ryan says, his gaze warm and steady. "What's the latest since we last talked? I know you had your court date. Get me up to speed." He takes a bite of his steak teriyaki bowl and wipes his mouth.

"Where do I even begin? I wasn't joking when I asked how much time you have," Piper says with a laugh.

"Tell me everything," Ryan says, leaning in.

"Okay, buckle up for the latest." She sets down her fork. "We had our court date, like you know. Hoover showed up with a high-profile attorney, which totally shocked me. I couldn't believe he thought he had a chance. He tried spinning a story that I'd brought it all on myself. It was awful to hear. By the grace of God, I ended up winning a one-year restraining order. The judge said he found Hoover fifty-one percent guilty, and I only won because he'd shown up at my work." Piper takes a sip of sparkling water.

Ryan's expression shifts. "Piper...I'm so sorry you had to go through all of that," he says softly. "I'm really glad the judge saw the truth. Have you felt any relief since then?"

"What's crazy," Piper says, "is you'd think I would have, but even after winning, I felt just as paranoid as before. Always looking over my shoulder, scared he'd find me." She pauses.

"Honestly, Ryan, I fell into a rut. I stopped caring about much of anything and let fear consume me. I'd go out with friends, drink until I didn't care anymore, and wake up hating myself for it. It was awful. I'm not proud of it. But living like that got old fast. Now I can see how God was chipping away at me, leading me right here."

"This is a judgment-free zone," he says gently. "I can't imagine everything you've been through. What do you mean by God was leading you to this moment?"

"I finally got tired of it all...of the hangovers, the emptiness. I felt God tugging on my heart and realized how far I'd drifted from my faith and how much I'd missed it. I decided I was ready to come to terms with my life." She takes another bite. "I kept wondering why God allows suffering to exist. That's what confused me the most. How could a God so loving allow such horrible, undeserved things to happen? Then I found a sermon series on Job, and it completely changed me. I learned that God uses suffering to refine us, to draw us closer. Sometimes He allows us to be undone, so He can rebuild us into something more whole in Him."

"Wow...Piper...you've been through so much," Ryan says, his voice gentle.

"It's like I became a new person overnight through that

message. God brought me back. But you won't believe what happened next."

"Given your story so far, I probably won't," he says, light-heartedly.

"A few days after I made that commitment, to myself and to God, and finally came to terms with my life, knowing Hoover would likely always be out there somewhere...he was killed. Hoover died in a hit-and-run car accident."

"What?!" Ryan stares at her, stunned. "He died? How did you find out?"

"Yes, he's gone. My dad called me at work, and at first, I didn't believe it. But it's been on the news. It's an ongoing investigation. It's been wild. I was at the lowest point of my life just weeks ago, and then this happened. It feels like the ultimate redemption, a second chance." Tears well in Piper's eyes as she speaks.

Unsure what to say, Ryan stands and moves to her side. He gestures for her to stand, then wraps her in a bear hug. "I don't even know what to say," he whispers, his breath warm against her hair. "I'm happy for you, for this new beginning. I'm sorry for everything you've been through, but I'm so thankful you're on this side of it, and that you're here, sharing it with me."

"Thanks. Me too," Piper says softly, pulling back and sinking into her seat again. "That's the latest with me. It's a lot, I know. Enough heavy stuff, tell me what's new with you."

"Nothing that compares to your story," he says with a soft grin. "My life's been pretty boring, actually. Work's finally settled into a more stable rhythm, which has been nice. I've finally been going to the gym in the mornings and keeping things low-key. I've been going to Northside about a month now, thinking about getting more involved there. It'd be good to meet more like-minded people." He pauses, looking at her intently. "You're one of the strongest people I know, Piper. I hope you realize that. I'm so happy you're finally finding real peace."

"Me too," she admits. "It hasn't totally sunk in yet. I keep reminding myself of everything to calm those nerves that keep popping up out of habit."

"That'll take time, no doubt." Ryan gathers their trays and drops them off nearby. When he returns, he smiles. "What do you say we get out of here?"

"Sounds good to me." Piper can't help but smile back. They walk out of the restaurant together and pause on the sidewalk.

"What's on your agenda the rest of the day?" Ryan asks.

"Honestly? Nothing. I'm pretty wiped. I was thinking about taking a nap, big plans today," she jokes.

"You want company?" he asks with a grin.

"As long as you're fine just hanging out, yes, I'd love that."

Piper drives them back to her apartment. When she parks, she's surprised to find Ryan already stepping out and opening her door for her.

They ride the elevator up together and step into her apartment. Piper's struck by how normal it feels, how natural this moment is.

Ryan walks toward the window, taking in the view of the Chicago River. "I don't think I noticed this last time I was here. What a view."

"It's what sold me on the place. Well, my parents, really," she laughs. "I love running along the river and lakefront. I haven't done it much lately, but after everything that's happened, I'm hoping to work up the courage to get back to it."

Piper sinks onto the couch, realizing just how exhausted she is after such an emotional day. Ryan sits beside her, and she finds herself leaning into the nook of his chest, just beneath his chin. He runs his fingers gently through her hair as she closes her eyes.

"You're going to put me to sleep if you keep doing that," she murmurs.

"If that's what you need, good," he says softly. "Sundays are for resting. I'd be honored if you fell asleep right here."

Piper's breathing slows, her body twitching slightly as she drifts off. Ryan closes his eyes too, eventually dozing beside her.

An hour later, they're jolted awake by a loud knock at the door. Voices carry through the hallway, someone announcing themselves, but the words are muffled, impossible to make out.

"Are you expecting someone?" Ryan stands abruptly.

"No. No one ever just shows up like this." Piper wipes the sleep from her face. Concerned, she hurries to the door with Ryan close behind and peers through the peephole.

"What in the world...it's the police."

She opens the door just enough to see who's there without letting them in. "Hi, can I help you? Is there an emergency?"

"Piper Hawthorne?" one of the officers asks. His name tag reads McGuire. He's built like a wall, his shaved head gleaming under the hallway light, his expression all business.

"Yes...that's me. Did something happen?" Ryan stands just behind her, protective but careful not to overstep.

"Ma'am, we need to discuss a few things with you. May we come in?"

"Sure, I guess. Come on in."

A second officer follows behind McGuire, a woman in her mid-fifties with a tight, slick bun and soft lines around her eyes.

Piper and Ryan lead them to the kitchen island in her studio apartment. They all stand in a loose circle.

"Is something going on? Is there something I can help you with?" Piper repeats, her voice uneasy. Ryan rests a hand on her back.

"Miss Hawthorne, I'm Officer McGuire and this is Officer Hodges," he begins. "We're familiar with your case...the reports you filed and the recent order of protection against Joseph Hoover. You're aware of what I'm referring to?"

"Yes, of course," Piper says sharply, crossing her arms.

"There have been some recent developments we'd like to discuss, as well as something we need to return to you," Officer Hodges adds.

"If you're referring to the fact that Hoover is dead, I already know."

"No, ma'am, that's not what we're referring to. Why don't you take a seat?" Hodges says gently but firmly.

Piper and Ryan pull out two stools at the island and sit across from the officers.

"Do you want him present for this?" Hodges asks, nodding toward Ryan.

"Yes, he's fine. This is my friend, Ryan. You can share whatever you need to."

McGuire exhales. "We're aware you've been through a lot with Joseph Hoover. We didn't realize the full extent until we found out where he was staying and searched his hotel room today. I'm not sure how much you know from the news. They tend to dramatize these stories." He pauses, choosing his words carefully. "The day after Hoover's death, we located his car a few miles from where he was struck. Inside, we found an explosive device...in plain terms, a bomb. Did you know anything about that?"

"A bomb? What in the hell?" Piper's voice rises. "No! Why would I have any clue about that?" Her pulse quickens. *Oh my gosh, are they questioning me?* She glances at Ryan, eyes wide. He rests his hand on her shoulder in reassurance.

"Maybe I'm saying too much," McGuire admits. "I guess this is just our lead-in to apologizing. We didn't realize the severity of your situation."

Piper tenses. "I'm sorry...I'm not following."

Officer Hodges steps in. "What McGuire means is that the

device in Hoover's car led us to obtain a warrant for his hotel room. What we found there was...alarming. It was enough that we felt it was necessary to come in person and to return some items of yours. His place was, for lack of a better term, centered around you. Finding you. Tracking you. He was obsessed, Ms. Hawthorne."

Piper blinks, trying to process. "You came all the way here to tell me that?"

"The main reason we came," McGuire says, "is that we found a box addressed to you. We opened it and cleared the contents. There was also a letter on his computer we're not going to have you read...it's disturbing, but we did want to return your belongings. It felt right to do that in person. What you do with them is entirely up to you."

He hands Piper a cardboard box about twice the size of a shoebox. Her name is scrawled across the top in black Sharpie, underlined twice in Hoover's handwriting.

"Thank you...I think." She hesitates, staring at it. "I don't think I want this box, but I appreciate you coming here. I don't need to know anything more than what you've already told me."

"Agreed, ma'am. This chapter, for you, is considered closed. Have a good evening."

With that, Officers McGuire and Hodges let themselves out.

"What in the world..." Piper says, trying to process what just happened.

"Piper...it feels like every time you come up for air, something else hits." Ryan looks at the box, then at her. "What do you want to do with it? Open it or get rid of it?"

Piper wants to scream. *Why is there always one more thing in this never-ending nightmare? When will it all just end?*

"I'm going to peek inside the box. I feel like I have to, while it's just sitting here."

She slowly opens it.

Inside lies a white, two-inch binder. A printed title page reads: *The Works of Piper Hawthorne.*

She flips it open, then snaps it shut when she realizes it's full of her class assignments. Beneath the binder sits a stack of photographs, at least a hundred.

She lifts one. It's a candid shot of her opening the door to her office in River North. Another shows her leaving the L station at Clark and Division. Another, leaning against her office window.

She looks away, pulse racing.

Something gold catches her eye. She reaches in and pulls out a thin silk scrunchie, her favorite hair tie, the one she'd worn on her left wrist nearly every day until it vanished. At the bottom of the box rests a framed photo of her and her parents.

She gasps. "This picture...it used to be on my dresser." Her mind spins, piecing it together. "I knew it!"

"He was in my apartment, Ryan. The night of your party... he was there. I knew it."

Ryan says nothing, just stays beside her, holding space.

Piper notices a small plastic bag at the bottom of the box. She picks it up and sees strands of something inside.

"Oh my gosh...is this my hair?" She claps her hands over her mouth to keep the nausea down and shoves everything back into the box.

"I don't want to know any more!" she cries.

"Gosh, Piper, I'm so sorry." Ryan's voice is steady but shaken. "What a deranged human he was. Thank God he's gone and out of your life forever."

A sudden resolve steadies her. "I know exactly what we need to do with this box," she says, meeting Ryan's eyes. She grabs his hand, presses the box into his arms, and says, "Come with me."

They ride the elevator in silence to the third-floor lounge, where the pool, grills, and fire pit are located.

"What are we doing here?" Ryan asks, looking around. The pool lies still as glass; a row of grills and empty lounge chairs line the terrace.

Thankfully, it's just the two of them. The night is so quiet you could hear a pin drop.

"This is it, Ryan," Piper says. "I need to put this to rest. Maybe this creepy, disturbing box of — well, me — is exactly what I need for closure. We're going to burn it and end this chapter of my life forever." Tears prick her eyes.

Ryan steps behind her, wrapping his arms around her. "I haven't been here for everything you've endured, but I'm grateful to be here now for the end of your nightmare and the start of your new beginning."

Piper intertwines her fingers with his, then pulls away. "Okay," she says, handing him a lighter from her pocket. "All I need is your help to light this thing."

Ryan kneels and turns the gas knob on. The round gray brick fire pit, usually meant for s'mores or warmth, should do the trick.

Once the flame catches, Piper opens the box with her name scrawled across the top. She pulls out the binder and tosses it in. The fire roars, climbing higher. Then she drops in the bag of hair.

Tears spill down her cheeks as she struggles to breathe through the release.

"Come here," Ryan says, pulling her into his chest. She breathes in his scent, letting him support her weight.

"Throw something in," she whispers, pulling back just enough to look up at him.

"Are you sure?" he asks softly. "This feels like something you need to do."

"I want you to, Ryan. It's all too much. I need you to."

He nods, picks up a stack of photos, and tosses them into the flames. The fire flares, igniting with urgency. Piper meets his eyes and mouths, *thank you.*

She picks up the frame with the photo of her and her parents and holds it to her chest. She sets it aside. *This is rightfully mine,* she thinks. *It belongs back in my apartment where it never should've left.*

She lifts the last item, the gold satin hair tie she once wore with her watch. The fabric slips through her fingers, familiar and soft. It had been her favorite once. She drops it into the fire and watches as it's swallowed by the blue-white core of the flame.

Finally, she picks up the cardboard box with her name written in Hoover's handwriting, tears it into three pieces, and throws it in.

She closes her eyes and whispers, "Thank You, Jesus, for my new beginning."

When she turns, Ryan is leaning against the brick wall, eyes warm as he watches the fire swallow the last remnants of her past. Piper steps toward him, closing the space between them.

"Thank you for being here. I couldn't have done this alone," she says quietly.

"You could've, Piper," Ryan murmurs. "You're the strongest person I've ever met. But I'm grateful our paths crossed today and that they led me back to you."

He leans in, his breath warm near her ear. "I know we're taking things slow, but...may I kiss you?"

Goosebumps lift across her skin, no longer from fear, but from something pure and exhilarating.

Piper looks up at him, a smile spreading across her face. "I've been waiting a long time for this moment."

Ryan tilts her chin toward him. "Me too. You have no idea, Piper."

His lips meet hers, gentle, lingering, while the fire crackles behind them, warm against the night. When they part, he tucks his forehead to hers for a moment, breath mingling with hers.

"This," Ryan whispers, "is the start of new beginnings."

AFTERWORD

Inspired by a true story, this book has been a decade in the making.

After my "situation" ended, when the sharp emotions finally faded and I stopped thinking about my own professor-turned-stalker every single day, I felt a nudge. God impressed on my heart that my story needed to be written down.

Nine years ago, I wrote a formal book proposal and attended my first (and only) writers' conference with my mom, eager to learn about the world of publishing and pitching my story. Back then, it was a book on suffering, and the way I planned to write it was, admittedly, quite boring. The real obstacle, though, was that I was pregnant with my first child. My husband, Dan, and I went on to have our three boys very close together. Once motherhood began, by the grace of God, it took over, and my book was put on hold. Truthfully, it was a relief. I wasn't ready to relive those moments.

As life went on, God's nudge on my heart grew stronger. For years, I felt it, acknowledged it, and then ignored it. I'd occasionally tell people I was working on a book, but I kept finding excuses to avoid actually writing. Eventually, I had to admit how hard it was to revisit the very memories that once broke me.

In 2022, I realized that if I went through life without putting my story on paper, it would be my greatest regret. God has given me a love for writing for as long as I can remember and entrusted me with a painful but beautiful story of redemption and hope. So, after all these years, I finally reached a place where I could go back and face my darkest days.

In 2023, I began formally pitching the book as creative nonfiction and received unexpected feedback from an agent: fictionalize it. At first, I was taken aback, but soon realized it was exactly what God intended. Thus, Piper Hawthorne was born, alongside the creative freedom I didn't know I so desperately needed.

It's my hope and prayer that as you read this story, you see how God undeniably works through suffering and struggle to bring about His purpose, draw us near, and mark our lives with His provision. Through Piper's journey, I hope you see how He's at work in your own life, too.

Thank you for being part of this story.

ACKNOWLEDGMENTS

First, I want to thank my Lord and Savior for gifting me this story.

It's an indescribable feeling to reach a place in life where you can look back on a truly challenging season, one where you were wading through deep waters, and not want to change it.

When I finally reached the other side of the season that inspired this book and grasped the hand God had been extending all along, I was a changed person. I can now see how that lengthy trial refined me and allowed me to navigate life afterward with a new lens — as a wife and mom, through future highs and lows — and how my faith was never the same. For that, I am eternally grateful.

I'm thankful that God whispered ever so gently and impressed upon my heart to write this book and that He kept nudging me for years, knowing His timing is everything. He was simply preparing me to write the book He always knew it would become.

A special note of gratitude to John Piper and the team at Desiring God. Several passages in *In His Sight* reference his 1985 sermon series *Job: Five Sermons on Suffering*, which deeply shaped both my character's journey and my own understanding of faith in hardship.

Excerpts from Job: Five Sermons on Suffering by John Piper, © Desiring God Foundation. Source: desiringGod.org.

John Piper is founder and teacher of desiringGod.org and chancellor of Bethlehem College and Seminary. For more than thirty years, he served as pastor of Bethlehem Baptist Church in Minneapolis. He is the author of more than fifty books, and his sermons, articles, and other resources are available free of charge at desiringGod.org.

To my mom and dad — thank you for always being there for me, encouraging me, and dreaming with me since the very beginning of this journey. From late-night pep talks to tackling "one shelf at a time," you've been my constant support system, my sounding board, and my reminder that no dream is ever too far out of reach. Thank you for dropping everything — always — to show up for me, and for loving me with such unwavering, unconditional love.

Mom, thank you for reading every version of this book (more times than I can count!) and for your thoughtful feedback along the way. You've always had a way of speaking truth and helping me see the purpose in every draft, every rewrite, every setback.

Dad, thank you for your quiet strength and ongoing encouragement, and for reminding me that faith and perseverance can carry you through anything.

To my family — Phil, Drew, Ellie, Shannon, Larry, Sue, Amy, and Davin, thank you for cheering me on and supporting me along the way!

To Kristen Kavan, my talented editor and dear friend — this book simply would not exist without you. I'll never forget the day God nudged me to reach out to you, and the rest is history. You have an incredible pulse for plotlines and pacing, and you were the guiding hand that helped shape this story into what it is today. I can't thank you enough, from the bottom of my heart, for your time, energy, enthusiasm, dedication, and patience.

To my former boss and dear friend (who's more like a sister), Kathleen Sarpy — thank you for teaching me to "act like you can," for taking a chance on me, and for standing by me through one of the hardest seasons of my life. Your belief in me reminded me of my own strength when I'd lost sight of it, and I'll always be grateful for your faith, mentorship, and friendship.

Thanks also to my former HC colleagues for standing by me during that wild season. I'm especially grateful for Caroline championing this book through the years. Special thanks to Alicia and Nick for being wonderful friends – we miss you and Chicago!

To my college girlies — Laura, Katherine, Amanda, Brooke, and Kristen — thank you for being there when life felt heavy and for staying connected even as miles grew between us. The memories and friendship we share will always be some of the sweetest parts of my life.

To my Lifeline ladies — Candace, Christina, Emily, Jenna, Kerstan, Laura, Lauren, Leslie, Morgan, and Sarah — your friendship has been an unwavering lifeline. Through motherhood, everyday chaos, and countless play dates and coffee chats, you've lifted me up, prayed me through, and cheered the loudest for this book. I'm beyond grateful for this sisterhood and for your constant encouragement and celebration.

To my biggest blessings, Sawyer, Holden, and Wesley — you are my world and the truest picture of God's grace in my life. Being your mom is my greatest honor. Thank you for your patience while I poured my heart into this project, and for filling my days with laughter, love, and purpose.

To Dan — there are no words sufficient to express my gratitude for you and to you. Thank you for your unwavering love, patience, and grace, and for believing in me even when this dream felt so far away. You've been my sounding board, my calm in the chaos, and the steady presence who kept me grounded through it all. Thank you for picking up the slack at home so I could write, for cheering me on when I doubted myself, and for never once letting me quit. You are my greatest supporter and my favorite chapter. I love you more than words can express.

Finally, thank you, *dear reader.*
 May *In His Sight* bless you and remind you that even in the midst of darkness, light always breaks through.

READER REFLECTION & FAITH DISCUSSION GUIDE

Inspired by the journey that shaped *In His Sight*.
Some stories stay with us long after the final page because they remind us of our own. Piper's journey is one of fear giving way to faith, of brokenness transformed by grace. These questions are meant to guide you toward reflection, healing, and renewed hope — a space to invite God into your story, just as Piper learned to invite Him into hers.

Trust and Control

- When have you tried to control something out of fear, only to realize it was never yours to hold?
- What would it look like to release that control to God today?
- Piper learns that trusting someone else can be an act of faith. Who, or what, is God asking you to trust Him with right now?

Fear and Faith

- Where does fear still have a voice in your life, and what might faith say back to it?
- Have you ever reached a point where surrender became your only peace?
- How can you remind yourself of God's presence when you feel unseen or unsafe?

Purpose and Protection

- Looking back, can you see moments where God was protecting or redirecting you, even when it didn't feel like protection at the time?
- Who has God placed in your life as a form of quiet protection or guidance?
- How do you usually recognize His presence in ordinary moments?

Healing and Redemption

- Piper believed she was too broken to be redeemed. Have you ever felt unworthy of grace?
- What has healing looked like for you — slow and unseen, or sudden and surprising?
- What does redemption mean to you personally — not as an idea, but as a lived experience?

Hope and Renewal

- The light in *In His Sight* becomes a symbol of hope breaking through darkness. Where have you seen light begin to rise in your own story?
- What does hope look like for you right now, in this exact season of life?
- If you could name one "sunrise moment," where God met you right where you were, what would it be?

Faith in Action

- Faith often means taking one small step forward

when the outcome is unknown. Where might God be inviting you to take that step?
- How can you be a reflection of Christ's steady love in someone else's storm?
- What would it look like to live in His sight — fully seen, fully known, and fully loved?

If your book club reads *In His Sight*, I'd love to hear what you think! Visit anna-powell.com to share your thoughts or drop me a note.

ABOUT THE AUTHOR

Anna Powell lives in Colorado with her husband, Dan, and their three boys. A lifelong lover of words, she writes stories that explore hope, resilience, and redemption. When she's not writing, you'll find her curled up with a good book, cheering rink-side at her boys' hockey games, squeezing in a workout, or soaking up time with her family. She believes deeply in the power of story to heal, challenge, and inspire — and hopes *In His Sight* does just that.

Connect with Anna at anna-powell.com or @theannapowell on Instagram.

www.ingramcontent.com/pod-product-compliance
Lightning Source LLC
LaVergne TN
LVHW041905070526
838199LV00051BA/2506